NOT ANOTHER
Christmas Movie

NOT ANOTHER *Christmas Movie*

A Novel

ASHLEY COWAN

alcove press

Published in the United States by Alcove Press, an imprint of The Quick Brown Fox & Company LLC.

Alcove Press and its logo are trademarks of The Quick Brown Fox & Company LLC.

Library of Congress Catalog-in-Publication data available upon request.

ISBN (hardcover): 979-8-89242-696-1
ISBN (paperback): 979-8-89242-697-8
ISBN (ebook): 979-8-89242-698-5

Cover design by Sarah Horgan

Printed in the United States.

www.alcovepress.com

Alcove Press
34 West 27th St., 10th Floor
New York, NY 10001

First Edition: October 2026

The authorized representative in the EU for product safety and compliance is eucomply OÜPärnu mnt 139b-14, 11317 Tallinn, Estonia, hello@eucompliancepartner.com, +33757690241

10 9 8 7 6 5 4 3 2 1

To the grandparents. Yours, mine, ours.

CHAPTER ONE

"This holiday season, good girl Annie Meyers is looking to get a little naughty," Annie Meyers said in her best movie trailer voice. She used one hand to swat and then rip down a piece of low-hanging mistletoe from the entryway and the other to balance the remaining contents of her Poinsettia Punch.

"What are you going to do with that?" Marsha Parsons asked, likely hoping to hear about some sort of romantic scheme her best friend was embarking on to spice up this mostly mundane holiday party.

"This stuff is poison," Annie sneered, holding the plant between two fingers.

"So is what you're drinking," Marsha said dryly. "Maybe we should get you something to eat before you finish that?" Annie raised a defiant eyebrow before chugging the lackluster and now lukewarm beverage. "Fine, well, I still want a snack."

"How much longer do we have to stay?" Annie whined when her cup was empty.

"Annie, it's our first holiday party in our first official office building. We should be celebrating," Marsha said, scanning the room for more food.

"I'm bored," Annie said, snapping back, her tipsy tone a tad too loud.

"We asked you both to join the party planning committee," an annoyed voice cut in. Annie and Marsha turned to see Grant Lee glaring their way, arms crossed, waiting in line to sit on Sexy Santa's lap. His impatient tartan-plaid-loafered foot tapped to the beat of "Dominick the Donkey," belted out by nearby karaoke singers.

"Grant, hi, I didn't see you there. Great party," Annie said sheepishly.

"Annie's not exactly the party planning type," Marsha explained as Annie silently mouthed "traitor" in her direction. "But count us in for next year!" Marsha exclaimed, and Annie audibly groaned.

Grant had gone to high school with Annie and Marsha in the quaint town of Simsbury, nestled in the heart of Connecticut, a quintessential New England destination. He kept two very active Instagram accounts, one under his professional name and another under his drag queen name, Peppermint Patti LuBone. Annie had inquired about rental space in the building after Grant had posted about it from his primary account, sharing that the marketing firm where he worked during the day had an open space. Annie and Marsha had signed papers for a year's lease just days later. Their new office was likely used as a storage closet before their arrival, but with Marsha's organizational skills, it quickly became a functional, albeit cozy, base for their mostly online business. It was Grant's second (and way more colorful and campy) account that made their tiny, adults-only operation feel welcomed there.

Grant was also quite proudly the self-appointed head of the building's party planning efforts. Considering the small allotted budget, he did an impressive job putting together events for everyone who rented offices, and they were always well-attended. And despite simply working within proximity of each other at entirely different businesses and knowing each other from childhood, Grant had gone from casual contact to a good friend over the past several months.

"And I saw you take that mistletoe, Annie. That was from my private collection. Give it back," Grant demanded, holding out his neatly manicured hand.

"Sorry, Grant," Annie mumbled, dropping it in his palm.

"You're lucky it's almost my turn to sit in Santa's lap," Grant told her. "He's cute, right? I found him on Facebook Marketplace."

Grant grinned as he leaped up and immediately straddled Sexy Santa, tongue at the ready to lick the red and green body glitter from his bare chest.

"Looks like you're on my naughty list." Annie heard Sexy Santa growl at Grant.

"Is it time for Santa Claus to 'cum' to town?" Grant panted. Annie and Marsha openly gawked at them, all ears and eyes taking in the unfolding scene.

"Are we on the set of a Christmas porno?" Marsha asked.

"Shhh, I'm watching," Annie murmured, wishing she had popcorn from one of those festively decorated tins to snack on. Grant whipped out the mistletoe he had taken from Annie and shot her a wink before planting a hard kiss on Sexy Santa's mouth.

"Oh, hey, I forgot!" Marsha squealed, grabbing her purse. "My mom gifted me some fancy cookies," Marsha lowered her voice and showed Annie a small red box. "They're from a place called Yes, You Cannabis."

"Say less," Annie whispered back, her eyes lighting up with delight. Marsha popped the top of the box open, revealing an assortment of holiday-themed treats.

"Let's try this one," Marsha said, freeing a chocolate crinkle cookie.

"Chocolate anything is the answer to everything," Annie said and nodded, welcoming the half that Marsha offered her. "Your mom is the best," she said, slowly chewing the soft cookie, allowing the taste of chocolate to take over.

"I think she wanted me to be a little more relaxed about meeting Pete's family. That and I think she feels slightly guilty for agreeing to work the holiday," Marsha said.

"How are you feeling about meeting Pete's family?" Annie asked. "Still excited?"

"Pete's dad designed a PowerPoint presentation for me about Hanukkah," Marsha said, the corners of her mouth unable to hide the delight longing to beam across her face.

"Stop."

"Seriously."

"No."

"Yes."

"Absolutely not."

"It's adorable. He wants me to feel included," Marsha gushed.

"PowerPoint," Annie said, pulling the word from her lips like a long-forgotten artifact of the past. "Did he dust off the old family PC to make it?"

"Yeah, I mean, that's probably exactly what he did," Marsha said. "He also spends hours selecting which DVDs he wants to receive in the mail from some tiny company that still offers that service."

"Like to use in an actual DVD player?" Annie asked. "What a legend. We must protect him at all costs," Annie murmured. "You need to marry into that family."

"Here's hoping," Marsha breathed out. Annie stared at her best friend in surprise.

"Wait," Annie said slowly, drawing out the word. "You don't think he's going to propose this week, do you?" Annie stared, watching Marsha's face bloom pinker. "Marsha! Is that on the table? The family menorah table?"

"No!" Marsha said, laughing and covering her face with her hands. "No. I don't think so, at least. Pete and I have joked about him 'putting a ring on it' after I removed my NuvaRing to go back on the pill—"

"Oh, that joke is dangerous," Annie warned, but Marsha continued.

"But I don't know, I don't hate the idea . . ." Marsha said, wiggling her bare ring finger in thought.

"I can't believe this is already happening," Annie said, struggling to keep her enthusiasm steady as a secret boulder surged to the bottom of her stomach. She knew she should be ecstatic for Marsha, that was her job as the lifelong bestie, but the truth was, Annie was terrified that her once inseparable pal would move on to marriage, drifting away into a new life, and leaving her behind.

"Let's not get ahead of ourselves," Marsha said.

"Says the chick playing around with her birth control," Annie teased, sustaining a cheerful facade. A thousand tiny needles prickled beneath her hairline, and an unwanted heat crept up her neck; already, her body instinctively itched to begin grieving the ending of their friendship era. Annie cleared her throat, trying to push the feeling away. "Marsha, I didn't know things were getting so serious."

"It's been a tough few weeks for you," Marsha said softly, her eyes displaying an earnestness that made Annie flinch inwardly. She was desperate to keep her vulnerability hidden. Annie found she functioned best when she was actively ignoring her feelings, especially those tied to some guy who had cut all their fraying strings.

"I'm fine!" Annie said quickly, trusting that, in true Indigo Girls' fashion, just because she spoke the words they'd be true. Especially if she *continued* to speak them. Marsha studied her until Annie had to look away. "I'm mostly fine," Annie added. She didn't want to think about this. Not here, all out in the open. Not at this silly holiday party. Not now. Thoughts about heartache were solely reserved for a couch and complete solitude.

"Annie," Marsha said, giving her a small nudge. "I've known you my whole life, you know you can talk to me about anything."

"I know," Annie said, unable to meet Marsha's gaze because she *did* know. This was her best friend, the person she had technically known in utero thanks to their mothers sharing an ob-gyn, crossing paths in the waiting room, and then realizing they both lived on the same street. The kid who had grown up beside her, weaving their childhoods together in an intricate, unbreakable bond. The friend who had now evolved into a partner within their unconventional business. The same person who had forced Annie out of bed to go to work when she wanted to consume nothing but her beloved Indigo Girls crooning on repeat and fed her actual food for meals. When Annie tried to drown her sorrows in too much coffee and wine and terrible TV after her latest heartache, Marsha had been a steady stream of substance and support.

Annie and Marsha saw each other almost daily and were in a constant text thread on multiple apps in case they couldn't be face-to-face. But while Annie knew she could console herself in Marsha's affection and attention, she couldn't bring herself to rehash this most recent breakup.

If one could even call what Annie had experienced a breakup. Chris had never been able to label her as his girlfriend, after all, and proof of their history had already been scrubbed from the (few and far between) twenty-four-hour stories on Instagram. He hadn't even been that nice to her, like, ever. None of her friends liked Chris or understood why Annie had marched alongside his endless parade of red flags. She didn't get it either. And yet her thoughts begged to replay every interaction, every word, every little thing, trying to make some sort of sense of why his absence from her life hurt so much. Chris continued to crowd her head, a song playing on a torturous roller coaster looping around her brain.

"Annie," Marsha repeated, her voice now full of concern. "I know this time of year is tough on you . . . How many years has it been now?"

"Sixteen," Annie breathed, the weight of realization registering; the moment that had impacted her so deeply was halfway between who she had been then and who she was now at 32. Marsha took Annie's hand and laced her fingers tight.

"Isn't it time to believe a happy ending is something you deserve too?" Marsha asked.

Annie's eyes prickled. From the idea of an actual happy ending waiting somewhere for her to find it and having no idea where to look? From imagining her best friend skipping off into the matrimonial sunset and leaving her behind, or acknowledging her personal history and complicated feelings surrounding the holidays? From the lack of snack options at this godforsaken event? Annie wasn't sure, but she refused to be the girl crying at the Christmas party.

"Can I have more cookies?" Annie asked instead.

"Is that a good idea?" Marsha answered, allowing Annie to change the subject for now. "Don't you have to drive to your parents' house later?"

"A tiny bite," Annie pouted. "Then I'll stick to stuff that sobers me up, like that Christmas tree cheese ball that's been left to cook under these flattering fluorescent lights."

"Maybe you can check in at home and then come spend the holidays with me," Marsha offered.

"Marsha, no, we've talked about this. I'm not sleeping on one of Pete's brothers' floors. And you don't need my bah-humbug tendencies to cast a shadow on what's sure to be a flawless PowerPoint presentation about the history of Hanukkah. Plus, can you imagine what my dad would do if I didn't fulfill each and every one of his handwritten house notes? He was already in tears at the idea of leaving the cat alone for too long. He needs me to cater to Arthur's every whim."

"I'm still shocked he agreed to abandon Arthur for Christmas," Marsha mused.

"Don't worry, he has plans to give the cat a special celebration upon their return. My dad is calling it 'Arthur's Meowy Clawsmas,' and my mother plans to make him a tiny Santa hat now that she's taken up knitting," Annie said, and Marsha laughed. "Neither mentioned having a postponed holiday for Elise or me, but what can you do?" Annie continued, thinking of her older sister who was also away this year, trekking across New Zealand with her girlfriend as a reputable environmental scientist. It had been several years now since her family had enjoyed a traditional Christmas celebration together, and Annie had no intention of changing that dynamic now.

"I guess I can't blame our parents for wanting to escape New England for warmer weather," Marsha shrugged. "My mom practically volunteered to work any flight stopping in a place with working sunshine and heat."

"And mine can't turn down a discounted Caribbean cruise with an unlimited drink package," Annie quipped, ignoring the pangs of abandonment that seized her muscles. There was something about her parents valuing her below a floating buffet catering to senior citizens for Christmas that had taken the wind out of her sails, and she tried to ignore the swell of emotionally shipwrecked emotions.

"They're there with the Laurels, right?" Marsha asked.

"Oh yeah," Annie answered. They both smiled, recalling the lively neighbors who had become close friends with her parents after nearly forty years of living next door to each other. The Laurels' house had been quite the destination for the kids of the street growing up as it was also the designated school bus stop. Mrs. Laurel always insisted that everyone wait inside when it rained and doled out warm Pop-Tarts she purchased for the neighborhood kids at any and every opportunity.

"Fine, you can go back home for a few days, but I'm still coming by on Christmas Day," Marsha insisted, and Annie swallowed the lump in her throat that appeared whenever someone said, "Christmas Day," refusing to let her mind return to her worst Christmas Day memory or how it had forever shadowed all the days that came after it. Marsha sensed Annie's familiar stiffening and changed tactics. "Oh! You should find someone to hook up with while you're there!" Marsha said, her excitement increasing at the idea.

"I'm sure Mr. Heartgraves is booked," Annie said drily.

"Ew, no, dummy," Marsha moaned, thinking about their cranky high school trigonometry teacher who had lived down the block growing up and had to be at least 100 at this point (and an acute point, at that). "Find someone who played on the high school lacrosse team—no, the crew team! Those guys were so hot, great arms."

"I'll see what I can do," Annie smirked, knowing full well she would not be leaving her parents' couch unless it was to retrieve a DoorDash order. Bravo wasn't going to just watch itself.

The karaoke machine let out a loud wail that pierced the room with sound.

"Oops, sorry, Grant!" Someone giggled, "I tripped over the cord!"

"We should get out of here before Grant goes batshit," Annie cautioned. But considering Grant and Sexy Santa were both missing, they obviously had more important matters to attend to. The first few notes of Mariah Carey's "All I Want for Christmas" boomed out of the small karaoke machine; a group whooped and cheered. Annie took a bite of her cookie and let out a deep sigh. There was only so much merriment she could pretend to muster at this point, and she had no intention of doing it clear-minded.

CHAPTER TWO

"Yup, that's disgusting," Annie said to her seasonal seltzer before sighing and finishing the can anyway. The audacity of including a boozy and bubbly peppermint flavor in the holiday pack was baffling. Annie grabbed for another spicy pizza-flavored Pringle to cleanse her palate. She accidentally nudged Arthur, her parents' orange tabby cat, who had been sharing the couch. He had originally been named after Arthur Weasley from the Harry Potter universe, but after J. K. Rowling's transphobic tweets and her unrelenting urge to continually double down on them, Annie refused to acknowledge him as such or include his surname when addressing him. Arthur shot over his best death stare side-eye and retreated upstairs. Annie shoved another Pringle in her mouth, wondering if it was time to transition to wine as her fingers itched to transition from the mindless doomscrolling to the deep dive into the darker corners, like every ex-boyfriend's Instagram account and their LinkedIn if she was feeling particularly naughty.

There was a boxed rosé on the living room table. Still, Annie didn't have a glass or any interest in walking the ten feet into the kitchen of her childhood home, knowing her father had likely completely reorganized the cabinets again. Annie looked down at the Pringle can and made the quick decision to dump the remaining contents into her mouth, shaking crumbs all over herself and the couch in the process. *That's a problem for future Annie*, Annie thought smugly as she shook the can one last time to loosen up any remaining morsels. She then poured the spout of the boxed wine straight into the can, praising herself for the quick ingenuity, and tossed back a large mouthful, taking in strong notes of marinara and malaise.

She had big plans to indulge in blatant, unabashed Internet stalking, and that was priority number one at the moment. True, it always filled her with both unrelenting dread and primal yearning, making her stomach twist in jealousy and remorse when she saw yet another romantic ghost from her mental graveyard announcing their recent engagement, marriage, or God forbid, sonogram pictures of their future spawn. Yet it was always too delicious to resist. Annie braced herself and searched Instagram for Chris's handle, @boner4musack.

It's not that she had been in love with Christopher Tinsel. There had been no plans to book a nail appointment, preparing for a Christmas ring finger photo shoot with this dude, and Annie had always pretended to have made her peace with that, rationalizing remaining present rather than face the reality of their future. But Chris had been the last guy she'd kissed who had meant something to her. She had liked him enough to want to keep seeing him, or at least keep hooking up with him, even when he had always been very clear that he didn't see Annie as any kind of long-term match or even someone he wanted to take out on a real date. The whole time they were "making moments" as Chris called it (which, yeah, looking back, was pretty weird), he was fairly active on more than one dating app. He also had a habit of openly dropping comments about how "hot and bangable" some of her friends were, including Marsha, her sister, her sister's long-term girlfriend, and, once, her next-door neighbor Nick Laurel. Chris had come across an old picture of a neighborhood "leaf blowing party" (a treasured tradition on their street where a group of neighbors worked together over the course of an autumn day to rake and blow all the leaves from each yard, subsisting on themed snacks at each house they hit). Annie learned years later that most of the adults had been consuming bottles of booze and encouraging the kids to do the majority of the actual leaf gathering, something that now she couldn't help but applaud and yearn to emulate. But when Chris saw the picture of the group of gawky teenagers, he shared his heartfelt opinion that Nick would make a beautiful woman. Annie had tried not to let it get to her that Chris had never once called Annie beautiful or any variation on the sentiment.

Chris did, however, make sure to remind Annie at any opportunity of his preferred type: "short, busty, and blonde." Again, Annie would try to shrug off those words from her broader-than-average shoulders while shifting her weight from one slightly taller-than-average leg to the other, crossing her hands over her average-sized chest, and throwing her mostly unruly dark hair back into a messy bun, telling herself it was fine, she didn't need labels, she was still in control of this.

He flagged her as "the marrying type," which Annie assumed was a pivotal step to becoming an official couple, but Chris had followed it up by asserting that he'd never want to be someone's husband. Annie would stifle her longing to find a life partner, a potential father to possible kids. For the first time in her life, that type of commitment from someone felt like something she desperately wanted. Yet Chris never claimed her as his in any real way, even going so far as to avoid ever being caught holding her hand in public. A piece of Annie had foolishly clung to the hope that maybe somehow, in some way, she could get him to change. If she kept up her cool girl demeanor and didn't pressure him, he'd finally wake up next to her after one of their nightly meetups, ready to be her official boyfriend. Instead, the final blow of their official end held some sort of bizarre power over her she seemed unable to break.

Chris had announced this decision the morning after Halloween, after a particularly colorful (both literally and figuratively) evening, by stating this would be their last "made moment." He was interested in someone else. Something that might have been nice to talk about the night before and not, let's say, while Annie was out of her very detailed "Fabio on a roller coaster after the goose incident" costume (inspired by the infamous 1999 inaugural ride of Busch Gardens Williamburg's Apollo's Chariot), shivering in Chris's cold, cream-colored, cheap cotton bed sheets, still wearing the long, blonde wig he had insisted she keep on. Worse yet, Annie still had the costume blood caked to her face because Chris hadn't wanted to wait for her to wash it off hours before. Chris had explained all of this shirtless while also clumsily strumming his guitar, which sounded pretty out of tune even to Annie's less-than-musically-inclined ears. He never bothered to meet her eyes or even walk her to the door to say goodbye. The memory still made her body feel like it was burning from the inside, singeing the discomfort into every inch of skin.

It had been a long November after that. It wasn't the first time she had fallen prey to the pitfalls of hoping a situationship would progress to a real relationship, but it had happened after her favorite holiday and just before the world ramped up on Christmas amphetamines. With Marsha's insistence and assistance, Chris had been promptly deleted from her phone contacts and strategically hidden on social media outlets to avoid any temptation to pay him attention. But he still managed to take up space in her brain in unruly bursts of fireworks, leaving heavy fog in their wake. Most of December felt the same, just with a more festive filter of glittery greens thanks to the distraction of holiday parties. Annie hadn't had it in her to get back on any dating or hookup apps, despite the constant pressure from every piece of media prioritizing falling in love this time of year. At this point, Christmas was a meaningless date on the calendar, something she had to endure until her cold heart decided to thaw or simply expire from lack of use.

Since her parents were out of town for the actual holiday, they hadn't bothered with any decorations (her father was still saving their now limited supply for his return, so Arthur wouldn't go without some fun and festivities) and Annie took some comfort in the house's escape from the constant Christmas celebration the rest of the world was screaming at every opportunity. Her childhood home looked how it always did, timeless and steady, a willing anchor she could cling to amidst any storm. Honestly, Annie was relieved knowing she wouldn't have to sit through another occasion with her prying relatives and have to explain once again that, no, she still didn't have a serious boyfriend and wow, thanks, a month's subscription to Match.com was indeed a great gift, no, she didn't plan to leave her "questionable and confusing" job to pursue a career in finance, and, yes, she would indeed probably die alone on her couch, choking on a highly processed and crumbly snack.

Annie took a deep, steadying breath, and her hesitant, hovering finger finally clicked on @boner4musack. Immediately, her phone screen was invaded by too many shots of Chris posed in mirror selfies from the gym (gross). But then she could see, starting in November, a collection of attempted artistic images with someone who Annie assumed must be his new girlfriend. Annie couldn't discern what she looked like, given that the images mainly consisted of their hands clasped together over a shared cup of hot chocolate with marshmallows or the faint outline of her coat behind a snowman, posed with a guitar, they had created together. Each also contained some sort of vague (but almost always a Phish) song lyric that added to the annoyingness of it all; she was pretty sure he had used "come waste your time with me" at least four times and "stay with me till time turns over" another three. Aside from the text captions, though, the pictures all looked bright. And merry. Annie hated every fucking one of them.

"Where do you think you are, a shitty made-for-TV Christmas movie?" Annie audibly rolled her eyes and let out a deep burp, her mouth still very much tasting of pizza chips and warm rosé. *Must be nice*, she thought bitterly, her eyes burning with unshed tears. Annie grabbed for the TV remote to distract herself from whatever this feeling was, marking her messy fingerprints along its surface. As if she had summoned it, a winter scene brightened the room with a beautiful, overly emotive actress in an impractical white coat and a generically handsome actor. They gifted each other weighted stares in a horse-drawn carriage like two real-life heart-eye emojis. Both looked familiar in that they must have once been teen pop stars and/or on some moody 90s TV show and had now matured to make a living doing seasonal made-for-television movies. Annie furiously tried to change the channel, shielding her eyes from the ridiculous, unbelievable scene, frantically needing anything else to land on, but the remote crashed to the floor, spilling its batteries under the couch.

Annie groaned. There was no way she had it in her to search for the pieces and then put the thing back together when she was rotting on the couch. So, against her better judgment, she let the movie play on. Worse yet, she found she couldn't look away.

Everything was so shiny and clean; no one ever made a mess. They orbited neatly around each other, and the only thing that threatened their humanity was the fear of losing the Christmas spirit, whatever that was. The lead character was a workaholic who never actually worked; rather, she busied herself in ridiculous holiday activities, apparently unaware that she was falling in love with the small-town, rugged lumberjack. It was like watching fast food, devoid of any true substance but mindlessly consumed. In this movie, no one sat home alone, tormenting themselves over someone's social media account. No one's parents left town.

No one actually lost the Christmas spirit. Utter disgust radiated from each and every one of Annie's eye rolls.

Before the movie could reach its cliché, predictable ending, Annie heard a series of loud bangs outside and remembered, from her father's meticulous notes that she still had to bring out the trash for its weekly pickup tomorrow morning.

Fuck. She would have to leave the warmth of the house to take care of it or risk the wrath of her dad in the form of an unbearable, weighted, disappointed side-eyed sigh. Assuming the noise had been another neighbor depositing their bin, Annie stood up and pushed the power button on the TV screen corner. She tossed a red throw blanket over her shoulders as a stand-in jacket when she couldn't immediately locate a coat. With the Pringles can rosé gripped by her teeth and one hand holding the last dark chocolate cookie Marsha had shared with her from Yes, You Cannabis, Annie used her free hand to drag the garbage can from the garage to the end of the driveway. It was a clumsy experience for all involved, but once the task had been completed, Annie rewarded herself with a small nibble of cookie and turned back to the house. But before she could take a step, another loud bang from next door caught her attention.

Always a horror movie virtuoso, Annie decided to sneak around the side of the house to get a view of whatever was happening while also avoiding being murdered. She soundlessly tiptoed closer to the Laurels' back door, where she saw a figure outside with a string of lights looped around each limb, giving them the appearance of a walking flare recently released from its gun. Annie crept closer, drawn like a moth rehearsing its introduction to a flame.

The person was focused on an enormous wooden chair. The backs of their socked feet were hanging out of a pair of leopard slippers, and under a knit hat, Annie could see earbuds in each ear and a head lightly nodding to what Annie assumed was music or a lively podcast.

"What's happening here?" Annie asked loudly to the person's back.

Nick Laurel startled, screamed, and jumped straight up and around to face Annie, the string of lights traveling with him. Nick's eyes were wide in surprise, and under each Annie could make out two pink, glossy patches. Despite the questionable fashion choices, she was mostly struck by how he didn't look like the little kid who used to annoy her with endless streams of questions at the bus stop, but how he looked way more like, well, a grown man. They had lived next door to each other their whole lives, Nick two grades below Annie, but besides waiting for the bus together and participating in various neighborhood activities throughout the passing New England seasons, they had mostly kept to their own social circles.

"I thought you were going to murder me!" Nick yelled in greeting, sounding like a sick bird and still clearly taken aback by Annie's sudden arrival. "Hold on, let me pause my music!" he yelled, fumbling in his plaid pajama pants for his phone. Once he had a moment to return his earbuds to their holder, he took a calming breath. "Annie, hi, sorry, you scared me."

"I can see that," Annie answered. "I'm surprised those under-eye masks didn't fly off," Annie said, unable to tame her teasing tone. Nick swatted at his face, remembering his choice of self-care skin routine, and quickly peeled them away.

"My mom's," Nick muttered. "They're snowflake winterberry scented . . . which doesn't make sense because winterberries are poisonous to humans," he explained, seemingly unsure why he was continuing to bring attention to the fact that he had been caught wearing his mother's pink under-eye patches.

"Sounds dangerous," Annie smirked. "I guess you've gone full bad boy these days, huh, Nick? And in leopard slippers?" Annie mock-gasped.

"Also my mom's," Nick groaned, obviously regretting all of his life choices.

"Oh, your mom. Forever a fashionista," Annie admired.

"I couldn't find my shoes, and she's got at least fifty pairs of leopard or leopard-adjacent slippers in the house," Nick said, and Annie nodded, knowing that wasn't an exaggeration. Even Annie knew how much the woman notoriously loved her leopard print, and her feet were never bare.

"What were you listening to so vigorously?" Annie asked.

"Lilith Fair Does Christmas," Nick said.

"I've never heard of that," Annie said, crinkling her forehead in thought. If she wasn't completely sick of holiday music, she'd definitely want to jam to that album. She and Marsha had spent many early childhood sleepovers in the musical company of most of the female singer-songwriters who had been a part of Lilith Fair during those fateful summers of her youth. Marsha's mom had taken them to see a show at the Meadows when they were kids. Annie still had the concert T-shirt she had bought with her hard-earned money (obtained after teaching herself how to set up an eBay account one summer and auctioning off household items, much to her parents' dismay but also reluctant awe). Subsequently, that summer likely played a part in her future career trajectory.

"It's a playlist I made on Spotify," Nick clarified. "I have Lilith Fair–inspired playlists for all the major holidays."

"That tracks," Annie smiled, remembering an impressionable child Nick asking Annie what kind of music she liked and studiously making a point to seek it out. It was endearing to know he had actually formed his own attachments to the lyrics and melodies that had been played as a part of her internal soundtrack. "So what's up, Nick? How long's it been?" She tried to remember when they had last crossed paths. It felt like a lifetime.

"Hoops and Hops the night before Thanksgiving. Six years ago," Nick explained, not quite meeting Annie's gaze. "But your high school graduation party was probably the last time we hung out together . . ." Nick trailed off.

"Hoops and Hops?" Annie asked, her face scrunching in surprise. "Why didn't you say hi?"

"You were with a bunch of other people. I didn't want to bother you," Nick admitted.

"I don't remember the last time I was there," Annie admitted. A visit to the local dive bar clearly hadn't cemented any lasting memory; she was impressed Nick had recalled that so quickly. "Whatcha doing out here in the middle of the night?" Annie asked, nibbling her cookie.

"I'm trying to set up a Santa display in the front yard," Nick said, and Annie took a few steps closer to examine what she had assumed was a wooden chair.

"Ew, why does that thing look like it's been stained with blood?" Annie asked.

"Fake blood," Nick said, like it was obvious. Annie stared back, eyebrows raised. "This is one of the barber chairs from a touring production of *Sweeney Todd*. They were going to disassemble it now that their run is over, but it was offered to me first."

"So you willingly drove that thing from Brooklyn to turn it into a Santa chair here?" Annie asked him, shaking her head in disbelief and wondering if her cookie was kicking in or if this was still normal Nick.

"I had to try," Nick shrugged. "My team constructed it, and I didn't have the heart to see it go. Plus, my parents didn't do any decorating this year. I have my work cut out for me if I'm going to get things ready in time for Christmas."

"What's the point?" Annie asked.

"What do you mean? It's Christmas," Nick countered, seemingly confused by her confusion.

"I mean, our families won't be home, why bother putting this stuff up? It's not like it's Halloween, which are the only kind of decorations worth the effort."

"It's the most magical time of the year. Annie, it's Christmas!" Nick gaped, staring with genuine, wholehearted conviction. Annie huffed and rolled her eyes. "Not in the winter holiday spirit this year?" Nick asked softly.

"Oh, I could be into some holiday spirits . . ." Annie said quickly, refusing to acknowledge any type of emotional baggage at this time of night while outside with the neighbors' kid and his weird, bloody Santa chair.

"It's okay, even Scrooge embraced the season eventually," Nick smiled, turning back to the chair.

"How dare you compare me to Scrooge, ew, he's so basic," Annie groaned.

"Here we go again, is it time for another rant about *A Christmas Carol*?" Nick asked with false surprise. "You do realize you've been sharing your strong opinions on this one since we were in elementary school and they brought in those local actors to perform it?"

"Well, it's so boring and overdone!" Annie complained, and Nick nodded at Annie's well-rehearsed argument. "And it's sad, considering the potential . . ."

"Oh, I remember, you want the ghosts to be scarier," Nick said.

"C'mon," Annie said. "Legit scary ghosts would be very cool. And don't even get me started on the boring time-travel bits. Such a waste," Annie finished, blowing air through her lips.

"I know you weren't a big fan of the holidays when we were in high school—" Nick began.

"I was full of so much angst in high school," Annie interrupted, still unwilling to acknowledge the one Christmas morning sixteen years before that had canceled all future enjoyment of the holiday.

"You were angsty?" Nick asked.

"Who wasn't angsty in high school? It was a requirement to graduate," Annie muttered.

"I always liked school," Nick said without a hint of sarcasm. They had only shared two years together in the building, Nick as a youthful freshman and Annie in her junior year, already wishing she could skip senior year and jump-start her life outside of high school. Annie remembered Nick as a friendly and eager kid, involved in a bunch of clubs, with a trajectory that had varied from her own.

"Most likely you remember me crying over some boy I had planned to kiss on New Year's Eve only to learn he was out of town with his parents or dating someone else," Annie stated, with more bite than she intended. "You had that girlfriend, though, right? What was her name again?"

"Bailey Jones," Nick answered quickly.

"That sounds like a dog's name," Annie said.

"I love dogs," Nick said, again, without an ounce of sarcasm, and Annie couldn't keep from laughing. "Watch out, Annie, this whole cynicism act may finally catch up with you and leave you haunted by your own ghosts one of these days."

"I wish!" Annie said, but she was cut off by the booming sound of a ringing bell.

CHAPTER THREE

"Can you hear that?" Annie asked Nick.

"Yeah, obviously," Nick answered, "It's very loud."

He tiptoed to get a better view of the street, his heels sticking wildly out of the slippers and his arms and legs still wrapped in lights. Annie shuffled next to him, and they walked up the driveway until their eyes found those of a man ringing a bell next to a red donation pail placed next to the stop sign and one streetlight, a few houses up the road. The rest of the street was completely dark, and upon closer evaluation, the man had both a bell and a beer in one hand and a green bong in the other. Even in the limited light, Annie could see he was wearing a red sweatsuit that looked stained by grease and a cream-colored powder and had a full white beard. She squinted toward him, trying to get a better look at his features. He looked like a mall Santa after a night of intense partying, eager to fuck stuff up. As she looked at him, the man gave her a small smile, revealing a gold front tooth, and he winked. Gross, that's not something people should ever try to do in real life, Annie cringed.

"Oh, wow, he's definitely holding a bong, huh?" Nick whispered to her.

"Respect," Annie mused. It was good to see Santa let loose and have a good time . . . though he risked being seen by Simsbury PD doing speed checks or worse, and way more likely, someone from the neighborhood Facebook pages, which would ignite the town keyboard warriors in a frenzy of comments and angry face reactions.

"What's he doing out here now?" Nick frowned. The man looked their way and continued to wave the bell, breaking every few rings to take a hit. The scene was strangely mesmerizing, and both Annie and Nick found themselves hypnotized, unable to do anything but stare. After a moment, Annie put the Pringles can back between her teeth to free her hand and stealthily turned off the flash of her phone to take a picture.

"What are you doing?" Nick hissed out of the corner of his mouth.

"Taking in the magic of the season," Annie told him, putting her phone back and returning the can to her hand.

"Hey, can I get a chip?" Nick asked, sticking his hand in Annie's Pringles can before she could stop him. "That's liquid," Nick said, shaking his wet hand into the front yard, shuffling back to the decorations.

"Rosé," Annie said, "Should have warned you. Want a sip?" Annie offered him the can. Nick made a disgusted face but took the can anyway and allowed himself a quick drink.

"Can I get some of that cookie?" Nick asked.

"What will you give me for it? It's a special cookie," Annie whispered.

"Why are you whispering? Are you scared stoned Santa is going to hear you?" Nick asked.

"Well, yeah, kind of," Annie admitted with a shudder. "I don't know his story, and I'm way too tired to listen to it."

"I'll trade you a boozy seltzer for it," Nick offered.

"If it's the peppermint flavor, you can go right to hell," Annie warned.

"Fair enough. Okay, what do you want then?" Nick asked.

"A bacon, egg, and cheese bagel sandwich with hot honey from the Coffee Spot. Oh, and a cold brew with chocolate cold foam. If I give you the rest of this cookie, would you drive over and pick it up tomorrow morning?" Annie smiled hopefully, batting her eyelashes at him.

"Fine. But only because I was planning on going there anyway," Nick sighed. Annie grinned and took one last small bite of the cookie before handing the rest over to Nick. "Now let's get inside and lock the doors."

"Santa doesn't use locks, Nick. Not when there's an open fireplace . . ." Annie said in a spooky voice before giving in to a yawn and turning to the wooden chair. "You're just going to leave this bloody thing out here for him then?"

"I'd rather enjoy this cookie," Nick admitted.

"Not going to lie, it's pretty weird I'm sharing my 'goods' with the kid next door. I feel like you're going to go tattle on me to our moms," Annie admitted, shaking her head.

"I think our parents will be too wasted this week to care what we're doing here," Nick said in a slightly defiant tone.

"Ha," Annie huffed, "Yeah, I saw a blurry picture my dad sent of the four of them on a formal night. Looks like they're taking full advantage of that drink package."

"It was nice seeing you, Annie," Nick said shyly. "Maybe we can catch up while we're both housesitting."

"Maybe," Annie shrugged noncommittedly. "Or I'll see you next week by the trash."

"It'll always be our spot," Nick deadpanned.

"And thanks again for my breakfast tomorrow, feel free to leave it at my doorstep if I'm still sleeping," Annie said with a wave, scurrying back to the warmth of her house.

"Night, Annie," Nick said after a sigh. He finished the remaining cookie in one large bite.

After locking up (and checking it twice), Annie posted an Instagram story with a heavily filtered stoned Santa and wrote, "Christmas magic." It wasn't much more than a blur of the man's red clothes, ringing a golden bell, and the bright green bong, but Annie had turned the live picture into a boomerang, bringing some of the absurdity they had witnessed to action. Right before she posted it, she added music so that Mariah's "make my wish come true, all I want for Christmas is you," timed along with the movement. Annie then made her way upstairs and found Arthur asleep on her teenage bed.

Her room was more like an old high school set, unaware of passing time. Which made her both nostalgic and slightly queasy, remembering the many nights she would spend crying into her keyboard over crushes who didn't know she existed, only to grieve by leaving some kind of emo song lyric in an AIM away message. Or adding yet another angsty poem to a journal showcasing a cover collage full of inspirational images and words she meticulously cut out from her sister's old Cosmo magazines.

Arthur woke suddenly, snapping Annie out of her daze, and hissed, claws at the ready. "Whoa, calm down, don't be an asshole," Annie said and turned her hand into a fist to allow Arthur to smell her and remember that she wasn't his mortal enemy and in fact just the person who would be feeding and watering him for the next several days. "That's better, you tiny demon," Annie murmured when Arthur nudged his small orange head into her hand, nourishing himself with a solid stretch and dramatically yawning. Annie let out her own yawn and sprawled across the bed, taking in the scent of her worn-out, well-loved quilt. She stared up at her familiar ceiling, forever cluttered with those ridiculous glow-in-the-dark star stickers. Actually, if Annie were being honest, she still found them to be very cool and would happily cover her apartment with them if they weren't so annoying to put up and remove. That and she didn't need the threat of stars standing in the way of getting back her security deposit.

On the wooden bedside table, her mother had neatly piled copies of her school yearbooks, and Annie sighed, wondering why they had been moved back up here from the basement. She contemplated at what point during this next week she would feel emotionally ready and physically tipsy enough to revisit their pages willingly. Knowing full well it would lead to looking up her old classmates online and chronicling the paths taken since graduation.

Annie saw her phone light up with a notification. @ boner4musack had liked her Instagram story. Whoa. Hold the phone. Literally. What did that mean? Likely absolutely nothing, but it still made Annie's limbs buzz restlessly, desperate for some sort of reason why. Chris rarely watched her stories and hadn't left any type of reaction to them since well before Halloween. Why this story? Why now?

Annie heard the sounds of Christmas music paired with conversation travel upstairs. It gave her a moment to pause her plan to overthink a stupid notification, as her pulse quickened, needing to investigate the noise. As she crept down the stairs, she quickly realized that the TV had turned back on and was playing another made-for-TV movie. Arthur was perched next to the screen, rubbing his head into the bottom corner.

"Did you turn the TV back on, you little weirdo?" Annie asked, relieved that it was only a dumb movie and not a serial killer. Annie turned the TV off again and returned upstairs, Arthur at her heels. Once she was back in bed, he walked up to Annie's chest and threw his body across her heart, purring loudly before closing his eyes again. The effect was enchanting. The calming repetitive sound, the familiar warmth of her bed, and Arthur's furry frame holding on to her like a tiny weighted blanket. Almost instantly, and before Annie could fight it, she was soothed into allowing her own eyes to close.

Of course, she didn't plan to fall asleep like that, but that's how these things happen. One must always heed warnings while resting alongside a tiny animal companion, after all. Annie swore she heard the sound of jingle bells right before she blinked her eyes back open to a warm, well-lit space.

Being so well-rested was immediately disorientating. She was most acquainted with waking up exhausted and blindly managing her morning in a cranky haze, desperately longing to go back to bed.

The room was suffused in a warm glow, and Arthur was now staring at her with a sparkly red collar around his neck that jingled with each small movement. It looked like he had been washed and fluffed, his orange fur catching a sunbeam and radiating brighter than before their catnap. Arthur was looking at her in such a sweet and serene way, his yellow eyes as big as a cartoon, and his expression just as broad. Annie gasped in surprise. Wait. Was this a different cat?

"Why are you looking at me like that? And where did you get that collar? Did you put it on yourself?" Annie asked him. He padded closer and purred into her face. "You're creeping me out," Annie said, sitting up. It took her a moment to realize she wasn't in her bedroom. Or, technically, she was in her bedroom, but it had completely transformed. "What's going on?" Annie asked the cat. He rubbed his loudly purring face against her arm.

The room looked like it had been staged for a furniture catalog photo shoot from another era—like, the late 1990s or early 2000s. The wonderfully worn blue quilt had been replaced with a red down comforter, and underneath her, the sheets had been changed to soft flannels with red and green snowflakes. There was a bright green garland covering the bed frame, and around her dresser white lights twinkled. A small tree decorated with colorful ornaments sat in the corner where the old popcorn tin had been growing dusty mere moments ago. Even the smell of the room seemed to have changed.

"Oh, wow, that's nice," Annie admitted out loud, taking in another deep breath. Her nose sparkled with cinnamon, orange, and pine. Annie looked down to see that she was wearing red silk pajamas. Like, fancy ones reserved for

Instagram influencers or wealthy housewives, or even Nick's mom, for that matter. And there was a big monogrammed "A" and "M" scripted in white thread across a pocket closest to her heart. Annie looked to the door and saw a beautiful leather suitcase with her initials stamped in a neat font in its corner. In a panicked moment of complete confusion, Annie leaped from the bed and opened the door.

"Mom? Dad? Are you home?" Annie asked, sticking her head out into the hallway. Was this some kind of joke? "Ellie?" Annie tried, wondering if maybe her sister Elise was to blame. But the house was still and quiet. Annie tiptoed down the hallway to see that it had also been decorated. Garlands had been laced across all available surfaces, wreaths placed on every door, and mistletoe hung above each frame. When she got back downstairs, she was greeted by another explosion of decorations, multiple trees and red ribbons, and white candles were burning in strategic spaces, creating an intimate glow.

"Who lit all these candles? Why are all the lights already on? And wow, there are multiple trees? This isn't safe!" Annie walked into the kitchen and saw a huge canister of Folgers coffee on the counter, and a full but otherwise pristine coffee maker. "Who made this?" she asked out loud again. She was unable to remove the glass coffee pot for further evaluation, and the coffee itself appeared to be unmoving. "Well, I take my coffee iced anyway," she muttered, squeezing her eyes shut. *Okay, this has to be some sort of bizarre dream*, Annie thought, moving about the space. *That cookie from earlier must have been stronger than I realized.* "Annie, wake up, I don't like this!"

She found her way into what was now a completely unfamiliar living room. Gone were the couch and its crumbs and in its place were two red velvet chairs draped with white, fuzzy throw blankets. They both had decorative, cringe-worthy pillows, one reading "Snowflake Kisses and Christmas Wishes" and the other "Believe in Magic." Annie found herself physically pained by the dorkiness. But she soon found the mounted "artwork" to be even worse. In one corner was a large wooden sign with the quote "Christmas is more than opening presents, it's about opening your heart," and she couldn't help but gag at the too-sweet sentiment.

Annie caught sight of a front window and screamed. Outside, everything was blanketed with snow. Well, everything aside from the brick-lined path leading to the sidewalk, which also looked completely devoid of the presence of winter weather. She ran to the front door to see if her car was still in the driveway. It was. At least, something resembling a car was there underneath a mountain of fresh white snow. Annie searched her pockets for her phone and came up empty. She frantically paced around the entryway, where she found a phone on a small, decorated table next to a nativity display.

"Help me, baby Jesus," Annie, never a religious woman, offered the tiny infant. Annie swiped it open, the phone recognizing her face, and was greeted with a beautiful picture of a lit Christmas tree as the wallpaper. None of her apps were on the home screen, though, and she couldn't open her contacts to text. Instead, a "no service" banner filled the top of the screen. When she couldn't access the internet or call out, Annie shook the phone and blew a puff of hot air into the charging port, hoping something would change. She turned it off and back on again, only to get the same result.

"No, no, no, wake up now, Annie!" Annie said, pinching her arm. "This dream sucks! You haven't even had your bagel or first iced coffee of the day yet," she whimpered. With each passing second that she didn't wake up, her heart rate accelerated.

The front doorbell rang out, playing an aggressive electronic version of "Feliz Navidad" and Annie yelped in surprise. It played again and she trembled, gripping the gold knob, unsure whether it was smart or safe to open the door.

"Annie?" A familiar voice called out. She couldn't place where she knew it from, so she opened the door to peek out. "Annie," the voice said again. Annie scrunched up her face. It was Nick.

"Nick!" Annie exclaimed, trying to figure out how to ask for help. "Something's going on—"

"I know," Nick said grimly.

"Know what? Why is the house decorated like this? The Christmas quote decor is killing me! And who made a huge pot of Folgers coffee?"

"I have a feeling we're not in Simsbury anymore," Nick said, cutting her off.

"What?"

"I think we're in a made-for-TV Christmas movie."

CHAPTER FOUR

"What are you talking about? Nick, what's going on? Was this you? Some kind of dumb prank or something?" Annie asked, her voice sounding more stretched and thinner the longer she spoke. "Ew, wait, did you change me into these pajamas?" Annie asked reflexively, crossing her arms across her chest.

"Absolutely not!" Nick scoffed. "And I could ask you the same thing, since I'm also wearing a pair!"

Annie realized now that he, too, was in pajamas—his marked "NL."

"The quality of the silk is exquisite, isn't it? Clearly, they've been handmade by a skilled designer," Nick told her, his eyes studying his sleeves in appreciation.

"Yes, they're incredible, and I'm in my Nancy Meyers postdivorce heroine era, get on with it already!" Annie scowled, gesturing for him to continue.

"I assumed it was the effects of that 'special cookie' last night," Nick started. "But when I woke up, the entire house had been decorated and warm cookies were cooling on the counter."

"Whoa, whoa, whoa, go back—" Annie demanded.

"To which part? When I woke up?"

"No—"

"The decorations?"

"No, the cookies," Annie hissed in annoyance.

"Huh?" Nick asked.

"I woke up to fake freaking Folgers coffee. I need a cookie," Annie said.

"Sorry, what? Like right now?" he asked.

"Yeah."

"Are you serious?"

"Yes," Annie said seriously.

"Yeah, okay, I'll wait to continue my assessment of this bizarre universe we've somehow shifted into and run back through the mysterious, likely CGI, snow to get you some cookies," Nick said sarcastically.

"Cool. Chop, chop then," Annie said and then sighed. "I need cookies before figuring out what the fu—" Annie started, but she was abruptly cut off by a loud noise. It sounded like what may have been designed to be a laugh but had since been warped and waterlogged after drowning in a haunted lake. "What the fu—" Annie tried again, and the sound got louder, drawing her attention to a three-foot-tall animatronic Santa Claus. "The fu—" Annie gasped in horror as a third, louder yet, "laugh" erupted from the demonic figure.

"Why can't I say fu—" Annie tried to whisper, but the Santa barked out a "ho ho ho" as if in warning. Annie's eyes grew wide, taking in the candle waving in Santa's waxy hand, now flickering to life, momentarily blinding her with its intensity. Santa's eyes stared unblinkingly, dead yet alive with merry menace.

"Oh, yeah, I discovered this one before I came over. Try to say another 'bad word,'" Nick smirked.

"No way, I don't want that thing coming more to life, what's happening?"

"Well, no swearing or indecent language here, ma'am," Nick offered, making his voice go into a soft Southern drawl.

"Under no circumstances are you to ever call me *ma'am* again, man," Annie warned.

"Noted," Nick nodded. "Well, as you observed, if you try to use a 'bad' word, it'll be cut out by some sort of loud sound. I tried it in my house, and the kitchen radio kept going off, playing Jessica and Ashlee Simpson's version of 'Little Drummer Boy' from the 2004 TV special."

"No!" Annie gasped, covering her ears in horror at the thought and feeling grateful she only had to endure a creepy child-sized mechanical Santa brought to life. Clearly, she would be watching her language for the foreseeable future.

"We're not in Simsbury anymore. Or, like, we're in an alternative reality of Simsbury. It's something like Simsbury. Based on my limited observations, we're now in a made-for-TV Christmas movie," Nick said.

"Why are you so familiar with made-for-TV Christmas movies?"

"I don't have to answer that," Nick said, crossing his arms, literally closing himself off to the question. "I have my suspicions on which network's universe this could be, considering the collection of ornaments on all of the trees and the blank holiday cards I found on our mantel," Nick said before Annie cut him off.

"I'm not mentally equipped to make sense of anything you just said. I need a cookie," Annie said. Nick rolled his eyes, realizing that she was not going to relent and walked carefully over the snow to his house. After a few moments he returned carrying a large cookie sheet. Annie hurried him into her house and leaned over to examine the goods.

"What the fu—" Annie started but cut herself off when she caught a glimpse of the expectant candle in Santa's hands. "What is that?" Annie asked instead.

"Cookies."

"Where's the chocolate?" Annie asked, grabbing a circular cookie to study.

"These are sugar cookies," Nick said.

"Plain sugar cookies are basically garbage," Annie said definitively. When Nick stared back blankly, she muttered miserably, "What's the point of a cookie without chocolate?" and tossed the pointless confection back on the tray. "Oh, hey, my phone isn't working, do you have yours?" Annie asked hopefully, changing gears.

"No, my lock screen is a cartoon picture of two snow people under mistletoe."

"Fu—" Annie started to yell in frustration but gritted her teeth. "Son-of-a-nutcracker," she said instead. "Let's check my parents' landline."

Annie raced into the kitchen, frantically searching for the cordless phone that had lived there for years. Instead, she found a black rotary phone placed in front of a cylinder piled to the top with shiny red and green round balls. Annie picked up the receiver, knowing before it reached her ear she'd be left helpless.

"Nothing," she said to Nick, her face full of frustration. Nick thoughtlessly moved the cylinder closer to him, eventually taking out the top three balls to hurl into the air. "What's happening here?" Annie asked, gesturing to the act.

"I'm stress juggling," Nick answered, his eyes never leaving the three balls as they masterfully went from one hand, into the air, and swiftly landed in the other before they were off again. "I went to circus camp, remember?" Nick said, and Annie swallowed a scream of exasperation. She was about ready to shake Nick to get him to knock off his nonsense in this incredibly nonsensical situation.

"I'm going to find my keys," Annie announced, unable to gather the patience to let Nick "stress juggle" a moment longer.

"Good luck. I couldn't find mine, and when I tried to brush the snow off my car, I couldn't do it," Nick told her, returning the balls to their cylinder and into the strange concept that a container of balls was considered a holiday decoration.

"What do you mean? That doesn't make sense," Annie said, shaking her head. She found a pair of red satin slippers in a basket near the front door and slid her feet in, jogging out to her car, incensed, on adrenaline, and ready to prove Nick wrong.

Annie saw Nick standing in the doorframe, his hands on his hips. Her arms were swinging before she even reached her car, which was still completely concealed under snow, but when her skin made contact, she didn't feel the cold; in fact, the "snow" didn't feel like much at all. It was like grabbing at clouds, and every time she scooped some away, more would take its place, making her attempts frustratingly futile. After about a minute, Annie was exhausted and breathing hard, her efforts completely unseen.

"Are we ghosts?!" Annie yelled over to Nick. "What's going on here?"

"I don't know . . ." Nick answered, deep in thought. Annie flew down the driveway. "Wait! Where are you going?" Nick asked, following behind.

"I have to get out of here!" Annie called back, landing on the clear sidewalk and resuming her powerwalk. She stopped in her tracks once outside Nick's house. The creepy Sweeny Todd barber chair was nowhere to be seen, and instead, the yard was full of inflatable reindeer and snow people. Framing the home, including all windows and doorways, were multicolored lights illuminating the morning snow. Annie was still gawking as Nick caught up to her.

"I didn't do this either, in case you're wondering," Nick said. Annie shot him a horrified look and raced to the next house on the block. It too was lit up and overly populated with inflatable creatures. Annie went up to the door and knocked on it for several seconds.

"Someone must be home, all the lights are on!" Annie said desperately, trying to get a look inside. When no one came to the door, she tried the house across the street and found the same thing: no one seemed to be home, and yet all their lights were on. She pounded on the door until she was breathless. She tried the next house, home to Mr. Heartgraves, and cried out his name to the lit-up front window. When he didn't answer, she walked back to the street.

"I don't understand. None of this makes sense," Annie said, finally feeling the ache of fear pulling at her muscles. "I'm scared," Annie admitted to Nick.

"Me too," Nick said, softening. "At least we're in this together, right?" Annie gave him a shrug in response. "Happy to have you here too, Annie," Nick sighed.

"It's not you, I don't want to be here at all. With anyone. I want to be alone on the couch, eating a bagel and drinking a cold brew," Annie said, returning to her frantic pace. "We need to find some answers. Let's go," she ordered, and Nick wordlessly followed. When they approached the stop sign, they both stopped in their tracks. There was a quaint wooden hand-painted sign reading "Main Street."

"Whoa," Nick marveled. Annie nodded, peering down the road. It was all lit up and bustling with people; perhaps that's where all their neighbors had gone. Streetlamps were covered in garlands, and she could see another handmade sign advertising Christmas trees alongside a series of colorful shops.

"What time is it? Why is it so bustling? Don't people have jobs?" Annie asked, and Nick shrugged. The familiar sound of bells caught their attention again, and they both turned to see a man wearing an impressive full Santa suit ringing a golden bell next to a red donation pail. "Stoned Santa!" Annie hissed at Nick as he scrutinized the man. "He's just cleaner here!" Annie pushed her way to Santa to confront him.

"Hey," Annie said.

"Ho, ho, ho!" the man said, full-jolly mode turned all the way up.

"No time for that! What's going on here? Did you do this?" Annie asked, pointing a finger at his chest. The man stopped ringing his bell to address her. He looked deep into Annie's eyes, and she had the uneasy feeling he was studying her soul.

"The snowstorm?" the man asked innocently. "No, dear, my magic can't compete with Mother Nature."

"Snowstorm?" Nick asked.

"Well, yes. It's closed the roads, and unfortunately, all communications service is out too," the man explained.

"That's not a thing," Annie said.

"Are you saying all the roads out of town are closed? And no one has the internet?" Nick asked.

"No phones either," the man said, looking unfazed by the situation.

"This is ridiculous," Annie told Nick. "Let's go talk to someone else."

"Everything you could wish for is right here," the man said, looking into Annie's eyes again and sending goosebumps across her whole body. Annie grabbed Nick's arm to move him up the street, now apparently called Main Street. Annie looked around and hurled herself in the direction of a store that appeared to only sell snow globes. It was packed with people and had a line out the door. Annie approached the waiting strangers.

"Hi," Annie breathed out, "I know this is going to sound crazy—"

"Why, little Annie Meyers! Is that you?" An older woman smiled. Annie studied her face, there was nothing recognizable to be found. "Oh, dear, so nice to see you! I've been so worried the storm had stopped you from coming home! How's Arthur?"

"The cat?" Annie asked, shaking her head, already bewildered from the interaction.

"I'm sorry, honey, I won't be able to let you cut in line, if that's what you're hoping for," The woman said, gesturing to the long line behind her. "I don't want to end up on the naughty list."

"Um, no, that's not what I'm hoping for," Annie started, still a mess of words piling on top of each other without direction. "Could I borrow your phone? I need to make contact with someone."

"You young people with your devices," the woman tsk-tsked. "I don't carry a mobile phone. Besides, the snow-storm knocked everything out."

"Right, the storm . . . so I'm to assume it was powerful enough to take out all means of communication but not strong enough to keep people away from waiting in line for snow globes?" Annie asked, and the woman stared at her blankly. "Why are there so many people out and about if there's a snowstorm? I don't understand," Annie tried, already sensing that this woman wouldn't be able to offer much more than additional confusion.

"Sorry, Annie, looks like they're letting a few more folks into the store; we can catch up later," the woman said, shooing Annie back toward Nick. Without a chance to think or try talking to another person, Annie wove them through the crowds of people, past the row of shops, until they reached what looked like a wall of snow at the end of Main Street. Annie tried to pass but was met by solid ice behind a curtain of thick white flakes. Not knowing what else to do, she ran back down the street (as well as she could in her satin slippers and pajamas) and tried to go the other way until she came to another wall of snow that was impossible to penetrate. Annie threw her arms up to the sky and spun around.

"What are you waiting for, huh? What are you waiting for?!" Annie yelled.

"Who are you screaming at?" Nick asked when she was done.

"You know, from *I Still Know What You Did Last Summer*? When Jennifer Love Hewitt screams, 'What are you waiting for, huh? What are you waiting for?' to the sky?" Annie asked, mimicking the movement again.

"I've never seen it," Nick shrugged, and Annie shook her head in disbelief before dissolving back into her whirl of panic.

"We're trapped. Maybe we're actually dead," she said, her voice cracking.

"Maybe," Nick said slowly. "But I'm still really, really relieved that I'm not experiencing this alone," Nick said in such a genuinely grateful voice that it took Annie momentarily aback and made her feel flustered. "I also don't know why we'd die and both be sent to some sort of Christmas snow globe that feels straight out of the made-for-TV universe."

"And why is this happening to us? Did you, like, make a wish in a fountain to be in a Christmas movie?" Annie asked. Nick let out a loud cough of surprise and quickly got a hold of himself.

"What? No! Did you?" Nick asked loudly.

"Yeah, like I would waste a wish on that," Annie muttered. "Is this because of Stoned Santa?" Annie asked. Nick's eyes widened at the idea, but he quickly covered up his surprise.

"We're stuck in Holiday Hollywood because some random man was ringing a bell and taking hits off a bong in public?" Nick asked skeptically.

"That guy knows something—I can tell. He said everything we could wish for is right here . . . let's go back and find him." Annie said, and the two walked back the way they came. This time, though, they reached their street without running into the Santa or his golden bell.

"He's probably back in his workshop," Nick joked awkwardly, and Annie glared at him. "Okay, why don't we change out of these pajamas and walk back into town to explore the stores and try to talk to more people," Nick suggested as they instinctively veered toward their homes.

"Could we have breathed in some kind of toxic gas?" Annie asked him, gulping the air as if to taste it and determine what was poisoning them. "Or, like, maybe it's an alien attack and this is how humans become extinct," Annie said, about to bite a cuticle out of habit before admiring how well-manicured her hands looked and resisting the familiar urge.

"But what a way to go, right?" Nick smiled, stopping in front of Annie's house.

"Eh," Annie shrugged. "Christmas is so cliché, you know?"

"Ah, glad to see Annie's bah-humbug routine made its way here too," Nick said, a small smile tugging at the corners of his mouth.

"You sound like Marsha," Annie groaned.

"Hey, did you see a suitcase in your room?" Nick asked.

"Oh, yeah, there was a bag with my initials on it. What's that about?" Annie asked him.

"Mine was mostly full of red and green turtleneck sweaters and peacoats," Nick said.

"Multiple peacoats?" Annie asked.

"Oh, and a few plaid flannel shirts too."

"Wow. Should we do a fashion montage moment of unboxing my suitcase?" Annie joked.

"Sure!" Nick grinned, eagerly nodding.

"I was kidding, but, yeah, we should check mine." Annie opened her front door and led the way upstairs. When Nick entered the room right behind her, she got a shy, nervous feeling.

"I don't think I've ever been in your room before," Nick said.

"Really? I guess your folks had most of the neighborhood parties and gatherings, huh?" Annie asked. *Is it weird that Nick's in my bedroom*, she thought. *He's like a true grown-up now.* But it's not like this was her real bedroom; this was some weird costume her childhood bedroom was wearing.

"I was scared to come to your house," Nick admitted.

"Why?" Annie asked.

"Your sister had that pet snake," Nick said with a small shudder.

"Oh, yeah, Elise had a real reptile phase for a few years. But don't worry, no snakes here now," Annie reassured him, reaching for the suitcase. It was much heavier than she expected. She looked toward Nick, hoping he'd lend a hand. He lifted it easily without saying a word.

"Where would you like it? Your bed?" he asked. Annie blushed and nodded. *Ew, why am I blushing?* Annie asked herself, unable to shake the nervous feeling floating around her belly. Once the bag was on top of her comforter, they both peered over it, like two children finding a treasure chest at the beach. "Open it!" Nick encouraged. Annie took a breath and unzipped the bag.

CHAPTER FIVE

"It's blinding!" Annie gasped once the suitcase was fully opened, pulling out white item after white item. A white coat, a white sweater, a shimmery white blouse, and a white hat with a white pom-pom on its top. Annie dumped out the remaining items. "Wait, where are the actual shoes? There are only heels in here." Annie looked at Nick as if he might know why this was her only footwear. He let out a sigh. "What is it?" Annie demanded.

"The women in these movies are always stomping around the snow in stilettos."

"No way. No. No one would ever believe that's a normal thing that actual humans do. And I don't do heels anymore, we're archenemies, and yes, that pun was intended," Annie proclaimed, high-fiving herself. "And I'm way too messy for all this white winter wear."

"Apparently, not in this alternative place. I think you're Made-for-TV Christmas Movie Annie now. And maybe this is exactly what you'd wear here. In any *case*, pun also intended . . . because it's a suitcase . . ." Nick grinned, holding his hand up, but when Annie didn't joyfully slap it, he moved to the door. "I'll let you get dressed. And I'll go change too."

"You're going to have to carry me there if I'm in these shoes!" Annie wailed, holding up a pair of red peep-toes. Nick laughed, and Arthur wove between his legs, making a figure eight of affection before jingling and jumping inside the open suitcase.

"Well, that's absolutely adorable." Nick pointed at Arthur as he slowly blinked. When Annie tried to shoo both boys away, she noticed an ornament tied to the top of her bag's handle.

"What's this?" Annie asked Nick as he turned back. She reached for it and untied it; it read, "Math puns are the first *sine* of madness." "That's horrific," Annie gasped, truly tormented by the gruesome geekiness. "Was this on your bag too?" Annie asked Nick.

"Mine had an ornament that said, 'You mean snow much to me' with two cartoon snow people sharing one red scarf," Nick said, but he seemed suddenly stiffer and wouldn't meet Annie's eyes. Before she could push him on it, though, he made another move for the door. "I'll let you get ready, see you in a few minutes."

Annie pieced together an outfit of pristine, high-cut, dark-washed jeans with silver buttons instead of a zipper, matched with one of the many white sweaters. She grabbed the hat and white coat and tried to pick the shoe with the smallest heel. Annie glimpsed the mirror and was surprised to see she looked quite pretty. Her hair fell in loose waves around her face, and she mused that it gave a redder impression than its usual brown, wondering if it was a trick of the light or another movie side effect. Her cheeks were pink and rosy with a pleasant glow that Annie hoped she could one day recreate with the right blush and highlighter. The pom-pom hat only further complemented her face. *I am freaking adorable*, Annie marveled. Well, dream, mysterious gas outbreak, and/or potential alien attack aside, at least she felt cute.

"Oh!" Nick breathed when he saw her again, waiting patiently outside her front door. He was wearing a crisp green flannel shirt topped with a dark emerald peacoat. His cheeks flushed and he looked down at his feet.

"What do you think?" Annie asked.

"You look straight out of a movie," Nick said softly.

"When in Rome and all that," Annie said, sweeping away his compliment while secretly inviting it to curl up across her chest for safekeeping. She didn't like that she was so desperate for a compliment from a guy that she would allow the words of Nick, her forever nerdy neighbor, to resonate so thoroughly, but it was still nice to hear. "Shall we?" Annie asked, gliding onto the front porch in graceful clicks.

Annie was relieved that while the ground (and her car) were covered in permanent fluffy snow, it still didn't feel all that cold; in fact, it was downright pleasant. She felt most comfortable with her jacket open, collarbone exposed. And she never once wished for the company of a scarf. But most miraculously, her heeled feet maneuvered with unusual ease, like Annie was skating on a supportive cloud.

"Let's start with the café. Are you hungry?" Nick asked once they could see Main Street in all its glory.

"Alarmingly, I don't feel very hungry. But, sure, I could always eat," Annie said. Nick nodded and led them closer.

"Déjà Brew?" Annie asked. "That's the name of the café?"

"It's a cute pun," Nick said, opening the door for them. The air smelled like thick apple pie slices fresh from the oven. There was an instrumental track playing that seemed vaguely familiar and festive, clearly some wordless off-brand Christmas song they could get the rights for. Next to a large, brightly lit Christmas tree, there was a bakery display full of decorated cakes, showcasing rows of red and green icing. The whole place was giving cozy but very early 2000s. When the door jingled closed behind Annie and Nick, everything halted, and everyone inside turned to look at the newcomers. For a moment, no one moved or said a word; Annie could feel their strange stares scorching into them.

"Nicholas Laurel?" a high-pitched, sugary sweet voice called out. Nick turned to look.

"Bailey Jones?" he asked, his mouth open wide. Annie was unsure why they were both inclined to include last names.

"I didn't know you were back," Bailey breathed. Nick seemed momentarily stunned as Bailey moved closer, and the two embraced in a slow-motion hug. Annie took a step back to take Bailey in. She was like a small bright light absorbing Nick and making him shine alongside her. Her hair was so blonde it was nearly white, with bangs that framed her heart-shaped face. Made-for-TV Christmas movie Bailey Jones looked like a doll that had come to life, or perhaps the Christmas angel on top of a tree, now staring up at Nick and asking him to please play with her.

"Whoa, are you a news anchor?" Annie asked, and both Nick and Bailey stared at her. Bailey let out a giggle that sounded more like a twinkling chime than actual laughter. "Your hair has real news anchor energy." Annie shrugged, and Nick and Bailey went back to making eyes at each other.

"I'm house-sitting for my folks. They're on a cruise," Nick babbled. "Do you still live in town?"

"I came back home to help my parents with the café," she smiled, gesturing around the room. "Business had been, well, a little slow," Bailey whispered to Nick. "But things seem to be picking up now that I'm here baking all the cupcakes and cookies," Bailey finished proudly. "Can I get you a table?" Bailey asked, glancing back at Annie. "Um, together?" Her eyes looked pained at the idea of Nick and Annie sharing a table for two.

"We're just neighbors," Annie assured her, not wanting Bailey to experience another moment of anguish that she was so clearly projecting all over her sweet baby doll angel face. Bailey bit down on her perfectly pink lip, smoothed her broadcast-ready hair, and smiled, leading them to a booth in the back corner.

"I'll seat you in the antique section," Bailey cooed, "It's my favorite spot in the café."

"This is also an antique shop?" Annie asked.

"We carry a few curated items. It's in honor of my great-grandfather, Wally Jones, who once owned this store. He was an avid collector and loved showcasing his special treasures for the town of Simsbury, especially during the Christmas season," Bailey explained. "See, here's a picture of him!" She pointed to a black-and-white picture of an attractive young man framed at eye level to their table. "Isn't he a dish?" Bailey sighed.

"A dish?" Annie asked.

"So handsome," Bailey said, looking fondly at the picture.

"Woof. Hard-on for ole great-grampy much?" Annie whispered to Nick, and he nudged her quickly in the ribs. Annie let out a sharp gasp of surprise, awakening Bailey from her trance.

"Well, I'll let you look over the menu," Bailey purred to Nick. Annie felt slightly stupefied by her big unblinking eyes and her breathy, high-pitched voice. "Can I start you with some hot chocolates? We have the traditional and peppermint cocoa blends today."

"What kind of iced coffee do you have?" Annie asked. There was a sound of glass shattering somewhere nearby. "Is it just regular or do you have other flavors?" Annie continued, ignoring the change in the air. "And what kind of milk alternatives do you have? Can I get oat milk? Wait, what brand of oat milk is it?" Annie asked, and Bailey looked increasingly horrified. Couples at nearby tables turned around to stare, mouths set in open O-shapes of terror.

"She's kidding!" Nick assured the onlookers. Some smiled, and some clutched their hearts and sighed in relief. "Oh, Annie, always the jokester!" Nick said through gritted teeth, emitting a loud forced laugh. Bailey joined in on his laughter and walked back to the kitchen, shaking her head.

"Nick. Are you telling me I can't get iced coffee here?" Annie asked fearfully.

"This seems like an exclusively cocoa town," Nick said, raising his eyebrows.

"I drink three or four iced coffees a day!" Annie whisper-wailed.

"Geez, try some water," Nick cringed, the idea of all that iced coffee clearly physically paining him.

"I mean, there's water in the ice . . ." Annie muttered.

"That still seems like an excessive amount of caffeine." Nick grimaced.

"Don't you dare judge me, made-for-TV Christmas movie watcher boy," Annie hissed. "I'm in a place called Déjà Brew and they don't have coffee? And what's the deal with your girlfriend? Was she always like that?"

"Honestly, the last time I talked to her, she was wasted on pumpkin beer near the butter sculpture at the Big E. I don't think she'd remember it . . . But back in high school? She was lovely, honestly, a perfect first girlfriend."

"I get it, she's hot." Annie nodded, assuming Nick's understandable attraction for his ex. "But also, like, clearly attracted to her ancestor. She's straight out of a horror movie. It's scary.

"What? No, she's a sweet, small-town girl . . ." Nick sputtered.

"Annie Meyers, is that you?" a voice sang out. "Oh my, with Nick Laurel? Are you two married now?"

"What? Ugh, um, big no," Annie answered quickly before she looked to see who she was responding to. "Grant?" Annie asked, studying the well-dressed man standing in front of them. His perfectly tailored, pristine white button-down shirt and navy dress pants looked like they had been specifically designed for his slim, small frame. His clean-shaven face radiated under a full head of thick black hair that looked even more lustrous and voluminous in this café lighting.

There was a youthful quality to his appearance that reminded her of elementary school Grant. He would make his presence known by trying to corral everyone on their bus route to sing "One Day More" from *Les Misérables* or

"Carrying the Banner" from *Newsies* under his lead before the bus driver inevitably yelled at him to "zip it." Clearly, growing up in Simsbury had helped pave the path to Grant's prominent standing within the Connecticut drag community.

"Grant! Oh, I've never been so happy to see you!" Annie squealed, so grateful to recognize a friend, and jumped up to hug him. In his ear, she whispered, "How did you get here?"

"Annie, hello," Grant replied a little stiffly. "It's so nice to see you both," Grant smiled at Nick.

"Are you back home for the holidays?" Nick asked.

"I just moved back—" Grant started.

"What?" Annie cut in, shaking her head in disbelief.

"I inherited my great-aunt's inn," Grant said simply. Annie's face clouded in confusion. Grant's parents had moved their family from Korea to Connecticut when he and his sister were kids, and this was the first time Annie had heard about a great-aunt or an inn associated with his family in Simsbury.

"But I saw you yesterday at the office party—" Annie began as Grant stared back at her blankly. "Wow, okay, we'll circle back to that. Can I borrow your phone for a second?" Annie asked. When Grant didn't reply, she added, "Look, I promise I won't snoop into your hidden pictures, or try to read all your recent notes again. I learned my lesson—"

"Sorry, Annie, my phone doesn't have a usable signal, so I left it at the inn," Grant said.

"No, you would never leave without it," Annie said, though Grant didn't appear to hear her.

"You run an inn?" Nick asked.

"Yes, the Nutmeg Nest," Grant answered.

"What's a nutmeg nest?" Annie asked, but again, Grant didn't hear her. "Grant, you can't be serious about moving back here. Are you going to leave your job? What about your party planning committee? And what's going to happen to Peppermint Patti LuBone?" Annie continued urgently—she could feel this familiar piece of the real world slipping away right before her eyes and there was nothing she could do to stop it.

Before Grant could answer, Bailey carried two large mugs heaped with whipped cream and generous portions of red and green sprinkles their way. "Oh no, she's heading back, protect me," Annie said under her breath.

"On the house. In honor of your house-sitting," Bailey said, batting her eyelashes in Nick's direction. "Oh, hi, Grant! Another cup of your usual?" Bailey asked.

"I'm taking it to go. I hate to say goodbye so soon, but I have to get back to the inn. Let's catch up later? They sure don't make hot chocolates like this in the big city," Grant smiled. Annie studied his eyes for any trace of the classic Grant spark, but that glimmer of mischief and adventure was lacking, leaving behind a flatness Annie found more than disheartening. Before Annie could grab him and try to shake the real Grant free, he waved and made a swift departure.

"Grant, wait!" Annie attempted, but he had disappeared, and Annie fought the desire to cry (or, honestly, simply scream) with frustration. For a moment, she thought Grant could be an exit out, not another road leading straight back to this madness. She turned to voice this to Nick, but he was locked in another staring contest with Bailey. Annie had no interest in watching them rekindle their love affair; she needed to brainstorm another way out.

"I'm going to go and um, freshen up. Re-tuck my sweater into my jeans, that sort of business," Annie said, waving two finger guns, but both Nick and Bailey seemed incredibly invested in their intense game of eye contact and didn't notice. Annie got up from her chair and ran straight into a broad man carrying perhaps the largest wreath in the history of humankind. Or from the props department of a made-for-TV movie, anyway. The collision sent Annie into an uncharacteristically graceful fall to the ground, her arm angled above her head like she was living out some kind of *America's Next Top Model* pose, already at peak smize. Above her, a chiseled, handsome face poked through the wreath's center.

Annie turned her head and blinked rapidly, trying to make sense of the man now standing over her, as if gallons of cold water had been suddenly dumped on her head. There he was, straight from the naughty list, in a well-pressed navy blue suit and wearing fuzzy reindeer antlers with bells, a look of surprise mirroring Annie's own.

CHAPTER SIX

"Chris?" Annie gurgled, part breath, part bark.

"Annie Meyers," Chris said, his eyes opening wide before a smile settled over his face, his long limbs striding to her in sweeping steps, his antler ears jingling lightly. Annie jumped up, allowing Chris to take her two hands, while still somehow holding the wreath, to squeeze her fingers.

"Ugh, hi," Annie whispered as the two of them took a pregnant pause to make quiet, strange eye contact. Annie shook her head and pried each finger back one by one, trying to focus. "Wait, what's going on? Why are you here?"

"I stepped away from my important business job in the big city to become an elementary school teacher and help out at my family's Christmas tree farm," Chris explained, his eyes twinkling. Annie scrunched her forehead in confusion. Chris had a job with some insurance company and lived in Middletown, Connecticut; in no world was it an "important business job" in a "big city." Annie studied him a bit more, struck that he was looking more clean-cut Canadian cute than the previous hot she remembered. "I'm sure that seems rather boring compared to your fashion background in the big city."

"What? No, I live and work in West Hartford." Annie reminded him. But when Chris didn't recognize the town, she continued, "You know, the one that's also in Connecticut and like twenty minutes away from here." Chris didn't react. "Okay, well, um, I guess you could say I work in apparel . . ." Annie started, nibbling the inside of her cheek, wracking her brain for any instances in which she had ever talked to Chris about her unconventional start-up. Chris stared back with a glazed look that could only be described as "dumbfounded mannequin."

"Annie, I can't believe you're really here," Chris said.

"Yeah, I don't know what to believe myself anymore," Annie said, examining his features.

"Seeing you again is bringing me back to all the memories and moments we made together," Chris said with an unfamiliar fervor. "What brings you to our small town?"

"Huh? I grew up here," Annie said in return, still unable to rationalize the person standing in front of her or any of the words coming out of his mouth. "What's up with the wreath?" Annie asked after a moment of Chris not saying anything. She tried to keep herself from clapping her hands together to see if Chris would blink.

"We're delivering wreaths to some of the local spots in town," Chris said proudly.

"Of course. Well, it smells great and it's so big. Like, so big." Annie said.

"Thank you!" Chris grinned, taking the compliment as if Annie had remarked on his own scent and size rather than the outstanding ring of foliage. Annie looked around to see if Nick would step in as backup; she wasn't sure how to navigate any part of these odd communications. But Nick was still wrapped up in his own Twilight Zone episode.

"I don't remember your family living in Simsbury. We didn't go to school together," Annie said, wondering if this Chris was anything like the one she had known in the real world or if this guy was someone completely new.

"We've had the farm for generations," Chris said, not answering Annie's question. Instead, he paused and squinted his eyes, like he was trying to fight a fire in his brain. "Now that I'm a teacher, my job is to direct the school's holiday play . . . though this year, most of our volunteer crew is stuck outside of town thanks to the big snowstorm. No one can pass Simsbury Mountain," Chris continued miserably. "As you know, each year the proceeds from the play are gifted to a local family business," Chris began.

"How would I know that?" Annie asked.

"And this year, there are so many worthy establishments that could benefit from those funds. Including our Christmas tree farm. We struggle sustaining the business in the offseason, which is about eleven months of the year."

"You're joking, right?" Annie asked, wanting to laugh. This was more unreal than the snow atop her car.

"I wish I were, Annie," Chris said forlornly. "It's a true crisis. The spirit of Christmas is in jeopardy. Especially because now the show is in danger of being canceled."

"Cancel the town's Christmas production?" an older man listening to their conversation interjected. "Why, it hasn't been canceled in over a hundred years!"

"A hundred years? I was never a part of a Christmas show when we were kids . . ." Annie mumbled.

"The show must go on, Annie. The whole town is depending on us. The spirit of Christmas is in jeopardy," Chris repeated, his voice urgent.

"The 'spirit of Christmas'?" Annie asked, furrowing her brow.

"Don't worry, Chris," Bailey said, suddenly standing right next to them and making Annie jump in her stilettos. "We'll all chip in and help."

"What? No, I couldn't ask you to do that," Chris said, his eyes growing misty as he connected with Bailey.

"It's the town's Christmas show! We have to do whatever we can! Right, guys?" Bailey asked.

"Is she talking to us?" Annie whispered to Nick, grateful someone with any kind of sense was in her proximity again, even if it was only her nerdy next-door neighbor. "Why the fu—" Annie started as a warped version of "The Little Drummer Boy" began on the old Victrola placed in the antique section. "Don't hurt me, ghost of 2004 Jessica Simpson," Annie breathed out, squeezing her eyes shut and silently promising to the whole Simpson family to watch her language. When the music stopped its warning, Annie turned back to Nick, "Why would we get involved in a Christmas show?"

"We won't let Simsbury down. It wouldn't be Christmas without the school production of *A Christmas Carol*!" Bailey cheered.

"*A Christmas Carol*?" Annie groaned, her eyes immediately rolling back into her skull.

"Count us in," Nick caved under the expectant stares. Bailey cheered and gave his shoulder a small squeeze. Annie punched his other arm.

"What is wrong with you?" Annie hissed in Nick's ear, dragging him back outside. "I don't want anything to do with some weird town play! They're probably going to try and sacrifice us to Santa on the stage after we all overdose on poisonous hot chocolate."

"Annie, what was I supposed to say? And, what else are we going to do?" Nick asked.

"I don't know, anything else," Annie cried out. "Literally, anything else!"

"We don't have access to our phones or the internet, we can't even watch TV or stream a movie," Nick explained.

"No TV? I'm going to die here!" Annie wailed.

"Maybe the way through this thing is just that, we have to go *through* it. It could be that we've been put here for some reason, so why not embrace all these clichés and maybe, by Christmas, all of this will go back to normal."

"No," Annie said, shaking her head. "I'm not at the same stage of grief as you are. How dare you already be accepting this! Grant doesn't own an inn and would never be caught dead without his phone. And that other guy I was talking to in there? The one that is apparently a town regular with a family who owns a Christmas tree farm and who is now directing the yearly Christmas play? I know him from my real life, and that's *not* him," Annie said, her head still shaking, trying to make any sense of what was going on.

"What do you mean?" Nick asked.

"Like, I *know* him," Annie said, gritting her teeth.

"He's your boyfriend?" Nick asked coolly.

"What? No!" Annie said. "He's someone I had, um, a 'moment' or two with," Annie said, still trying to keep her voice to a whisper. "I haven't talked to him since Halloween."

"Since you were 1999 Fabio on a roller coaster?" Nick asked.

"Well, technically, I was Sexy Fabio on a roller coaster post goose," Annie started.

"Yeah, that goes without saying." Nick smiled.

"Wait, you remember my costume? How?" Annie asked. Nick turned another shade of pink as Annie reminisced over the long-sleeved, blue, button-down shirt she had painstakingly altered by hand and the small stuffed goose she had proudly sewn the word "silly" on with black thread. The Fabio wig had gone into a Goodwill donation bin right after she left Chris's apartment for the last time. It conjured too many ick-filled memories for Annie to ever consider wearing it again, but she hoped that perhaps another kindred spirit would find it and use it to fulfill a mutually satisfying sexual journey outside of the truly lackluster experience it had provided for her.

"It was a good costume," Nick mused, "theatrically speaking . . . I remember your Instagram picture . . . and the silly goose," Nick added with a small appreciative laugh.

"Oh. Okay. Thank you," Annie said, her cheeks feeling a bit flushed. "I put a lot of time into it."

"I could tell," Nick said.

"Listen," Annie said, refusing to be distracted by a compliment, "I don't want to be a part of any of this. Can't we just go back home and drink until we black out?"

"I need to tell you something," Nick started.

"No," Annie said in a whisper, already anticipating what he was about to say.

"I'm pretty sure there's no alcohol here," Nick said, confirming her worst fears.

"What? No, my parents have a full bar at home, and your folks had quite the stash too if memory serves." Annie laughed, but there was a nervous edge to her voice. Nick shook his head sadly.

"Not anymore," Nick admitted. "I haven't been able to find a drop of anything anywhere. Remember that pack of seasonal seltzers in my garage? They vanished. Even the peppermint ones."

"They don't drink in made-for-TV Christmas movies?" Annie asked, tugging on her hat so it covered her eyes for a needed moment.

"Rarely, and it's maybe like a sip of celebratory champagne after a victorious town event and only at the very end of the movie."

Annie ripped the hat off her head and flung it at Nick. When that wasn't a satisfying release of her feelings, she grabbed a handful of snow, sculpted it into a quick ball, and hurled it at Nick's face, letting out a scream of frustration. She grabbed another fistful when Nick ducked and slipped, grabbing Annie's jacket as he fell, carrying her down with him.

"Nick!" Annie yelled once the two had landed softly in the snow. Nick laughed. "It's not funny! I'm still in these fu—no, I need a new word, stilettos!"

"Look! They're making snow angels!" a young voice called out in glee. "May we please join the fun?" Annie looked up to see a noticeably well-dressed group of children marching closer in a united line of red and green. "Hurry, help me up!" she gasped. "They're coming for us!"

"We're not in a horror movie, Annie," Nick said while giving the kids a friendly wave. Once the group was closer, they each gracefully fell into the soft snow and began moving their arms and legs.

"This really is the best time of year, isn't it?" one child said and grinned at Nick.

"I'll carry these memories in my heart forever and cherish them for all of my days," another child added.

"We're so fortunate to live in a place that celebrates and honors this special season," a third child said and smiled.

"Why are they talking like that?" Annie whispered to Nick.

"Like what?" Nick asked.

"Like they're old people or something. It's creepy as f—," Annie said, cutting herself off and clearing her throat. "Okay, clearly I use that word more than any other profanity, I need a workaround . . . creepy as . . . truck," she finished, smug that she hadn't set off a sound nightmare.

"They're sweet," Nick told her, diving back into the snow to make his own angel.

"You're beautiful," a little blonde girl said, staring up at Annie.

"Oh, thanks," Annie said, softening just a little.

"I hope I look just like you when I grow up," the little child sighed. Annie emitted a nervous huff and gave the girl a small smile.

"You're beautiful too," Annie told her truthfully.

"You kind of look like my mom," the little girl started.

"Really?" Annie asked.

"My dad really misses her," the girl said simply.

"Where did she go?" Annie asked.

"She died," the little girl said through now tear-filled eyes.

"Nope, nope, nope!" Annie said, shaking her head. She refused to engage in this one. Even if she wasn't the holiday movie expert that Nick was, she recognized the popular trope. She wanted nothing more to do with this adorable little girl and her heartbroken father.

"Holly!" a voice called.

"Hi, Daddy!" the little girl yelled. Annie turned to see Chris heading their way with a huge smile.

"I see you've met Annie!" Chris grinned.

"You have a child?!" Annie gasped at Chris. "Why didn't you ever mention that?"

"Annie has come to save the day. She is going to help us with the play!" Chris proclaimed, missing Annie's complete shock, and Holly hugged Annie's legs, almost knocking her back to the ground.

"Is it true?" Holly asked Annie. Annie let out a small, choked cough in response.

"She's going to be in charge of the costumes. Father Christmas was watching out for us. Sending in someone with a big-city fashion background." Chris smiled warmly at Annie.

"Or maybe it was Mommy," Holly said to Chris. "She's always looking down on us," Holly said softly, and Chris nodded. "This is going to be the best Christmas ever!" Holly cheered after a moment. "Well, the best Christmas since we lost Mommy," Holly added, suddenly somber again. The yo-yo display of emotion was making Annie incredibly uncomfortable, but Chris, looking toward his daughter, his face now crestfallen, made it almost too much to bear.

"I hate it here," Annie said into her hands before looking around for Nick and not the guy who had dumped her in a dingy bedroom, who apparently now had both a dead wife and a child.

"Who is that?" Holly asked her dad, pointing over at Nick, who was still making frantic motions in the snow with the other children.

"Nick!" Annie yelled to him. He jumped up like a happy puppy, his pants coated in snow, a huge grin on his face. "Come introduce yourself to Holly," Annie said, her teeth glued together. "And then, we should probably get back home. I think I left a cinnamon-spiced candle burning!"

"Annie, you're so funny, you can't go home yet, the snowman competition starts in ten minutes!" Holly laughed.

"So?" Annie asked.

"I thought she'd want to be on our team," Holly said, looking toward Chris. "She doesn't want to be on our team, Daddy?"

"I'm sure Annie is busy; she's a very successful big-city businesswoman," Chris said, unable to meet Annie's questioning stare. Holly let out a sad whimper and grabbed her dad's hand.

"Don't make the kid cry!" Nick said to Annie, now standing beside her. "Can I be on your team too?" Nick asked Holly.

"I hate you," Annie mouthed silently to Nick.

"No such thing as hate here," Nick muttered back, "you mildly dislike me at the moment." Annie shook her head in annoyance and looked up to the sky. It had turned a beautiful cotton candy pink color, lighting everything in sight in a warm haze.

"Wow," Annie whispered. Nick looked up.

"Yeah," he said.

"It's like it's been filtered. I wish I could make this into an Instagram story . . ." Annie murmured, her hands itching for the weight of her familiar phone and its many functions.

"Let's take a selfie!" Nick said. "The camera is the only thing that sometimes appears and actually opens on my phone."

"Huh?" Annie asked, but Nick had already whipped out his phone. Annie saw a flash of the mistletoe and snow couple cartoon and couldn't help but laugh at the ridiculousness of it.

"Got it!" Nick said.

"Ew, no, take it again! I wasn't even looking the right way!" Annie scolded him. Nick obediently held out his arm to take another picture, waiting for Annie's nod.

"Are you guys okay?" Chris chuckled cautiously. Annie and Nick turned toward him, remembering he was still standing there.

"Capturing some holiday memories," Nick smiled and tucked the phone back into his coat pocket. "So, Holly, can I be on your snowman team?"

"Do you also have a fashion background?" Holly asked, her tone playfully scrutinizing.

"Well, no, but I do have a lot of theatrical, scene construction experience. I help build sets for various Broadway touring shows," Nick said.

"Broadway shows?" Annie asked.

"Yeah," Nick shrugged.

"That's actually pretty cool," Annie said. "I thought you were like a weird roadie or something."

"A weird roadie? Ouch," Nick said, shaking his head. "Um, no. Being a tech theater kid in high school can have a pretty cool career trajectory," Nick said rather proudly.

"Nick is also helping us with the town holiday show," Chris explained to Holly, and her already big eyes grew larger before she hugged Nick's leg. He looked way more excited by the attention than Annie had.

"Thank you, thank you both! It'll be the best Christmas ever!" Holly smiled. "Now let's go win a snowman competition!"

CHAPTER SEVEN

Chris offered Annie his arm. She stood dumbfounded for a moment before realizing she was expected to link her own through his so he could lead them to this snowman event. For so many late nights after meeting at bars, waiting to catch a ride back to his apartment, Annie had yearned for him to take her hand. She had even grabbed his once, only for him to immediately drop hers like it was on fire. Chris had always hated that type of public intimacy, at least with her.

This must be how we lady folk walk around town in these movies, Annie thought, *our feet in heels and our arms linked to some man*. Though even as it made her internally roll her eyes and want to thrash wildly against the heteronormativity of it all, a part of her reveled in the simple warmth and support of someone walking beside her. She gave in to it and wove her arm into the space. Annie tried not to overthink the last positions their bodies had taken together and did her best to silence any feelings of wanting to recreate them again, knowing this was not the same man she was used to. Annie turned back to see Nick and Holly behind them, already engaged in a deep discussion about snowman design.

"Holly seems like a great kid," Annie said after a moment of silence.

"She truly is," Chris gushed proudly. "She thinks the world of you."

"What? She literally just met me . . ." Annie stuttered uncomfortably.

"Annie, look at you," Chris said, stopping mid-step to stare at her. Annie was sure she was blushing now. "You're extraordinary." Chris said it so earnestly, so easily, and Annie had the weirdest sensation that she was going to burst into tears. The force of a simple, genuine compliment like this, so foreign to her, especially from a person who had never before offered more than a fleeting spot in his bed.

"Thank you. That's very sweet," Annie told Chris, her voice guttural, trying to fight the emotion of the moment. She felt pathetic, allowing a basic acclamation to take her breath away. "And you seem like a wonderful dad," Annie added after clearing her throat. Whoa, this was a lot. Chris had always made Annie feel like she was asking for more than he was willing to give; he had never once presented as the "fatherly type." In fact, he had vehemently rejected that idea. And yet here he was, modeling it like it had been his life's calling.

"That's the best compliment there is," Chris smiled before taking on an emotive, faraway look. Annie had only ever seen Chris this emotional after making her listen to forty-five minutes of a bootleg Phish concert on one of the first nights she had gone home with him.

"So, what are we in for tonight with this snowman contest?" Annie asked, trying to lighten the mood as they approached what looked to be a gazebo set in the middle of a squared-in, snowy park. Small groups of people cluttered the decorated perimeters, their winter gear blending in with the red banners and small white lights, preparing for what appeared to be a well-populated event.

"You're in for 'snow' much fun!" Grant chirped, suddenly popping up from a crowd like he was about to deliver his showstopping musical solo. Annie let out an involuntary gasp of surprise. "How are your trivia skills?" Grant grinned.

"Ugh," Annie uttered before clearing her throat and trying to speak. "I'd say I'm an expert in all things Bravo."

"Bravo?" Chris asked curiously, trying the word out in his mouth like it was an unknown bite of food.

"I mean, pop culture?" Annie pivoted, unsure how her already limited trivia knowledge would translate in this weird world.

"Hmm, pop culture." Chris murmured, his forehead wrinkling in deep thought.

"I'll be the master of ceremonies tonight, and I have a list of Christmas-inspired trivia questions," Grant interjected.

"And what's more popular in our culture than Christmas? Annie, you'll be an asset!" Chris cheered in relief.

"I thought this was a snowman decorating contest," Annie said, narrowing her eyes at Grant in question. "Why are we overcomplicating that with trivia?"

"Well, once the competition officially begins, I'll be ringing the trivia bell announcing a new question. If your team answers correctly, you'll win another prop to use in your design," Grant beamed.

"Oh, what fun," Annie said flatly.

"—it is to ride in a one-horse open sleigh, hey!" Chris sang out loudly, drawing smiles from onlookers ready to sing along with him.

"Looks like someone is ready for the Christmas music round," Grant winked at Annie as he turned to welcome another group of participants.

"So every single question is going to be Christmas-themed?" Annie asked, grimacing at Nick.

"Annie, you're so funny. Of course, it's Christmas-themed," Bailey giggled, abruptly popping back into their small group. "Too bad we can't all be on a team together," Bailey sighed, gazing at Nick. "I'll be competing with my family, of course, in honor of Great-Grandpa Wally and the bakery. But win or lose, drinks on me! Can I grab anyone a beverage?"

"Wait, did you say something about drinks?" Annie asked Bailey hopefully.

"It's going to be hot chocolate again, Annie," Nick said so quietly that only Annie could hear it.

"I can whip us up a fresh batch of cocoa," Bailey chirped.

"Bailey," Annie said urgently, "I have to ask. Is there, um, anything stronger you can add to my hot chocolate?"

"Stronger?" Bailey asked, her eyes growing again to that glassy doll stare.

"Yeah," Annie nodded. "To boost it up a bit?"

"More than marshmallows?" Bailey asked.

"More than marshmallows," Annie confirmed. Bailey's face crinkled in deep concentration for a few moments.

"Well, I have heard of a recipe, but, no, that's simply too crazy . . ." Bailey wondered aloud, nibbling on the corner of her pink heart lips.

"What's too crazy?" Annie inquired back. "I would really, really love to know what you think is too crazy, Bailey." Annie could feel the tension radiating from Nick and knew she was pushing some delicate boundaries with her inquisition.

"It's an . . . ethnic recipe," Bailey began, her voice quiet like she was afraid that if she continued, she'd be arrested for speaking so boldly.

"What the truck." Annie shook her head, cringing. "How is she allowed to say that? Why isn't a scary sound cutting her off?" Annie asked Nick, who could only offer a small shrug. "I mean, please, go on," Annie said, stepping closer to Bailey.

"It's called a 'Mexican hot chocolate'!" Bailey said, and a hush came over the group.

"Wow!" Chris said, looking like an eager child.

"So a hot chocolate with a little cinnamon and chili powder?" Annie asked, her voice now chagrined.

"Yes!" Bailey squealed, clasping a hand over her mouth like she couldn't quite believe it. "How did you know that?"

"She's from the big city," Chris said sheepishly, "She probably drinks stuff like that all the time."

"The only drink I need from Mexico is tequila," Annie complained to Nick, and he shot her a death stare, obviously wanting her to leave things alone.

"Chili powder . . . in hot chocolate! Can you imagine?" Chris asked Bailey, still shaking his head in awe.

"I can't!" Bailey giggled, covering her face in her hands.

"Fine, yeah, I'll take it," Annie told Bailey. "If you can make me one, I would love to try it." Bailey stopped laughing immediately.

"Seriously?" Bailey asked, terrified.

"Annie," Nick said with a sharp edge of warning.

"Ugh, fine," Annie told Nick. "I'm kidding, I'm kidding!" Annie said, holding up her hands, and Bailey let out a huge sigh of relief. Chris laughed in utter merriment at the whole scene.

"Oh, my goodness, you got me that time!" Bailey laughed, shaking her head and moving back toward the café, muttering about chili powder.

"Nick, I'm about to chew on glass and chug whatever cleaning products I can find," Annie said, and Nick put on a big exaggerated smile.

"It's true, your sense of humor is unlike anyone else," Nick said loudly. "Why don't you help me secure a spot for our snowman, you silly comedienne?"

"Great idea, I'll help Bailey with our drinks," Chris said, taking an extra beat to stare warmly at Annie. "And maybe I can get us some cookies too."

"Oh, he still likes you," Nick noted once they were alone.

"Who?" Annie asked.

"Who do you think?" Nick asked, glancing around the lit square for an open spot.

"Santa?" Annie asked innocently.

"You wish. Chris, obviously," Nick said.

"He dumped me," Annie said, half-heartedly gesturing to an unused space. "And I am not his type, he made that very clear," Annie muttered, the pangs of the rejection resurfacing before a startling realization passed over her face and she gasped. "Wait. Is that why we're here? To fall in love with these low budget movie actors and, what, save the spirit of Christmas?" Annie could feel a swirl of panic tingling her toes and stretching across her body. "Nick. Please tell me you're just as terrified as I am about being stuck here. You're not, like, secretly hoping you can stay forever, right?"

"No, I'm not secretly hoping that," Nick said, walking over to claim their snowman staging station, but Annie wasn't totally convinced.

"I can't wait to see your design!" Grant exclaimed, returning from his rounds, his hands flying across his chest and lingering near his heart. "It's such an honor to be this evening's host."

"Sounds like you've been busy since you got back to town," Nick remarked.

"You know me, I love being busy!" Grant smiled at Nick.

"And we know you also love gettin' busy," Annie joked, trying to wink at Grant. He didn't pick up on her tone at all.

Annie winced, wishing once again that the Grant she knew would reappear. She thought fondly of that Friday before President's Day, right after Annie and Marsha had moved into the building, when she had crossed Grant's path at the elevator and he had invited her to grab a drink at a nearby bar. Two shots of Mount Rushmore Rum and they made a bet on which one of them could first kiss a man who looked like a past president. It had been inspired by the tall, bearded stranger they had both fallen in lust with while watching him pile loaded nachos into his mouth.

And, sure, he could sort of pass for a relative of Abraham Lincoln. Luckily for Annie, this loose lookalike had allowed her to kiss him first, which led to the technical win. Later that night, though, he had gone home with Grant and gotten Gettysburg undressed. Unfortunately, after their hookup, he promptly passed out and wet the bed before emancipating himself from the presidential suite. But the experience had solidified Annie and Grant's friendship like only a dude peeing your bed can. This Grant would never engage in such blatant tomfoolery.

"It's such a special time of year," Grant continued, unaware of Annie's silent lament. "It's just nice to be back home. There's no place I would rather be than right here." Grant concluded, and Nick nodded.

"Really, Grant? I feel like I could think of a few places you'd prefer . . . oh, and I'm dying to know what happened after the party. Did you take Santa home with you?" Annie prodded, committed to cracking him. Grant gave her a puzzled look, but Annie was determined to poke a hole in this man's costume if he insisted on wearing Grant as his disguise.

Chris broke Annie's investigation, swinging a full tray of steaming hot chocolates and sugar cookies in their direction.

"I got some for you too, buddy," Chris told Grant affectionately.

"Are you trying to butter me up?" Grant asked playfully. "Hey, y'all, Chris is trying to butter me up!" Grant said loudly, grinning.

"*Y'all?* We're in Connecticut," Annie said, wondering why everyone seemed so eager to weave in and out of stereotypical Southern charm. "You know Grant's imagining Chris rubbing butter all over his chest," Annie told Nick.

Chris reached for a sugar cookie and took an enormous bite; the sound of sugar cracked and echoed in Annie's ear. Her stomach flipped in response, desperately wishing for anything other than the current offerings. Not because she was especially hungry, the made-for-TV Christmas movie haze must be delaying her usual voracious appetite, but because the thought of only existing on hot chocolate and sugar cookies made her uneasy. Where was Marsha with her purse always full of snacks and quick dinner options when you needed her? The thought of her best friend made Annie ache. What she wouldn't give to have Marsha nearby, for so many reasons, and instead she was stuck with Nick and a bunch of weird pod people.

"I'm going to finish setting up," Grant smiled. "You better clear those ears out, because our first trivia question involves music lyrics," Grant winked and mimed locking up his mouth and throwing an invisible key into his cup of hot chocolate. He grabbed a pair of reindeer antlers and welcomed another group of participants.

"Don we now our gay apparel . . ." Annie murmured.

"Annie, we haven't started yet!" Bailey laughed, appearing by Nick's side.

"You're a natural at this," Chris told her reassuringly. Annie sighed and took a sugar cookie to dip into her hot chocolate.

"Fa-la-la la-la la-la-la-la!" Annie sang, directing her voice at Nick, her mouth now crammed with cookies. Nick grabbed a cookie, keeping strong direct eye contact, and gingerly placed the entire thing in his mouth.

"Troll the ancient yuletide carol," Nick grinned back with small bits of cookie across his front teeth, and despite herself, Annie smiled.

Grant's voice, which was now mic'd and coming from multiple speakers surrounding the town square space, directed everyone's attention to the small stage where he waved a large flag on a pole. Annie couldn't quite make out the mass of text on it.

"Welcome to the Annual Simsbury Snowman Shaping, Sculpting, and Styling Spectacular Showcase Soiree! Yippee!" Grant managed to get out the tongue twister without stammering and all within one breath. "The Annual Simsbury Snowman Shaping, Sculpting, and Styling Spectacular Showcase Soiree is a true town favorite, and I'm thrilled to be your master of ceremonies." Grant bowed proudly as the crowd cheered.

Once they had finally calmed, Grant continued in a softer, more serious tone, "I know how important the Annual Simsbury Snowman Shaping, Sculpting, and Styling Spectacular Showcase Soiree is to our festive community. This truly is the most magical time of year. Teams of four will compete to create a unique design capturing the joy of the season, but I already consider us all winners of the Annual Simsbury Snowman Shaping, Sculpting, and Styling Spectacular Showcase Soiree for simply being here tonight. When I ring my golden Christmas bell, one member of your team will be sent to grab four props from a designated table. Some things will be bundled and others will be single items. And the other team members can handle the balls."

Annie let out an involuntary small choke of laughter at Grant's earnest usage of "balls." Nick shot her a warning stare before rolling his eyes, and Chris looked on quizzically, unsure what that sound was or why Annie had made it.

"Remember, every five minutes, I'll ring the bell with a new question, and if your team answers correctly, you'll win another prop to use in your design! How is everyone feeling? Are we ready to have 'a ball'?" Grant asked and the crowd let out more cheers. "Have an 'ice' time and I wish you blizzards of success! Ready! Set! Snow!" Grant chanted, rapidly waving the flag and a bell in unison.

Holly squealed in delight, and Chris wrapped an arm around her. Nick glanced at Annie as if waiting for her direction.

"Do you want to start on the snowman, and I can get the props?" Annie suggested. It's not that she had any real interest in participating in this absurdly titled event, but she did have an appreciation for accessories and a deep curiosity about what she could uncover. More importantly, she knew her talents did not lie in snow construction.

Her team nodded, and Annie set off for the tented prop area and its tables at a steady pace. Somehow, though, she wasn't quick enough. When she walked in, the space was empty and most of the items were already gone. How everyone else had managed to secure their items before Annie had walked in seemed suspicious. "Snowman sabotage," Annie muttered, trying to quickly assess her very limited options.

She saw a basket of large pieces of sheer cloth and grabbed it. Next, she saw a ginormous tub of cellophane and white wire, and placed the basket on top, planning to carry out her four items in one go despite their size. She couldn't find a traditional black top hat, but she found a red beret and put it on her head before snatching a lonely orange carrot that had fallen off a table and shoving it in her mouth to bring back to their spot.

Annie knew she must look ridiculous carrying the basket on top of the tub while wearing a beret and lightly keeping a carrot steady between her teeth. But the current of competition raced through her veins. Annie shuffled forward, unable to see much before her and trusting she'd get where she needed to be without much fuss. It should have come as no surprise when her body and all of the items she was carrying collided with three large balls of snow in the process of being transformed into a man, and all of the props went flying into the air.

In the nanoseconds before she went down, Annie saw the sheer fabric pieces escaping in different directions, and for one glorious moment, she was performing an elaborate ribbon dancing routine at the Olympics. She also made out the blur of a rogue, medium-sized, shaggy dog wearing a green bandana who caught the carrot midair in its mouth before immediately bolting from the scene. Just when Annie thought she'd finally found the ground, two arms grabbed for her jacket and softened her landing. The beret slid forward and covered her eyes, momentarily taking away Annie's sight, leaving her blindly unaware of her rescuer.

CHAPTER EIGHT

"Fancy meeting you here," Chris said, lightly moving the beret upward on Annie's forehead with a warm thumb as he held her close. Annie stared up at him open-mouthed (and carrot-less), unable to speak or move.

"Finish this lyric!" Grant's voice sang out around them, "I don't want a lot for Christmas—"

"There is just one thing I need," Chris finished, his unblinking eyes still locked on Annie in his arms.

"Yay, Chris and his team win a special prop from our trivia winner's collection!" Grant cheered as Chris guided Annie back to her feet.

"You saved me," Annie breathed out.

"You should see the other guy," Chris joked, gesturing to the giant snowballs that had once been stacked on top of each other. Nick was trying to gather more snow to round them out, but Chris took large strides over to the fallen balls and lifted the middle-sized one into the air as if it weighed nothing and gingerly placed it on top of the larger mound.

Annie watched, marveling at his impressive strength and skill. Nick let out a small huff before gathering the props Annie had dropped to the ground. Holly was already picking up the colored fabrics as if she, too, were in her own Olympic routine.

"Are you alright, Annie?" Chris asked kindly, turning his head back to her.

"Oh, yeah, I'm more embarrassed than anything. Is our snowman going to be okay?" Annie asked.

"He's perfect," Chris soothed, lifting the third large snowball on top of the other two, effortlessly setting it in place.

"I should have known those hands could handle large balls," Grant encouraged Chris, admiring the progress he had made so far. Annie let out another choked cough of surprise.

"You can't handle them too roughly or you'll risk sacrificing their firmness," Chris nodded. Annie let out a tiny squeak, finding it increasingly difficult to keep her impulse to giggle silenced.

"These balls look like they've been polished," Grant said, stepping closer to their emerging snowman to get a better look. "Am I getting too close? I'd hate for my breath to warm them—"

"Chris! You should go pick out a prop!" Annie yelped. She was sure if this act kept up, she would not be able to contain the crazed scream and/or laugh currently clawing its way up her throat.

"Great idea. Holly, want to join me?" Chris asked.

"Yes, Daddy," Holly smiled, putting her small, gloved hand into Chris's.

"We'll be right back," Chris said, leading Holly to the exclusive prop table. Annie hoped they'd have more luck than she had and turned her attention back to Nick. His fingers moved rapidly with large pieces of white wire and the roll of cellophane.

"Whatcha making over here?" Annie asked.

"I thought we could create a snow globe and place our snowman inside," Nick explained as he worked.

"Oh, wow," Annie considered. "That actually sounds pretty cool . . ."

"Thank you," Nick said, finally pausing a moment to catch her eye before returning to his task. "Glad to see you're okay after that fall," he added, and Annie nodded her thanks.

"What if we used some of the fabric to make it look like that sunset?" Annie asked him after a beat, picking through some of the pieces and pulling out the pink and orange hues. Nick's face brightened, and he gestured for her to keep selecting sunset shades.

By the time Chris and Holly returned carrying a basket containing a red scarf, big black buttons, and a spool of thick black ribbon, Nick and Annie were well into their creative groove, and the foursome worked wordlessly in a shared understanding, pausing only to hear Grant's trivia questions.

The mysterious dog with the bandana returned to the scene of the crime with the carrot intact and dropped it at Annie's feet before running back into the night right before they were ready to close off their snow globe, sealing their man inside of it. Annie handed it to Holly, allowing her to complete his face.

"Did that dog look like Dougie to you?" Nick asked once things had settled and Grant was reviewing the entries.

"Dougie!" Annie said, taking her hands to her heart. "The most pathetic and perfect rescue dog in the world."

"Your grandmother walking the block with Dougie and singing your praises to every neighbor that passed her way is pretty unforgettable. And her bright orange visor—"

"Safety first!" Annie said, imitating her grandmother's voice every time she put on her walking gear and lecturing anyone within a fifty-foot radius on the importance of staying vigilant and cautious, which as a true-crime girly, always resonated.

Annie and her family had fostered Dougie, a mostly blind and mostly deaf senior long-haired Chihuahua mix after finding him abandoned at a rest stop on the way home from a summer vacation to Maine. He had been malnourished and shivering, but Annie had wrapped him in a beach towel and refused to get in the car unless the dog came too. Once they had arrived back in Simsbury it only took a few visits from her grandparents to decide they couldn't live without the little guy and had to have him as their own. They had spoiled him endlessly with homemade meals and beautifully crafted knit clothing items to keep him forever warm and fashionably cozy, and her grandmother had tenderly carried him everywhere when they left the house. Whenever they visited Annie's home, Annie's grandmother would proudly parade Dougie and his latest apparel around the neighborhood, gushing equally about her sweet pup and beautiful grandchildren to any and every person who crossed her path.

"I can't believe you remember Dougie," Annie said softly, turning toward Nick, her body tingling with something she couldn't quite define. She didn't have the chance to think much about it before Grant skipped over to admire their work.

Their entry was truckin' phenomenal. The snow had been easy to mold while never feeling too cold to handle, yet their snowman gave the impression of unflinching stone. The end result was a design that surely defied the laws of nature but was absolutely stunning. Unfortunately, they still lost.

"That contest was rigged!" Annie seethed at Nick through clenched teeth once the winning snowman had been crowned, and the crowd dispersed. Her hands were all fists and fury.

"Oh, my gosh, wasn't that so much fun?" Bailey asked, skipping over. "You guys did such a great job, this is gorgeous, Nick," Bailey said, her big eyes fixed on him.

"Congratulations on your big win," Nick grinned at her. "I love how you made your snowman into a baker. The tray of snow cookies shaped like snowmen was a great touch."

"Thank you, Nick. My great-grandfather, Wally Jones, is looking down on us with pride, I just know it." Bailey smiled, and Annie let out a tiny groan she tried to cover with an exaggerated yawn. "We're going to make snowman cookies at the café tomorrow. But those won't be made of snow," Bailey joked.

"Great. Another non-chocolate cookie," Annie muttered miserably.

"Would you like me to escort Holly home?" a deep voice questioned from behind them. The man had a huge white beard and wore a crimson coat.

"Santa?" Annie whispered as Nick gave her a nudge. Annie couldn't stop staring at the stranger. She was almost certain it was the same man who had been ringing that golden bell with a knowing stare that morning.

"Are you sure, Uncle Felix? I don't want to put you out," Chris started.

"Nonsense, 'tis the season for you young folk to enjoy some holiday cheer!" Uncle Felix chuckled merrily.

"Yes, 'tis the season!" Bailey cheered, her doll eyes still focused on Nick as she batted her eyelashes up at him. "Would you walk me home too?" Bailey asked softly, refusing to blink until Nick nodded.

"Uncle Felix, can you make me some of your famous candy cane cocoa?" Holly asked in a small voice, tugging gently on Felix's coat.

"Holly," Chris warned, but he smiled at his daughter warmly. "Just one cup. And thank you, Uncle Felix. I won't be home too late. I want to make sure Annie gets back safe and sound."

Felix looked toward Annie and winked before turning back to Holly.

"He winked at me!" Annie gasped at Nick and dug her fingers into his arm before Nick shot her a look to take it easy.

"Ready?" Chris asked Annie, offering his arm. She nodded as Nick and Bailey linked up, heading in the opposite direction.

Chris and Annie walked the short distance back to her house, making small talk about their snowman until they reached Annie's doorstep, and he stopped to stare meaningfully into her eyes. It was the stuff of romance movies. But Annie realized, to her dismay, that this may be the first time she had ever soberly taken in his full face. Seeing him like this, so open and present, was nothing like any of their past interactions. For starters, previously they had always been at a tipsy baseline. All her memories of Chris were slightly blurry, and he only ever revealed pieces of himself. The arch of an eyebrow, the defined cut of his jaw, in between the messy make-outs that inevitably transformed into messier "made moments." If Annie was being honest, almost all of their sexual encounters had been confusing and chaotic, and every single one had come with a regrettable hangover. If she were being even more honest, maybe Annie could admit that she couldn't make a good decision when it came to Chris, and she didn't actually like the version of herself who was so desperate to be in his company anyway.

But here she was, completely sober, staring back at another variation of the Chris she had previously known after the closest thing to a date the two had ever experienced. And, okay, sure, the Annual Simsbury Snowman Shaping, Sculpting, and Styling Spectacular Showcase Soiree hadn't been the harrowing affair Annie had originally expected, but she wouldn't exactly have described it as fun. She kept waiting for Grant to showcase some of his legendary pageantry, but, even as the event host, his performance was muted and tame. This was the kid who had once put on a one-man show of *Oklahoma!* in his parents' garage and had his sister sell Girl Scout cookies before and after it so she could meet her quota, for goodness' sake. Annie was still haunted by his interpretation and delivery of the dream ballet sequence and thought of it every time she sank her teeth into a straight-from-the-freezer Thin Mint.

Just like this new version of Grant, Annie was struggling to balance the memories she had of Chris with his made-for-TV Christmas movie counterpart. She kept waiting for the mask to slip, for him to make some inappropriate and blatantly sexual comment or joke that Annie would pretend to find clever and not at all offensive. But so far Chris was committed to this G-rated character.

"Annie Meyers," Chris sighed, snapping her back to the present.

"That's me," Annie said, and when Chris didn't follow that up with any further commentary. "I wasn't expecting to see you here today, like this, it's been . . . well, weird."

"You've only gotten more and more lovely in the time we spent apart," Chris began. Annie was happy to hear she had gotten hotter in the weeks since Halloween. "I should have shared more about my past," Chris concluded in earnest, seeming to take the weight and full responsibility of their previous dynamic.

"Um, about you having a kid? Or a dead wife? Or owning a home in this economy? Yeah, that was all pretty surprising," Annie answered. It still stung to think about how Chris had reacted to his own assumption that Annie was the kind of person who wanted things like a spouse and children in the future, the sentiment never earning her any of his esteem. Sure, maybe she did want those things at some point, but those were secrets she barely let herself consider, let alone topics of discussion with Chris.

"I'd love to share this magical season getting to know each other better," Chris said hopefully. Annie could only stare back, her mouth open, unable to complete a thought, never mind a word. Chris smiled and squeezed Annie's hand. "We're all so grateful to have you and your outstanding talents here. I'm not sure I'll be able to sleep tonight; I'm so delighted to have you at rehearsal tomorrow."

Annie's pulse quickened. Was he hinting that he wanted to "not sleep" together? Should she invite him inside so they could fall back into their normal routine? Except nothing about this was normal. For one, they were both completely sober without the hope of booze to blanket some of the awkwardness. And two, Annie's feelings were complicated. Here he was, this walking heartbreak, saying things she had only ever dreamed about, and Annie was terrified to trust it. She didn't want to make herself vulnerable to the inevitable ending hiding in this holiday haze.

Then again, she didn't have her phone to distract her, and she didn't really want to go back inside alone. Her body longed to lean into his familiar warmth. Annie smoothed her hair, giving Chris a small and, she hoped, seductive smile.

"Should we talk more inside?" Annie asked, opening the door and gesturing for him to follow.

Chris grabbed for her hands again, clutching her fingers and bringing her closer. Annie looked up at him, and his eyes bore into hers, causing her breath to catch. *He wants me to kiss him*, Annie thought, allowing her body to inch closer to Chris. Annie closed her eyes and angled her mouth in his direction. If they made out a little on the front porch, she was sure she could convince him to stay.

"Oh, I would, but I need to get back home to Holly, I know she'll be trying to get another hot chocolate out of Felix," Chris said. Annie's eyes opened wide in surprise. "Good night, Annie."

CHAPTER NINE

Annie's heart dropped, instantly feeling his rejection and spiraling into another tornado of confusion. She watched Chris retreat onto the street until his figure had disappeared, twisting the Santa hat in her hands in pure frustration, a small scream escaping.

Without thinking a moment longer, Annie marched over to Nick's house and pounded on the door. She didn't care if he had managed to lure Bailey back and they were in the middle of making a moment of their own.

"Nick!" Annie yelled at the door, using her fists to take turns banging.

"Hi?" Nick asked, opening the door. Annie barged in and glanced around for Bailey.

"You're alone?" Annie asked.

"Um, yeah? I walked Bailey home and just got back," Nick said. "What's wrong with you?"

"Did you and Bailey have sex?" Annie asked bluntly. Nick choked on his saliva and dissolved into a coughing fit.

"What?" Nick sputtered.

"Tell me!" Annie hissed.

"Of course not," Nick said.

"Did you make out?" Annie asked.

"Annie, why are you asking me this?" Nick asked.

"Answer the question!" Annie yelled.

"No, we didn't kiss," Nick told her. "Happy?"

"No!" Annie yelled back, pacing down the front hallway before turning to Nick abruptly. "Chris didn't kiss me; he didn't even try . . . he said a bunch of nice stuff, but then he left! Was he kidding? Is this some sort of cruel joke?"

"Well, okay, if you follow the recipe for made-for-TV Christmas movies—" Nick offered.

"The recipe?" Annie interjected immediately.

"Yeah, they all fit a similar format," Nick explained.

"Which you mysteriously somehow know by heart," Annie said, but urged him to continue nonetheless.

"Two romantic interests have to first have an 'almost kiss' before a real kiss, and that usually only happens at the end of the movie anyway," Nick told her.

"Chris wouldn't even come in for a hug," Annie complained. "He, like, delicately squeezed my fingers after he walked me home. It was so formal and awkward," Annie shut her eyes, squirming at the memory. "Okay, wait, let's go back to the recipe stuff."

"Which part?" Nick asked.

"What if we tried to speed up some of those movie milestones you mentioned? Could we expedite our stories and move things along?" Annie spat out, her thoughts spinning wildly. "Maybe that's the key to getting out of here—we hurry up and just check off every stupid step so we can get out of here."

"I'm not sure; like I said, I don't know how any of this works—" Nick said.

"Go over the general outline. Tell me the whole formula," Annie demanded. Nick let out a sigh and ran a hand through his hair. Annie couldn't help but notice it was looking thick and lustrous.

"Um, well, we have an introduction. Usually, it's a female lead, living her life when, bam, some kind of new opportunity comes up—like, maybe, she has to rush home to her small town from the big city to save the family business right before Christmas. Then we meet the romantic interest. Often they're reintroduced to someone from their past and suddenly, they're seen in a flattering holiday light," Nick said, smiling at his interpretation.

"Keep going, what comes next?"

"Some sort of complication or something to raise the stakes—"

"Like the play or the snowstorm?" Annie asked, and Nick nodded in thought.

"Yes, and usually the lead is, um, a bit begrudging to agree to their involvement," Nick added, peevishly glancing her way.

"Perfect, I'm nailing that," Annie said proudly, and Nick let out a huff of laughter.

"Next, we get introduced to some supporting characters who are there to back the budding relationship blooming between the two romantic leads."

"When do things get spicy?"

"Annie, this is a made-for-TV Christmas movie. Things go from bland to mild, at best. Let's keep our expectations in line. These movies are supposed to let people escape and distract themselves from the stress of everything else in their world. They're like the movie equivalent of putting on cozy socks or getting a nice warm hug," Nick continued.

"A hug? Boring! These are supposed to be romantic, right?" Annie asked.

"Sure, but it's more about the long glances and soft sighs, a pure and simple love. But, yes, you're right, this would probably be the point that the lead characters have that 'near kiss' I was talking about," Nick explained, using his hands to note the "near kiss" quotations.

"Yeah, explain some more about the 'near kiss.' I don't understand how or why that would happen so frequently, why can't they stick their tongues down each other's throats?" Annie asked.

"Okay, usually it's like"—Nick moved closer to Annie to demonstrate his point—"they're just about to let their lips meet," Nick said, his face only inches from hers. Annie could feel her eyes dilating at his sudden proximity. Annie's limbs tingled in anticipation, like they were about to die of thirst and Nick was a glass of water they yearned to reach. This surprising reaction to him was paralyzing. *Yikes. What was that?*

"But something comes along to break the tension and they're interrupted," Nick finished, his mouth close enough that she could feel his warm breath. But then he stepped back, completely unaware of the heart he had unexpectedly stopped in Annie's chest.

"Honestly, sometimes, I find those moments more romantic than the final kiss," Nick admitted as he continued his assessment. Annie rolled her eyes, resetting herself, relieved to find her default snark returning.

She breathed out the tension in her muscles, attributing her strange physical reaction to Nick's closeness as a quirk of their circumstances. That had to be it.

"After that, we need some sort of mix-up, like there's a miscommunication and someone overhears something that they misinterpret. The lead has a reawakening where they reevaluate their circumstances and how they feel; they realize they've found a new happiness they didn't know was possible and a love they never knew they needed, that kind of thing. They have to have a moment to overcome the fear of getting hurt and assert their acquired understanding. Often, both romantic leads have to overcome this step so that they can finally reveal their honest affection. Sometimes it's thanks to one of those supporting cast members—"

"I call Santa Felix," Annie interjected, and Nick looked like he wanted to say something about that but instead continued.

"Oh, and usually one of them will say 'Merry Christmas' to the other romantic lead but, like, in a sad way as they slowly walk away. When they think there's no way for them to be together, and it's all over."

"Such dum-dums," Annie said, throwing her hands up.

"It often ends with a proposal, and there's a nice closing moment of the leads sharing a modest kiss surrounded by the town as it snows."

"I'm sorry, the norm is having a proposal with a 'modest kiss'? And viewers willingly believe that two characters who have never banged or experimented at all sexually are now going to spend the rest of their lives together?" Annie asked, aghast.

"I don't think the intended audience is thinking about that," Nick said.

"What if one character has a secret kink that the other can't handle? Or like, she loves latex, but he's allergic? Does it ever not work out because they weren't sexually compatible? Do we ever get some kind of update?"

"About a secret kink? No, sad to say, I haven't seen that pop up," Nick said dryly. "Sometimes a movie will do like a 'one year later' epilogue moment in the end with the characters getting married or something," Nick shrugged.

"Do you think they have, like, holiday-themed lingerie? Like when they finally get it on?" Annie asked, her mind wandering.

"Annie, are you okay? You seem overly curious about the sex lives of fictional characters," Nick said.

"They're not fictional now, they're us!" Annie retorted with a loud groan before whipping her head back to Nick, realizing she had used "us" when referring to their sex lives. "We have to trick the system before it tricks us. We need to hurry up and get our *almost kisses* out of the way so we can move on to the next steps and escape back to normal . . . Wait. What if we kiss? Like, right here, right now?" Annie asked.

"What?" Nick spluttered, instantly reddening.

"Oh, sorry, do you have a real-world girlfriend or something? Or were you looking forward to kissing Bailey again?" Annie asked, uncomfortably unsure which way she wanted him to answer.

"I don't have a real-world girlfriend, no," Nick said, his cheeks pinkening as his eyes focused on the floor.

"Cool, so let's kiss and get it over with. Is that okay with you?" Annie asked, taking a step closer to Nick. Her breath caught, nerves betraying her. Silly, since it wasn't supposed to even mean anything.

"Um," Nick looked as rigid as a reindeer caught with a mouth full of cookies from Santa's secret stash.

"Can I kiss you?" Annie asked. Nick looked up, and after a moment, his face only growing redder by the second, slowly nodded his head. He licked his lips in preparation, and it sent a zing through Annie's body. "Okay, I'm coming in," Annie announced, trying to move through the awkward energy. This could be their ticket out of here, why was she even hesitating?

Annie inched even closer until Nick was millimeters away. She steadied herself, tilted her head and closed her eyes, preparing to quickly tap her mouth against Nick's, but when she tried to move her lips any closer, they were met with an unseen barrier. Annie widened her eyes to see that Nick had closed his. His expectant expression made Annie actually want to kiss him even more. She tried again, but still something blocked her way.

"I can't—" Annie started and Nick's face changed into one of hurt and horror. "No, no, I mean, I physically can't. Try to kiss me," Annie urged, puckering her lips. Nick looked perplexed but bit down on his bottom lip before moving closer. He let out a small gasp when he too was unable to kiss Annie. Just like the wall at the edges of Main Street, neither could cut, or kiss, through the space between them.

"Let's stick out our tongues and see if we can touch them," Annie suggested. Nick made an exasperated face but complied. They both darted a tongue out, reaching for the other. No luck. Their tongues circled near each other but never met. Annie groaned into her hands and had a new thought. "What's the situation . . . downstairs?" Annie asked Nick, examining his crotch area before meeting his eyes again. Nick looked bewildered. "I mean, like, are we dealing with a Ken situation or do things work as usual?"

"What are you asking?" Nick asked, shifting his weight uncomfortably.

"I don't want a creepy sound going off, so I'm not sure how to word this," Annie considered. "Can you get . . . hard?" Annie asked, cautiously looking around the room. When no sound alerted, she let out a sigh of relief. Nick looked stunned. "Well, can you?"

"I don't know, I haven't exactly experimented with that," Nick told her, looking flustered.

"We should figure this out," Annie said. "For research. Think of something sexy," Annie ordered, staring at his pajama pants for movement.

"Annie—" Nick breathed out in exasperation. Annie got an idea and started taking off her sweater. "What are you doing?" Nick sputtered.

"I'm trying to test things," Annie said. She lifted her sweater up and something snapped into place around her torso. When she looked down, she could see the sweater back in place. She tried it again, only to get the same results. Nick moved closer.

"It's like you're a GIF, your clothes keep looping," Nick said, marveling.

"You try—take off your pants," Annie ordered, breathy from her attempts. "Do it!"

Nick, knowing he couldn't refuse her, unbuttoned his pants. He had unzipped his fly, and Annie brought her head down to his pelvis to get an up-close view. When the pants moved down, they too were immediately replaced and looped back on. She let out a frustrated huff and stood back up.

"Let's turn our backs and see what happens when we look past our underwear," Annie said, turning around and unbuttoning her pants. She hadn't paid attention earlier that morning when she changed, as she had kept on the basic white undergarments. When she looked down at her sweater, she gasped. She thought maybe she was having a seizure. All she could see was a pixelated blur. "No, no, no," she groaned, trying her pants and getting a similar image.

"It's censored?!" Nick cried out in surprise, his back to Annie. When he turned to face her, they both looked shell-shocked.

"Okay, okay, this is just another part of being here. And another reason we have to get out," Annie said, trying to convince herself more than anything. She paced in nervous thought. "Back to the storyline recipe. We've had our introduction, a timely opportunity, reestablished some sort of something with past flames, and we've got this awful play and other holiday activities to do . . . We still need a near kiss, more mix-ups, a reawakening, someone saying a sad 'Merry Christmas,' and then a proposal. Did I get everything?" Annie asked Nick, and he gave a small nod. "Right. Okay, so we can assume from . . . that," Annie said, gesturing to the missed kiss left unspoken and unanswered. "That you're here for Bailey and I'm here for Chris?"

"You're probably right," Nick agreed. Annie couldn't get a read on what he was thinking or feeling. "Okay, let's meet outside tomorrow morning. We'll walk over to the inn and see what town event awaits before rehearsal," Nick said, and Annie made a face, clearly not interested in attending the rehearsal. "That's where Chris and Bailey will be."

"Should we assume the made-for-TV Christmas movie time will wake us up and we'll both be ready and outside ready to go when we're supposed to?" Annie asked, realizing Nick was suggesting she leave.

"That's sort of what I'm assuming, yeah," Nick said, walking her to the door. "Wait. Should I walk you home?" Nick asked.

"Nah, I'm fine, this is probably the safest place to be a woman walking home alone at night, right? Might as well enjoy it while I can," Annie said and waved, leaving Nick to watch her go.

Back at her house, things were more or less as she had left them. Arthur was pleased to see her and greeted her at the door.

"Do I need to feed you?" Annie asked him, and Arthur led her into the kitchen, where he rubbed against a timed feeding device that spat out a handful of dry cat food. "Well, that was good timing. Enjoy, bud!"

After triple-checking that her phone still wasn't usable, Annie tried not to make eye contact with her own censored nudity and put on the silk pajamas and cuddled under the quilt's festive fabric. *Please let me sleep*, Annie pleaded to the made-for-TV Christmas movie gods. The last thing she wanted to do was lie awake scheming about how she was going to get her ex to almost kiss her. *Or let me go back to my life*, Annie tried to bargain. *I'll stop being such a Scrooge or whatever landed me here in the first place.* Luckily for Annie, the made-for-TV Christmas movie gods granted her the former.

CHAPTER TEN

It was the sound of bells that woke her from a notably dreamless sleep, still very much not in her real life. Or at least, Annie thought it was bells. But when she opened her eyes, the only sound came from Arthur, who was purring loudly, apparently ecstatic that Annie was now awake.

Annie searched the room for a sign that things were back to normal, but it was all as it had been the night before. She grabbed her phone from the side table, knowing before she checked to confirm it that it would indeed still be wearing the "No Service" banner across the lit Christmas tree.

The suitcase appeared to be glowing under its own ring light, inviting her to explore today's outfit and needed toiletries. Another white sweater, this one with delicate pearls sewn into the shape of snowflakes paired with black leather leggings. "How edgy," Annie said to the pants and grabbed travel shampoo and conditioner bottles from the cosmetic bag.

Annie's current real-life rental only had a shower stall, so it was a pleasant surprise to find her bedroom now contained an en-suite complete with a bathtub lined with glass jars of what Annie assumed must be bubble baths. Compared to the cramped bathroom inside her small apartment, the concept of a warm bath in a pristine tub sounded so luxurious and clearly something the made-for-TV Christmas movie Annie would embrace.

Twenty minutes later, Annie was blissfully submerged in bubbles when Arthur pushed the bathroom door open. He placed himself on the bathmat, purring loudly again.

"You're going to let cold air in, you jerk!" she yelled in Arthur's direction. Already, she noticed the temperature of the room changing and her bathwater losing heat. Arthur didn't move and continued to gaze at her without blinking. "Ugh, fine, I guess it's time to get out," Annie muttered, carefully stepping out of the tub and avoiding Arthur's obnoxiously flicking tail.

She wrapped a thick towel around herself, marveling at how luscious it felt against her skin, relishing its softness and full coverage. Annie glanced at herself in the mirror above the sink. Her face was dewy and rosy and, once again, she regretted not having access to social media to document this thirst trap because, dang, this made-for-TV Christmas movie natural beauty filter was nice.

When she met Nick outside, her hair now hanging in soft waves across her shoulders (mainly thanks to the magic hair dryer that had somehow managed to style her hair in seconds) and dressed in her leather leggings, Nick stopped in his tracks and his jaw dropped.

"You look like Sandy at the end of *Grease*," Nick applauded and Annie laughed. There didn't seem to be a trace of awkwardness apparent after last night's tongue touch attempt, but Annie couldn't help but wonder if it was also on Nick's mind. "Ready for another big day? I'm curious what town event awaits and how today's rehearsal will unfold," Nick said. Annie let out a loud groan, remembering the stupid play.

"Those creepy children performing in an already lame story are going to haunt my dreams," Annie said.

"Isn't that kind of the point of the show?" Nick asked as they walked onto Main Street. He looked left and saw a sign for the Nutmeg Nest and pointed. "Wow, that was even easier than I thought it would be." Annie and Nick approached the inn and stopped outside the big white staircase leading to a large porch covered with holiday decorations. On the large red double doors was a huge wreath.

"Looks like Chris has been here," Annie said, gesturing at the greenery. "This place is legit. I wish my old dead aunt had left *me* one of these. Oh, or a vineyard. Is that ever a thing in these movies?"

"Maybe, but I imagine the winery part would consist of people who actually spit out the tasting wine so they don't risk getting tipsy," Nick mused.

"That's offensive. I guess I'll stick to inheriting a giant mysterious inn then," Annie said.

"Maybe in the sequel," Nick said, giving her a small smile. "Need any help up these stairs in those stilts?" He asked, his dad joke game strong and steady.

Annie was pretty sure she could maneuver the heels alone but allowed Nick to take her arm anyway. When they reached the door, they could see Grant waiting by the window. He threw the doors wide open and flailed his arms in excitement, ushering them closer. He was dressed in a formal tuxedo with his hair slicked back.

"Oh, wow, that's a choice," Annie whispered.

"I'm so glad you could join us for breakfast!" Grant gushed.

"We love food," Annie shrugged, and Grant let out a loud, hearty laugh.

"Annie, you're so funny." Grant smiled warmly at her.

"This place is impressive," Nick said, glancing around the front hall.

"I'm glad someone thinks so," Grant sighed to himself.

In the corner was a reception desk where an older woman sat wearing a Santa hat and broadly chuckling into a bright red phone. Annie was about to maul her to make a call out when she saw the phone wasn't plugged in.

"She's practicing." Grant smiled as if sensing Annie's interest. "Phone lines are still out. No calls in or out from the big city," Grant quipped. The woman continued laughing as she took notes in a large red notebook with an oversized pen shaped like a candy cane. There was a tall Christmas tree near the grand staircase, decorated with red ribbon and white lights. The decorations were classic and thoughtfully displayed, giving the room a feeling of welcoming warmth and simple elegance.

Annie saw a man standing near the staircase, wearing dark sunglasses, hiding half his face. He was completely bald, but Annie silently questioned if it was because of an ill-fitting bald cap. More than anything else, he wore a serious expression while his black clothing camouflaged most of his presence. Still, there was something that seemed so familiar.

"What's up with that guy?" Annie whispered to Grant.

"That's Ferguson," Grant whispered back. "He's on security detail for one of our guests," Grant continued in a hushed tone. But before Annie could ask a hundred follow-up questions, Grant was back to his normal showman-like voice. "Let me escort you to the dining room."

Nick took a big step forward, and Grant teased, "Oh, you two just missed the mistletoe. Don't worry, Annie, it's all over the inn, I'm sure you'll get another chance."

"Wait, what? Mistletoe? More like mistle-no, am I right?" Annie said, forcing out a fake laugh, feeling her face flush. She couldn't meet Nick's eyes.

"How long did you say you've been running the inn?" Nick asked.

"Three days," Grant said.

"And you just had that tux ready to go?" Annie asked.

"The letter from my great-aunt's estate came just last week," Grant continued as if he hadn't heard Annie's question.

Annie wanted to laugh, knowing full well that in reality Grant had spent most of last week planning the office party in between "auditioning" sexy Santas. "I could never abandon this special place. So many priceless memories. And not right before Christmas! We've had some investors offer obscene sums of money to take it over. All from the big city, of course. One of them is actually still stuck here because of the big storm." Grant cringed. "Sorry, Annie, I know that's where you're from, but those people don't have the small-town community values that we do. So, here I am! Running this beauty and helping out with the school's Christmas show; I'm in charge of ticket sales."

"And you're also the host of all these town events? That's a lot of stuff to accomplish in three days' time . . ." Annie mock-marveled.

"I'm so inspired by the holidays. It fuels me," Grant smiled.

"And actual human people are staying in the inn? Like, right now? Other than that Ferguson character, I mean?" Annie asked, still not believing that "security detail" was necessary in the made-for-TV Christmas movie Simsbury.

"Well, yes, thankfully, we were blessed with reservations before the winter weather and some because of it . . ." Grant trailed off in a dreamy trance. "I have a spot for you two right here at our community table," Grant said, and Annie's eyes latched on to those of a familiar stranger.

"Why, hello there!" Felix said, looking up from the table. "It's so nice to see you on this beautiful morning." Annie locked eyes with Felix for a moment, and a spark rang through her. *He's got to be Santa*, Annie thought. "You both look ready for your close-up." Felix finished, and Annie thought she caught a flash of meaning behind it.

"Good morning!" Nick said loudly, breaking Annie from her introspection and catching the attention of the woman sitting across from Felix. She appeared to be somewhere between sixty and ageless with her silver hair neatly confined in two tight braids, each tied with a piece of green yarn. Wearing bright red cat eyeglasses with rhinestones lining the frame and earrings that jingled every time she moved her head. Which was often. *Arthur would dig those*, Annie thought, eyeing them swing back and forth. Overall, the look screamed, "quirky eccentric", and Annie thought she played the part well.

"Are we interrupting you?" Annie asked.

"Not at all, please sit down! Your presence is a treasured gift," Felix said in his fiercely jolly voice, gesturing for

Annie to sit next to him. Annie looked at Nick, but he was fixated on the woman at the table.

"Sorry, it's just that you look so familiar . . ." Nick said, pulling out a chair.

"Well, of course she does. This is Noelle, the owner of Twinkle Twinkle Little Treasures!" Felix grinned. "She's famous!"

"Oh, yeah?" Annie asked.

"I don't want to boast," the woman started.

"You must!" Annie encouraged, more curious than ever about what this woman could be famous for.

"My store is the largest exclusively Christmas snow globe collection shop in New England," Noelle said proudly, her cheeks looking like two bright, gleaming, red apples.

"Wow," Annie said, her face locked into a forced smile that couldn't reach her eyes.

"That's exciting," Nick told her, kindly. "We walked by the shop yesterday and things seemed very busy."

"I've been blessed with the best customers in this beautiful town," Noelle said, putting a hand to her heart.

"So are you two . . . together? A couple?" Annie asked playfully, wiggling her eyebrows. Nick shot her a look of surprise, which Annie returned with an air of fiery mischief. Why not try and throw a little spice into the conversation and see what happens?

"A couple of cronies," Noelle said with a tight-lipped smile aimed at the table.

"Cronies?" Annie asked. "You look pretty cozy to me," she encouraged.

"Felix has been a wonderful friend to me for many years. After I lost my husband, he was a great beacon of support," Noelle continued.

"Oh, I'm so sorry to hear about your husband," Annie told Noelle more softly. "I'm sure it's not easy around the holidays." Nick stared at Annie again with a look of surprise, but this one was different, and she couldn't put a finger on why. "What?" Annie snapped at him.

"Nothing!" Nick said quickly. "I'm also sorry for your loss, Noelle. But it's wonderful you've found a friend in Felix."

"We have a lot of fun," Felix chimed in.

"Oh yeah? What kind of trouble do you two crazy kids get into together?" Annie asked.

"We like to take a nice long drive every Sunday after church to the loveliest little bakery," Felix said, a faraway look of contentment in his eyes.

"Now we're talking," Annie encouraged. "Go on."

"They have the most outstanding oatmeal cookies," Felix continued.

"And?" Annie prompted and when Felix didn't elaborate, she asked, "You take a long drive for oatmeal cookies? On purpose?"

"They're oatmeal raisin cookies, dear," Noelle explained as if this would explain everything.

"Raisin . . . ? That's somehow even worse," Annie murmured to herself as she shuddered in horror. She could think of nothing more terrible than all of the times she had bitten into an oatmeal raisin cookie thinking it was a chocolate chip and the cruel disappointment that morphed into rage upon that discovery.

"Sounds like someone is getting hungry," Felix knowingly smiled at Nick. Grant waltzed back to the table, his black dress shoes squeaking with each step, and dropped off two mugs of hot chocolate in front of Annie and Nick.

"Your aunt would be so proud of you," Felix said, his eyes glistening. "Stepping up and continuing her legacy." Felix stopped himself to take a long slow slip of his own hot chocolate and gaze off into space.

"I miss her dearly," Grant said after a beat of pointed silence.

"We all do," Noelle added. "This inn has been a Simsbury staple, especially during the holiday season." The three settled into the heaviness of the moment, hypnotized by its spell, and each in a fog of their own creation.

"Has it?" Annie asked, eager to break whatever weird emotional trance enveloped the table. This was certainly news to her.

"Of course, dear girl! Haven't you ever attended the annual Christmas Ball?" Noelle asked, snapping back to stare at Annie.

"Can't say that I have," Annie replied.

"Oh, Felix, isn't that the saddest thing you've ever heard? What a travesty! You big-city people can get so lost in the hustle and bustle of it all, always on the go, staring at a screen, you forget to look up at all the joy and happiness right in front of you!" Noelle exclaimed, adjusting her glasses.

"Annie, you must come this year. Black tie formal required, of course," Grant smiled, scurrying back toward the kitchen.

"Um—" Annie began, but she didn't know how to finish the sentence because she was afraid that if she admitted she didn't own a ball gown, Noelle would suggest a shopping montage moment at some downtown boutique catering to dated fashion trends, and that was a step further than she could reasonably handle.

"It's on Christmas Eve, after the Christmas play and once the local business is awarded their funds," Felix explained.

"Wow, sounds like quite a full day," Annie said, purposely eyeing Felix for a reaction because that day would indeed be a busy one for Santa.

"Okay, my merry friends, I hope you're hungry," Grant sang out, carrying a big tray of food and another pot of hot chocolate. "Wait until you try my candy cane pancakes! Old family recipe," Grant exclaimed. He dropped two plates in front of Annie and Nick. On top of the red and green sprinkled pancakes were two mini candy canes shaped together to make a heart.

"Great presentation," Nick said to Grant, and Grant let out a little squeal of delight and shimmied his shoulders. It was the closest Annie had seen of the real Grant, and it gave her a small shot of unexpected joy. She happily took a big bite but stopped chewing when a particularly pointy piece of candy cane became lodged in her back molar.

"Ouch," Annie said, trying to use her fork to loosen the piece.

"Don't you love it when a piece of candy cane gets to stick around a little longer?" Noelle asked.

"That's one way to put it," Annie grunted, still trying to get it out, but to no avail.

"It's like a little kiss of peppermint; your breath will be fresh all day!" Noelle said as Annie finally dislodged the errant shard and gave herself a high-five in celebration. "Aw, too bad, maybe next time it'll stay. I'm keeping one in now!" Noelle made a loud sucking sound with her teeth for emphasis.

Annie looked to Nick for confirmation that Noelle was seriously praising a piece of stuck candy cane in her mouth.

He looked at her, grinning, his own teeth purposely plastered with tiny pieces of red and white.

"Fresh breath all day, Annie. In case you get caught under the mistletoe!" Nick told her.

"Exactly!" Noelle exclaimed, but when she caught Felix's curious eye, she returned her gaze to her pancakes.

"You never know when the moment may strike," Felix smiled.

"Well, it's never happened to me before, but I'll certainly keep it in mind," Annie answered back.

"She says that, but she caught me under one many years ago," Nick casually told Noelle and Felix.

"What?" Annie barked out a laugh. "No, I did not."

"You did," Nick said.

"When?" Annie demanded.

"Um, a few nights before Christmas. My freshman year of high school," Nick said, clearing his throat.

"Nick, what are you talking about?" Annie asked.

"You kissed me under the mistletoe," Nick said.

"No, I didn't! I would never do that!" Annie said, putting her fork down. Nick's ears had grown quite pink.

"You kissed me," Nick repeated softly, the back of his neck racing to match the pink hue of his ears. Noelle and Felix looked on, their eyes flickering with excitement.

"No way," Annie said, shaking her head, but when Nick refused to yield she stared back at him, trying to read his face. "Nick, I didn't do that, did I?" Annie asked, her voice nervously trembling.

"You and Marsha had experimented with peppermint schnapps and chocolate syrup . . . and some old wine coolers that night," Nick whispered so only Annie could hear him. "Our parents were all at that annual neighborhood

Christmas party down the block, and all the neighborhood kids came over to my house to watch movies. I had mistletoe under my bedroom doorframe, kind of as a joke, kind of because I was already a hopeful romantic." Nick shrugged with a small self-deprecating laugh.

"Oh, Nick, I didn't like, force myself on you . . . ?" Annie asked, clutching the table.

"No, no, nothing like that. It was very consensual!" Nick reassured her, but Annie only loosened up a little. "It was a passing moment, our, um, lips barely brushed each other. I think you may have planned to kiss me on the cheek, and I swerved my head . . ."

"Oh my," Annie whispered, "I'm so sorry. We were probably snooping around upstairs, trying to get into your siblings' rooms or your mom's closet, we had no right to be there—"

"No, please don't be sorry. It was my first kiss, if you could even count it as one, which I absolutely did," Nick said, a small smile flirting with the corners of his mouth. Annie groaned and covered her face in her hands. "I was this nerdy theater kid, and you were this cool, older girl. It made my Christmas," Nick admitted.

Annie peeked an eye out from her hands. "Really?"

"Most definitely," Nick said meaningfully.

"And you never mentioned it to me?" Annie asked.

Then an awareness came over her. If Nick had been a freshman, Annie had been a junior.

She had no idea then that, within a few days, her stance on holiday parties would change forever.

"I'm mentioning it now," Nick smiled softly.

Annie considered Nick's face. It was so familiar but held something completely new. He looked so handsome, so rugged. Was his facial hair coming in thicker today? Annie studied Nick's defined jawline, now with a very complementary five o'clock shadow, and had an impulse to bite down on his chin to know what it would feel like to hold it between her teeth. The realization came over her like a punch to the gut, and she desperately tried to think it away. Annie looked away and tried to ground herself. She needed to focus on how to escape this place, and sexy musings regarding Nicholas Laurel were not going to do her any favors.

"Dear lad, may I trouble someone for more hot cocoa?" Felix asked, sensing that his assistance might be able to ease the tension.

"Another cup? Are you sure, Felix?" Noelle whispered, her voice full of concern.

"Let's get the man another cup! He's not driving!" Annie shouted and turned her hands into finger guns. And then, committing to the bit, made "pew-pew" sounds.

"What was that?" Nick asked once she finished. Annie shrugged, unable to justify anything that had come out of her mouth or her fingers.

"Today's the Annual Simsbury Jolly Holiday Skate and Snack with Santa Extravaganza Celebration, and we'll be heading over to the ice rink in a few minutes if you want to walk together," Noelle suggested. Annie pinched Nick's arm, horrified by such an event title and immediate lack of enthusiasm to participate.

"Ow!" Nick cried, rubbing the spot. "You're a walking weapon, woman," he muttered as the sound of a crash came from the lobby. Annie jumped at the chance to investigate and also remove herself from Noelle's invitation.

From the door, Annie could see an exasperated Grant, clinging on top of a ladder, and the cold stare of Ferguson in the corner. At the bottom of the ladder was a cardboard box full of garlands and a man in a tailored suit, head tipped back and gazing quizzically at Grant. Annie froze mid-step, craning for a better view when Nick barreled into her. The heat of his breath against her neck made her turn, her gaze tipping up to him just before the sweet, sharp scent of candy cane pancakes carried her down.

CHAPTER ELEVEN

When Annie opened her eyes again, she was on the ground, and Nick was on top of her. He gave her a half smile.

"You okay, partner? I can't take you anywhere," Nick said warmly, sending a shock of electricity through her body, landing in an unexpected spark between her legs. Annie squirmed in confused arousal, wanting both to keep Nick's weight firmly on top of her and to run screaming from this scene.

"I blame the pancakes," Annie said dumbly. Nick laughed and swiftly made his way up, giving Annie a hand to help her off the ground. When they were both situated, Grant was off the ladder, casting nervous glances toward the man.

"What's wrong with the pancakes?" Grant asked, making his way to Nick and Annie.

"Nothing!" Annie said. "I was kidding. I heard a sound and saw you on the ladder—are you alright?"

"Oh, phew, you had me scared something was off with the recipe," Grant sighed.

"Nothing so serious," Annie assured him when she placed the man as he approached them. "Sexy Santa!"

"Annie, this is Perry," Grant started stiffly.

"Chipperton Clement III," Sexy Santa interrupted as Grant's cheeks flushed at the correction. "Senior Director of Asset Realignment and Divestiture with Northpoint Capital Group," he finished proudly, offering Annie his hand to shake.

"That's a lot of words," Annie said as he continued to hold her hand.

"My company sent me, but the snowstorm kept me," Perry explained, his eyes focused on the now broken box of garlands next to the ladder.

"Relatable," Annie nodded.

"That looks like a safety hazard," Perry warned.

"I know what I'm doing," Grant said, gathering the pieces. His dejected tone sent a sad shiver through Annie. The last time she had seen these two they had looked ready to go make a sex tape.

"They have you working on the play too?" Annie asked Perry.

"Play?" Perry asked.

"Why doesn't he have to help with the show?" Annie asked Nick.

"I do have a background in dance," Perry shared tentatively, unsure if he should dare reveal more.

"You do?" Grant asked as Annie clutched Perry's arm.

"Join us," Annie ordered with an intensity that caused everyone to raise an eyebrow. Annie sensed she had perhaps gone too far and backpedaled. "I mean, if you want! Think it over!"

"I don't think Chipperton Clement III would be interested in our community events, given the nature of his task here," Grant said curtly, taking the box and its contents to the front desk to be checked for damage. Perry watched him, a look of hurt passing through his eyes, before he turned to Annie and Nick.

"It was nice to meet you both," Perry said tightly. Annie and Nick watched as Grant stole glances at him as he made his way back upstairs.

"All of his best parts, all of my favorite things that make Grant Grant have been dimmed or completely shut off," Annie said when Grant returned to check on Felix and Noelle. "These made-for-TV movies are boring beige when they could be a vivid rainbow. It's a tragedy." Annie finished, heading back outside.

"You know what might make you feel better?" Nick asked once they were on the street.

"If you say going to that ridiculous ice-skating event, I'm going to pinch you again," Annie warned, turning her fingers into menacing pinchers.

"It's the Annual Simsbury Jolly Holiday Skate and Snack with Santa Extravaganza Celebration, but I was going to say, we should probably discuss this kissing thing," Nick said and Annie's face heated. Was this about her actions in high school or last night? Or how her body had betrayed her brain just moments ago? "How are you planning to get Chris to almost kiss you?" Nick asked.

"Oh!" Annie exhaled. Right, of course, Nick was referring to today's mission and not at all calling her out for obviously wanting to bone him back there. "We know we can't skip to an actual kiss but how hard can an almost kiss be?" Nick considered the question. "It's going to be pretty hard, huh?" Annie asked and Nick winced. "Okay, what do I have to do?" Annie demanded.

"You'll have to build some rapport. Make Chris feel comfortable. In this case, you'll likely have to get in Holly's good graces so that you can warm his wounded, widowed-dad heart," Nick said.

"What's your plan for Bailey?" Annie asked.

"Maybe I can help her in the bakery, and we can have one of those food fights with buckets of flour?"

"That's going to make her almost kiss you?" Annie asked.

"Honestly, yeah, that could do the trick," Nick shrugged. "And ice-skating may help us lay the groundwork."

Annie groaned, knowing Nick had a point. She wouldn't get any closer to almost kissing Chris if she didn't spend enough time within kissing distance of him.

The town of Simsbury was also the home of the International Skating Center of Connecticut. The destination became rather famous thanks to gold medal winner Oksana Baiul, who, according to nineties pop culture, put Simsbury on the map when she moved to town after her Olympic success. All of that didn't mean much in this made-for-TV reality, though. This skating rink, which seemed to only exist for the Annual Simsbury Jolly Holiday Skate and Snack with Santa Extravaganza Celebration, was outside and conveniently located next to the Christmas tree lot on Main Street.

When Annie and Nick left the inn, they only had to walk a few feet before they were greeted with a cluster of animated townsfolk worked up and talking at double speed.

"Oh, thank heavens you're here!" Noelle cried, her voice cutting through the crowd.

"Hi, Noelle," Nick said in surprise. "Wait. How did you beat us here?" Nick asked and was immediately silenced by Noelle's hushed voice.

"There's been an accident," she breathed.

"What happened?" Annie asked. Despite Noelle's serious tone, she was relatively confident that nothing too stressful could actually happen in this universe.

"Felix twisted his knee," Noelle said sadly. "He's not going to be able to play Santa for today's event."

"When? We were literally just sitting with him. Is he alright?" Annie asked. When her eyes found Felix, he was sitting at a nearby table, grabbing a doughnut, and he offered her an animated and friendly wave. "Um, he seems fine to me?"

"Oh no, he definitely needs to sit this one out," Noelle continued.

"But wasn't he going to *sit* and be Santa?" Annie asked.

"Nick, we need you," Noelle begged, her voice dropping low. Felix winked at Annie, and she let out a sharp exhale.

"He winked at me!" Annie gasped.

"You need me to fill in as Santa Claus?" Nick asked, like he had been fully expecting this twist.

"Yes!" Noelle cried. "You're our only hope!"

"Nick's the only hope? What about all those older dudes over there?" Annie said, gesturing to a group of older men who were double-fisting doughnuts decorated with red and green sprinkles and holding steaming cups of what Annie could only sadly assume was hot chocolate.

"We need Nick," Noelle said resolutely.

"Sure, makes perfect sense. Okay, Nick, have a blast cosplaying Santa. I'll see you when you're done," Annie said, patting Nick's back and stepping toward the doughnut table, ready to fill her own two hands with whatever sugary concoctions were available.

"Not so fast, young lady," Noelle said.

"Who, me?" Annie asked innocently, still slowly creeping closer to the food and beverage station.

"Yes, you. I certainly can't play Mrs. Claus now; that wouldn't be appropriate. We'll need you to take on that role."

"Wait, huh?" Annie asked, her mouth stuck in an open, shocked expression.

"You heard her, you're going to be my Mrs. Claus," Nick said rather smugly.

"I'm sorry, are you happy about this?" Annie snapped to Nick. "Why on earth am I needed? No one is here for Mrs. Claus. Let's let Nick be the star of this show—" But Noelle cut her off and steered her and Nick toward the small equipment shed.

"The costumes are hanging inside on hooks. Get a move on changing, would you? The kids will be arriving any moment!" Noelle gushed before retreating to Felix.

"Nick," Annie said. "We don't have to actually do this, right? This is way out of my comfort zone here. Noelle must be joking; there's no way I'm necessary to this whole thing."

"C'mon, Annie, it could be fun. Plus, I want to see what you look like as an old woman!" Nick said, grabbing the costume bag marked "Santa" and gently handing her the one marked "Mrs. Claus." "Pretend it's a Halloween costume?"

"Imagine doing a walk of shame dressed as a hungover Mrs. Claus," Annie said.

"See, that can be something you can aspire to," Nick said, heading to a small stall inside the shed. "I'll go in there and you can change out here. Let me know when you're done and I'll come out, or like, zip you up or whatever." Nick let the stall door close, and Annie let out a groan. She angrily unzipped the bag and pulled out the heavy red velvet dress cuffed with white fur. Upon first glance, she had to admit, it was nicer than she had expected. *Huh, maybe I'll be a hot Mrs. Claus,* Annie thought hopefully. *Perhaps I'll be the best "ho-ho ho" in town.* When Nick stepped out of his stall, Annie shrieked in amusement.

"Oh. My. Gosh. You look like Felix! Like Santa!" Annie marveled, walking closer to Nick and tugging on his white beard. "It's so soft! Like a wolf."

Annie stepped back to further inspect Nick's costume. She had another unusual flush of feeling aroused by Nick in his red velvet pants and black suspenders until she reminded herself that being attracted to Santa in clothes that Felix last wore went against all laws of nature. But Nick looked good. Really good. Like, hold the "o" in good for longer than necessary, gooood. He was still wearing a basic white T-shirt, his look awaiting the big, signature jacket, and his face was mostly covered by a white beard and a pair of glasses. "I like you in glasses," Annie said, her voice a bit huskier than she intended. She cleared her throat. "I mean, you look good in glasses," she said, trying to cover her obvious drooling.

"And you look . . . pretty. Like, so pretty," Nick told her honestly.

"Good thing you can't get hard here," Annie joked, finger gunning toward his crotch. She instantly regretted it. Nick's eyes widened. "I mean, because I'm an old lady, and that would be weird—" Annie stammered.

"Yeah, that's the weird part," Nick cracked a smile. Annie let out a relieved breath, hoping to quickly move past her awkwardness.

From what she could tell, the Mrs. Claus dress was surprisingly flattering. The tailored bodice hugged her curves, the skirt flowed out, and although it was toasty, it didn't feel unbearably heavy. The costume included a small pair of spectacles and a white wig of curly hair, complete with a red bonnet on the top. The neckline of her dress was flattering and showcased her collarbone in an almost, dare she say, mildly sensual fashion. Lastly, Annie had a small cape covering her shoulders, and all in all, she didn't hate the look.

"Do you need help buttoning that?" Nick asked, voice gruff and low. It was painfully sexy, sounding like it could bruise her if it wanted to, and Annie thought she might beg it to.

"Yes, thank you, I can't reach," Annie admitted. Her heart quickened as Nick stepped closer, and her breath hitched when his fingers found the line of buttons, beginning to work the first one. They moved with such precision and power her brain couldn't help imagine what else those fingers could do to her body, her thighs already squeezing together at the thought. Annie tried to block it out, but as Nick moved up the dress, she found herself desperate for him to fist her hair with one hand and rip the dress off her with the other, pressing himself firmly behind her so her own hands could reach back to explore everything under his Santa pants until he was panting her name with each stroke—

Wow. She had to get herself under control and get back on track. This event was an opportunity to connect with Chris, not Nick. She was supposed to be game-planning how to almost kiss him, not daydreaming about getting railed by Santa in a supply shed.

As he was finishing fastening the last thick black button, Annie turned back, facing Nick again, who was standing tall, eyes locked on her. Their heads were only inches apart now, and Annie could feel Nick's candy cane breath. It made all the hairs on the back of her neck stand erect, and Annie could feel her pulse racing. Her body clearly had a plan immune to anything rational, and she was sure Nick could read every dirty idea that Annie was trying to hide. When a breath skimmed her lips, she had to restrain herself from backing him against the wall and grinding her body against his, desperate for the heat and friction. Annie didn't want to just kiss Nick, she wanted to devour him. But before she could move, the shed door banged open with a thud, shattering the moment.

CHAPTER TWELVE

"Hope I didn't interrupt anything," Noelle tutted with the smallest hint of mischief in her voice. "Let's get going, kids. We need you out there ASAP. Why aren't you wearing your skates?" Noelle scolded.

"What's that?" Annie asked; she was sure the record-scratching sound from her head was loud enough to be heard all the way to the real North Pole, instantly killing the lustful desires still heating her skin.

"Your skates," Noelle explained. "We have Santa's chair already placed on the ice."

"You're expecting us to ice-skate? In these costumes?" Annie asked, shaking her head.

"Well, Santa will sit," Noelle explained, "once he's been situated."

"And what am I supposed to do?" Annie croaked.

"You'll help guide the children over to him, of course," Noelle said.

"I think it's pretty problematic that you'd assume I know how to ice-skate!" Annie gulped.

"Honey, you're from Simsbury. Of course you can ice-skate, no need to be modest," Noelle told her, handing each of them a pair of black skates. "I'll walk you out when you're ready!"

"Nick!" Annie whisper-shrieked.

"I think it's going to be okay. Everyone is always a strangely good skater in these movies," Nick explained thoughtfully.

"You're not scared?" Annie asked.

"I have all this padding in case I fall," Nick grinned and stuffed his shirt with a small pillow meant to round out his belly.

Annie had been so distracted by Noelle's entrance that she hadn't had a chance to make sense of what might have happened if they had been left alone a moment more. Would they have been blocked by another barrier? She had been more than ready to climb into that Santa suit with him. What was happening to her? Were these feelings real or another fatal symptom of the made-for-TV sickness currently consuming their lives? Annie had no idea, honestly. Instead, her mind drifted to Nick's lips or if she might actually taste those candy cane pancakes once his mouth touched hers . . .

"Annie? Are you okay? You look flushed," Nick asked, his voice full of concern. "Don't worry, I'll be there on the ice with you in case you need help."

"I don't want people to assume Mrs. Claus needs Santa for everything," Annie pouted. "For this portrayal, I'll be channeling an unapologetic feminine confidence," Annie covered, relieved that Nick hadn't caught on to her obvious horny face.

"Remember, stay in character while you're out here," Noelle told them through a tight smile once they were out of the shed. "Everyone is counting on you two," she warned and helped lace up their skates before walking them to the entrance. "As you can see, Santa's chair is in the middle of the rink. Mrs. Claus will skate you there and then bring the kids over one by one to sit on your lap. We have some elf helpers who will be taking pictures," Noelle said, waving at Bailey and Chris, who were skating laps around the rink in bright green costumes. Annie thought they looked like a perfect pair of competitive ice dancers.

"Not sure why poor, overworked, and underappreciated Mrs. Claus has to skate around when Santa has elves to help. Maybe I can go take care of Rudolph or something?" Annie asked, pleading with Noelle.

"Nonsense! Santa needs his Mrs. Claus!" Noelle chided.

"Yes, Mrs. Claus. Santa needs you," Nick smiled at Annie.

"I hope you're aware of how full-on creepy and not normal this is," Annie whispered to Nick.

"You're right, Mrs. Claus, it does look like a wondrous day for a skate!" Nick said loudly in his deep Santa voice. Annie did a double-take in surprise, and Noelle gave them a big thumbs-up of support.

"Why don't you do a nice slow loop around the rink together and hand out candy canes to the families? Then we'll begin!" Noelle said. Annie took the basket of candy canes from Noelle and sighed, looking at Nick. He stepped out onto the ice and offered his hand to Annie to help her get her footing. Annie's first moves were trepidatious, but Nick steadied her and didn't let go as they took a slow first glide. When Annie didn't fall, she looked at Nick and beamed.

"I'm skating!" she said, her cheeks colored with delight.

"I knew you could do it," Nick said quietly but still using his Santa voice.

"I wish we could have had this event as kids," Annie said, looking around at all of the people walking around outside of the rink waiting for their turn to talk to Santa and share their secret wishes for the season. The air itself was thick with unspoken cheer, and Annie pulsed with an unexpected pride for her hometown. Even when it wasn't starring in a made-for-TV movie, Simsbury was charming. A place committed to honoring its historical heritage while also showcasing an active appreciation of modern culture set inside a pocket of local farms and scenic hiking trails. *Such a lovely place to raise a family*, Annie mused, grateful for her upbringing and trying to ignore the ache of wanting a future where she could confidently plant seeds destined to grow until their happy ends. "I'm skating so well," Annie said, plucking herself from the daydream. Her body was easing into the rhythm a bit more each time one of her feet hit the ice. "I'm, like, really good!"

Two figures making rapid movements across the rink caught Annie's attention. Bailey and Chris were each performing a series of tricks on the ice to the cheering of the children. Bailey spun with her arms above her head so quickly that she became a beautiful green blur of movement, like some sort of fairy on fire, or possibly, just absinthe itself. Chris, meanwhile, was attempting to speed skate and jump over large decorative boxes of presents.

"You should join them! You're, like, really good," Nick teased.

"Geez, is there anything those two can't do? They're unstoppable," Annie said. Annie narrowed her eyes. Chris's body was much more muscular and taller in this reality. The elf costume looked particularly strained as he gracefully jumped over a silver package, and Annie swallowed, ready to focus on the task at hand. "First person to get an almost kiss wins an iced coffee in the real world," Annie whispered quickly to Nick, sending a big wave in Chris's direction. Before Nick could respond, Bailey called out to him, finishing her spin with a flourish.

"It's Santa!" Bailey boomed.

"Looks like that elf may try and sit on your lap too, Santa," Annie said as Bailey gracefully glided toward them. "Or your face," Annie smirked, and Nick let out a choke of surprised laughter.

"Santa, let me help you to your chair!" Bailey said in a loud, high-pitched elf voice. "I'd hate for you to break a bone, Mrs. C., considering you're so much older and frailer than I am!" Bailey said, directing her words mostly to Nick. Annie's mouth hung open in surprise, momentarily too stunned to retort. Bailey let out a loud whistle with her hand and signaled Chris to join them. "Brother Elf, can you help Mrs. Claus find her way? I'll take care of the big guy over here," Bailey grinned, playfully poking Nick's prop pillow belly. "You are the cutest Santa ever," Bailey whispered into Nick's ear. Annie's chest warmed. Was it annoyance? Jealousy? Before she could think about it, Chris glided closer and forced her to refocus her feelings.

"Anything for you, Sister Elf!" Chris told Bailey, nodding as she took Nick away. "Hi, Mrs. Claus," Chris whispered, smiling at Annie. "I must say, I've never seen such a pretty Mrs. Claus in all of my many days working at the

North Pole." Chris kept his eyes on Annie. He seemed so sweet and sincere. Annie wanted to remark on the weirdness of Chris and Bailey calling each other "brother" and "sister," but she was pretty sure this was the closest thing to flirting she had experienced so far with Chris, and she needed to push it as far as it would go.

"Who me?" Annie said, batting her eyelashes up at Chris. "Oh my, is that a candy cane in your pocket?" Annie asked him, curious if he would pick up the sexual innuendo she was laying on as thickly as possible.

"It is!" Chris beamed, handing her a wrapped candy cane. "Would you like it?"

"Would I like to have a lick of your candy cane . . . ?" Annie asked, taking a finger to tap her lip like she was deep in thought, again overdoing it to the point of absurdity. Chris looked confused.

"I'm not sure, would you?" Chris asked. "Oh, you silly goose, you have a basket of your own!" Chris said, gesturing to the basket of candy canes.

"Yes, but I think I would much prefer to have your candy cane inside my basket," Annie told him, slowly emphasizing each word.

"Okay!" Chris said obliviously as he gently tossed the candy cane into her basket. Annie sighed, unsure which tactic to try next.

Nick had now been placed in the center of the rink, and Bailey was skating around his chair as a line of children formed outside the enclosure. A speaker in the corner of the rink turned on, playing a wordless, familiar-sounding holiday song Annie couldn't place. She guessed it was another one of those off-brand, made-up songs made-for-TV movies used so they didn't have to get the rights to the actual popular stuff. Annie and Chris made their way to the entrance of the rink, escorting kids to Nick, Annie's mind in desperate need of redirection. She could not think about how she had almost mauled Nick in the ice rink's shed. She needed to charm Chris.

Thankfully, the time passed in an easy haze of slow skating, candy cane sharing, and general holiday merriment. When the last child, a patient Holly, had whispered her Christmas list into Nick's ear, Chris took his daughter's hand to enjoy the free skate portion of the event and opened the gate for the town's skating community to join them. Annie set off over to Nick, where Bailey was fawning over him and fixing his beard.

"Sister Elf!" Noelle bellowed from the entrance, beckoning Bailey over with broad arm motions.

"Is she okay?" Annie asked.

"I'll check!" Bailey chirped. "Be back soon, Santa!" And with that, Bailey completed one of her signature twirls and sped off to Noelle. Annie turned to look at Noelle, who gestured at her to help Nick up and do a few laps around. It was an impressive amount of information she was able to convey with only her eyes and some rather theatrical movements.

"How you doin', Santa baby? Did you have a nice time away from the North Pole?" Annie asked sweetly.

"I did. The kids all asked for, like, the cutest stuff, like snow on Christmas morning or for their families to all be together."

"What did Holly ask for?" Annie asked.

"A new mother and a new wife for her dad," Nick said with a grimace.

"No!" Annie gasped. "We have to get out of here so that none of that can be real and Holly can return to the made-for-TV bubble of oblivion," Annie said, shaking her head. "Alright, then, can I give you a hand, old man?"

"Sure," Nick said, standing and holding on to Annie. "Let's give these costumes a few more moments, shall we?" He offered an arm to Annie so she could link hers through it, and once joined, they skated in sync. They slowly passed a few townspeople until Annie spotted the gentleman she had seen earlier at the inn. The one who was apparently on security detail. Annie squinted at his frame, again finding something familiar in his stance she couldn't quite put her finger on. He kept his dark glasses on, so it was hard to discern specific details of his face, but even at their distance, Annie still questioned if he was wearing an ill-fitting bald cap.

"Hey, there's that security guy from the inn. Does he look familiar to you?" Annie asked, trying to get a better look. She wasn't looking where she was skating and ended up colliding with Chris. Annie dropped Nick's arm as her hands went up protectively, running into Chris's broad chest and causing her right skate to catch. Before she could fall, though, Chris had caught her in midair.

"Funny meeting you here," Chris said suavely.

"Chris!" Annie said, trying to right herself. "I'm sorry! Thank you for saving me . . . again," Annie breathed out, flushed from the close call.

"Are you okay?" Chris asked, revealing a small dimple on his cheek that Annie had never noticed before. "Do you need to sit down?"

"I can take you, Annie, if you need," Nick said with a look of concern.

"No, no, I'm fine," Annie said.

"Then could I interest you in a skate around the rink together?" Chris asked shyly, and Annie nodded, giving

Nick a victorious smile, her sights set on winning that iced coffee. Nick gave her a hesitant thumbs-up before jumping back into his Santa character, skating away with a series of loud "ho ho hos."

Annie allowed herself to be pulled in close, taking in the scent of pine wafting from Chris, even in his elf costume. Their linked arms didn't charge her with lust, but it was indeed comforting. A pleasant place to catch her breath. She tried not to question why she had wanted to kiss Nick earlier when the whole point of her being here was to kiss Chris. Wasn't he the rightful answer to this movie puzzle?

"Have I mentioned that you make a lovely Mrs. Claus?" Chris asked Annie.

"You did, but happy to hear it again," Annie smiled at him. "Who knew you'd make such a cute elf?"

"Well, I have been playing the part for years," Chris said proudly.

"Of course," Annie conceded.

"I know your fashion job in the big city is so important, but I sure am glad the snowstorm gave us a chance to enjoy some small-town holiday fun. You know, before you have to head back to the big city for your fashion job," Chris said.

Annie scrunched her eyebrows in contemplation. She would have loved to share this sentiment with Marsha, considering they worked together on this "fashion job." In the past three years, they had gone from conducting business out of their West Hartford apartment to a garage in Newington and, finally, to renting an actual (though tiny) office space courtesy of Grant's connections.

Annie had been employed as a personal assistant to a monstrous man who ran a local travel website. While she had often enjoyed the perks of featuring new places in the Farmington Valley and surrounding areas, no amount of free food could make up for the late-night calls Annie had received from her boss, screaming at her to deliver yet another highly personal item to his home or the barrage of rageful texts he'd explode her phone with when a rose ceremony on *The Bachelorette* didn't unfold the way he wanted (which, spoiler alert, was every time). Marsha had been working as a store manager for Bath & Body Works. A job she had fallen into after having worked there during her college breaks from UConn. She had come to completely despise it. She hated being directed to micromanage the staff of mostly older, exclusively part-time women, who would knit on their breaks, while under constant scrutiny and pressure from the off-site corporate offices to sell more A Thousand Wishes body splash.

After a particularly brutally cold and cruel New England winter and a messy breakup on Marsha's end (that had actually unfolded in the Bath & Body Works break room and resulted in a few sympathy knit items), Annie had suggested selling their used underwear for money to put toward visiting a warm beach, with an unlimited cocktail package to survive the season. The actual suggestion had come out of an exceptionally bothersome evening when some frozen pipes near their washing machines had flooded the apartment building's basement, making it impossible to do laundry. Annie had even gone so far as to put up a detailed and very descriptive ad on Craigslist, assuming they'd get a good laugh reading a response or two while taking another spoonful of peanut butter and handful of popcorn for dinner and debating which of their parents would be more helpful in lending them access to their washer and dryer.

What followed were fifty-three emails of interest within the hour. After a quick trip to retrieve a six-pack of Bud Light Lime (the beverage of choice at the time for sharpening their minds and loosening their morals), Marsha and Annie drafted a proposal that would eventually become their business plan.

It hadn't been the easiest road during those early years. Until they could hire people to help them with it, Annie and Marsha had to oversee all of the customer operations, website design and maintenance, and ensure quality content. No, they never sold their own underwear; they were merely the middle women of the operation, but most of their friends and family thought they were absolutely insane. When Annie and Marsha were both able to go full-time with LaundryBae after a year of steadily and safely simplifying sales between used underwear sellers and satisfied buyers, they celebrated with an all-inclusive vacation to Mexico featuring an elaborate food and drink menu.

Marsha met Pete Cohen in line for iced coffees and sour gummy worms before even boarding the plane. Pete was heading to the same resort for a bachelor party, and Annie eagerly enjoyed harmlessly flirting with all of his (mostly married and all agreeably dorky) friends at the gate. It had been love at first flight, and Pete had proved to be the perfect souvenir for Marsha to bring back home after a week of tipsy bliss. Within a few months, Marsha had moved in with Pete, leaving Annie in the one-bedroom they used to share. For the first time in her life, Annie was living alone. But it allowed them to conduct their business in Pete's garage before they had the means to move to an office. Aside from spending their days focused on the best practices and policies for facilitating the sale of dirty panties to (mostly) men in need, it all felt rather professional and grown-up.

Annie blinked back to the present, catching Chris's expression. He seemed suddenly more serious, his eyes dark and debonair. He slowed down so they were almost at a standstill and was about to say something when Annie's skate caught a rogue candy cane on the ice, sending her body into another graceful, slow-motion fall. This time, Chris caught her and allowed her to stay momentarily suspended, his arms holding her up and his face mere inches from her own. And then when he glanced at her lips, Annie almost choked in surprise. Wait, was this their almost kiss? Was it happening right now? *What do I do*, Annie wondered, instinctively seeking out Nick, hoping he could guide her through this, but instead of Nick's eyes, she landed on a much more familiar pair, and her heart stopped.

CHAPTER THIRTEEN

"Marsha!" Annie yelled, breaking free of Chris and blindly skating her way through a small crowd. She knew those eyes from the deepest depth of her soul—she had seen Marsha! This was it, her best friend was here to save her, save Christmas, save everything. "Marsha!" Annie called out again, desperately trying to get another view.

She stopped mid-skate when a movement caught her attention. Annie marveled at a woman performing a series of axles and spirals on the ice. She was dressed in a lilac-colored coat and a matching knit hat. When she completed what looked to be another double axel, she found Annie's eyes. Again, Annie could see it was Marsha. Well, her face looked like Marsha, but the woman was clearly wearing a wig of strawberry blonde curls.

"Marsha!" Annie said for a third time, but her voice wavered in confusion now. The woman cocked her head to the side.

"Hello, have we met?" the woman asked kindly, skating closer, Marsha's familiar "professional" smile plastered on her face.

"Marsh, are you in on this whole thing? Was this some elaborate prank?" Annie asked, skating closer to meet the woman.

"Oh, are you Annie? I've heard all about you from Grant. He says you're very funny," the woman said. "I'm Eve," Eve continued in an accent Annie couldn't quite place. It was sort of British, but it sounded like the attempt of a formal, stylized voice more than anything else.

"No, I'm not doing this," Annie shook her head. "Marsha, stop, please," Annie begged.

"I'm sorry, I don't know what you mean," Eve said. "Are you alright?"

Annie didn't know if she should laugh or cry. She looked at Ferguson and now it clicked why he looked familiar. Ferguson was Pete, Marsha's boyfriend, wearing his own weird wig and costume.

"Pete?" Annie asked, looking up at him. He stared back, unmoving.

"You okay, Mrs. Claus?" Nick asked loudly, skating up behind her. "I saw you almost fall . . . again . . . and then rush off. I wanted to make sure you were okay," Nick continued more softly.

"Nick, that's Marsha. And her boyfriend Pete," Annie urgently confided; she needed Nick to make this stop, to make sense of another absurd ornament on their farcical tree. Nick gave Eve a scrutinous glance, his eyebrows furrowed in thought.

"I can certainly see a resemblance," Nick murmured to Annie. Annie wanted to argue and insist that the person standing with them was her lifelong best friend and that she practically knew her face better than her own. "Your skating . . . It's incredible. Are you an Olympian?" Nick asked Eve in an attempt to uncover their true identities.

"Oh, you're too kind. No, but I did train with our country's Olympic coaches from an early age as part of my exercise regime," Eve said as Ferguson offered an encouraging nod.

"Your country? Where are you from?" Nick asked.

"May I please formally present Princess Eve from the kingdom of Wintermore," Ferguson said in his low baritone voice. Eve committed to a deep, graceful curtsy on skates, showcasing impressive flexibility. There was an awkward moment when Nick and Annie were unsure if they were supposed to do the same; they silently eyed each other until they wordlessly agreed to attempt their own curtsies on skates. Nick moved slowly, first tucking his head, and managed to pull off a half-decent bow, all things considered. His right skate glided gracefully enough behind his left, and using his right arm to cross his center, he folded downward. Annie's venture was another story. She quickly tried to get one leg behind but hurled her body too quickly and was about to topple forward when Nick wrapped both arms around her.

Annie was so startled by the movement that it almost caused them both to go down hard on the ice, but thankfully, perhaps with the extra heft of the Santa suit, Nick centered them, and they made their way back to a standing position.

"I'm oh so very grateful the storm landed me in such a lovely, quaint American town," Eve cooed, as if she hadn't just witnessed the completely ridiculous scene. "When my private plane was forced to land here in the snowstorm, I thought it would be the worst Christmas of my life," Eve explained.

Ferguson took an ornate handkerchief from his coat pocket to give her, and Eve dabbed at dry eyes, crying on cue without a single tear. "But the people here have truly taught me the importance of the holiday season!" Eve finished with a flourish.

"I'm sorry, what? What's happening right now? What is this?" Annie asked Nick. She was baffled but not in the mood to entertain this ridiculous charade. Nick could only offer a small shrug. "Why are they here? Why are they like this?" Annie hissed angrily. She had no intention of simply accepting that her best friend was here being introduced to this world under the guise of a new character.

"Movie storylines often include a best friend," Nick considered. "They usually show up to, like, give a boost of encouragement or give some advice without overshadowing the protagonist. And often, they're introduced as a 'Christmas cheerleader' who also doubles as an emotional anchor—"

"She's my Holiday Hype Queen?" Annie asked, desperate for an answer.

"Oh, I'm not a queen, I'm a princess," Eve bashfully interjected. When Annie turned to her, desperation practically dripping off her face, Eve skated backward, ready to escape this strange interaction.

"Wait, you can't leave me. When can we see each other again?" Annie asked, not wanting to sound so manic but completely unraveling into unhinged. Even if this version of Marsha was not the one she wanted right now, Annie needed her best friend.

"Perhaps we'll cross paths again at one of tomorrow's holiday offerings?" Eve asked with a hopeful smile that couldn't quite hide her need to retreat from Annie's fervent energy. "Ta-ta!"

"All okay, Annie?" Chris asked, skating closer as Eve exited. "Looks like you could use a hot chocolate."

Annie's heart sank as Eve offered a finger wave, turned her back, and made her way off the ice with Ferguson. When Annie turned back to Chris, it hit her that she had also missed a chance to almost kiss him. This entire event had left her feeling even more defeated and deflated. How did Marsha now fit into this whole thing? Why was she here in disguise? And why couldn't Annie have gotten the princess storyline?

"We should probably get changed if we're going to make it to rehearsal on time," Nick said, sensing that Annie was about to burst—whether into tears or flames, neither of them was sure.

"Yes, of course." Chris nodded his head enthusiastically. "Thank you both again for volunteering your time for such an important production. Holly and I will see you at the theater," Chris grinned, putting on a voice to emphasize "theater."

"We don't want to be late for our first rehearsal," Nick said without a hint of sarcasm.

"Oh, I absolutely want to be late, very late in fact," Annie countered.

"I don't think time works like that here," Nick said. "How're you doing, really?" Nick asked her gently.

"Aside from my best friend not recognizing me and me becoming a clumsy, falling mess?" Annie asked, crossing her arms to her chest.

"Now you listen to me, young lady! Even if we're horribly mangled, there'll be no sad faces on Christmas," Nick said in his best Jim Carrey as the Grinch impression.

"That's not bad," Annie admitted.

"I spent a lot of time perfecting various Jim Carrey character impressions," Nick said proudly.

"That tracks," Annie said dryly, immediately recalling Nick's childhood obsession with Ace Ventura.

"Let's de-Santa ourselves and then I can jump into another character," Nick offered.

"What can you show me from *Eternal Sunshine of the Spotless Mind*?" Annie asked as Nick led their way off the ice.

When Annie and Nick approached the elementary school's cafeteria a few minutes (and impressions) later, they noticed Perry was outside and eagerly waiting for them.

"Hope it's alright I came, I thought I'd take you up on the offer to volunteer," Perry said.

"I'm sure they'll be happy for the help," Nick nodded, holding the door open.

"Grant kick you out?" Annie asked.

"What?" Perry asked, shocked and hurt. "No, I, um, didn't want to be in the way of his decorating. Thought I could be more useful here," Perry said, not quite meeting Annie's prying eyes.

When they entered the large cafeteria/gymnasium, everyone was already gathered in chairs in front of the wooden stage. Despite the emotional roller coaster that had been her morning, the sense of soothing nostalgia unexpectedly blanketed Annie, so cozy and comfortable. It wasn't the smell of what she remembered from school cafeterias, no rectangle pizza mixing with the aroma of kids fresh from gym class here, thank goodness.

"You look . . . happy," Nick said, looking her over. "That scares me."

"Shh," Annie murmured, trying to conjure the scent again.

"Welcome!" Chris boomed from the corner of the room, interrupting her smelling attempts. "We're so grateful that Miss Annie and Mr. Nick are here."

"We brought Perry," Annie called over to him. She hoped maybe Perry could take on some of the volunteer assignments intended for her.

"Let's welcome them, shall we?" Chris asked the group of children.

"Good morning, Miss Annie. Good morning, Mr. Nick. Good morning, Mr. Perry" the group of children sang out in perfect unison.

"Creepy," Annie whispered.

"I'm going to introduce myself to the director," Perry said, already an air of professionalism escorting him through the room.

"Nick!" Bailey called, running over to them, all trace of her earlier elf costume gone. "Annie, you're here too?" Bailey asked, barely looking at Annie before giving Nick all of her attention. "Oh, Nick, thank you so much for coming, you're always such a blessing," Bailey cooed. "I'll be taking over as stage manager, but you'll be fully in charge of all the tech stuff, of course. We'll be working side by side. Let me show you the booth first and then I'll take you backstage to see the set pieces." Bailey finished, taking Nick's arm and leading him away. Annie gave Nick a pointed glare, reminding him to get going on his almost-kiss mission.

"Hi, Miss Annie," a small voice said. Annie looked down to see Holly. She was wearing a green corduroy dress with a headband in the same color. Okay, maybe this is what she needed, the time to charm the mysterious child so she could lure her dad to an almost kiss . . . Yeah, that didn't sound like a creepy fairy tale villain at all.

"Oh, hi, Holly, how's it hanging?" Annie laughed nervously.

"Hanging? You mean the mistletoe?" Holly asked in a confused tone.

"How are you?" Annie asked instead. "Did you enjoy ice-skating?"

"I had an enchanting time," Holly smiled. "And I'm ever so pleased to make your acquaintance again, Miss Annie."

"Err, okay. Cool, cool," Annie said, looking around for Chris. She wanted to make sure her efforts with Holly were not going unnoticed.

"Do you want to see the costumes?" Holly asked.

"Will your dad be joining us?" Annie tried.

"He's about to start warm-ups," Holly said, taking Annie's hand in hers and leading her to a room behind the stage. It was a strangely intimate moment holding this little child's soft hand, like Holly's fingers were embracing a tiny piece of her heart that Annie hadn't been aware of until now. *Stop that*, Annie thought, *that's got to be the made-for-TV movie brain hard at work and I can't afford to be so susceptible to its powers.*

When Annie walked into the costume room, she nearly lost her breath at its depth. The walls were lined with rows of shiny silver clothing racks full of pristine pieces arranged firstly by item type and then by color. Annie spun around to get a 360 view of the space, yearning for a soundtrack to instigate her own trying-on-costumes montage, her fingers already twitching to touch every item.

"Do you like it, Miss Annie?" Holly asked hopefully.

"Yes," Annie answered with genuine affection. "It's all so beautiful."

"I'm sure you must see a lot of impressive clothing in your big-city fashion job," Holly said shyly.

"I do indeed work with a lot of, um, impressive items," Annie admitted, thinking of one of their more memorable customers who sought out underwear specifically worn while their owner competed in local baking competitions, asking that the pair please be packaged with some sort of used cooking utensil. *It's always bread week somewhere*, Annie thought before returning to Holly, unwilling to go into the nuances of her job with this small child. "So what exactly do you guys need my help with here?"

"We need to ensure everyone has the proper costume. Here's the cast list and what each character should be wearing in each scene," Holly said, handing over a neat and color-coded tabbed binder.

"Got it," Annie said. "So I can go through what we have here and help organize some options. Then I'll pull kids individually to confirm things fit before setting the rack."

"Wow," Holly whispered in complete awe.

"What?" Annie asked.

"You're so professional, Miss Annie. You know how to do everything," Holly marveled.

"I think you're giving me way too much credit," Annie smiled and hid her reddening face behind a rack of tweed jackets.

"We're so happy to have you and Mr. Nick here, helping us," Holly said. "And I know my dad is really, really glad you're here, Miss Annie." Annie looked back at Holly and she was giving her a significant stare. It made Annie's insides squirm, unsure what to say—was this kid going to be her wing-woman? Annie brought her hands into two waving big thumbs-up and grinned at Holly.

"I am happy to be here," Annie said, sort of like a robot that had been programmed to say that. Holly didn't seem to notice. "Thanks for showing me around. Will your dad come to check in on things back here soon?" Annie asked awkwardly, still feeling icky about trying to use Holly to lure Chris within kissing distance as soon as possible.

"I'll run along and check!" Holly beamed and returned to rehearsal, leaving Annie with a moment to further inspect the racks of impeccable, child-sized garments. She found herself escaping into a cloud of relaxation as she examined her list and started organizing the pieces, her thoughts never returning back to Chris or his whereabouts.

Instead, her trail of concentration found a path back to her grandparents. It was something about the warmth and the scent combination that brought her right back to their house. Annie's eyes prickled like they always did when she thought of them, and her heart squeezed with feeling. It had been over sixteen years now since their deaths, but their absence still ached in Annie's bones. They had loved the holiday season, more than anyone else she had ever met. Her grandfather's love of Christmas had been contagious, a pillar for their whole family's relationship with the yearly celebration. When her grandmother passed first, the magic and joy of the holidays had been in jeopardy of vanishing like the smoke from a forgotten fire, but her grandfather had emptied his grief into keeping the Christmas spirit alive. For all of them. Up until his last breath.

Normally, when her brain tried to replay memories of her grandparents, she'd do everything she could to stop them in their tracks. It felt too emotionally risky given how much she had adored them and how hard she tried to work daily to silence the ache of their absence. But there was a strange safeness working alone in this warm haven that disarmed her, and Annie allowed herself to recall the day her grandfather had moved into their family home, shortly after her grandmother's passing.

He'd only had about two suitcases worth of clothing, toiletries, and trinkets of his past eighty-plus years, but his Christmas menagerie had required the rental of a small U-Haul. Her parents had humored him, partially to ease their own grief and wanting to do everything in their power to lessen his, and Annie had made it her mission to make sure every item her grandfather wanted made it safely from his home and found a space in hers. The act of moving her body with a purpose kept the tears at bay and, even in her teenage state, she built a wall around her true feelings, broadcasting a strong presence to the world. Only her grandfather could see right through her, crack her open, and delicately nurture the pieces back together. In the handful of months they had spent living under the same roof, he had taken care of Annie in ways she hadn't realized until he too was gone, the void he left behind excruciating and endless.

When the first knock came from a child waiting to solidify their character's look, Annie blinked, wondering how long she had been in this room and if she could take that kind of incredible professional focus back with her to the real world forever.

Like she suspected, even after years of claimed use, the pristine costumes fit and flattered each child like they had been created just for them. Annie merely hung the pieces on new hangers and made labels with each character's name and scene. She also helped to create an established prop table, outlining each prop with masking tape so that it had a defined place to go when it wasn't onstage. It had been a small idea borrowed from the limited theatrical experience she had endured in school, but, boy oh boy, the praise was endless. Annie had to turn a blind eye when she caught Chris flagrantly blubbering at the back of the auditorium, a handmade handkerchief dancing around his face. Everyone was so dang grateful to have her there, and it made her uncomfortable because it didn't feel genuinely earned.

"Have they all been seen? The kids will be reviewing their songs," Bailey said once Annie had finished meeting all of the characters on her list.

"This show has singing in it?" Annie asked, already not a fan of whatever strange musical component awaited them.

"Of course!" Bailey said. "And we're so lucky, Chris is showcasing more of his talents and doubling as our musical director!" Bailey exclaimed, and Annie's brain pulled up that unfortunate image of Chris talentlessly plucking at guitar strings. "And now that Perry is here, he'll be taking over the choreography, what a visionary . . ."

"So Chris doesn't need me out there? He still hasn't come back here yet," Annie interrupted.

"He's handling so much with the play . . . and the family Christmas tree lot," Bailey said, oozing with admiration. "But I'm sure you'll see him soon enough," Bailey smiled and fluttered out the door.

Apparently a trained and skillful pianist, Chris was kindly and patiently leading the kids through a vocal exercise. And somehow time passed easily and unremarkably. It wasn't just the delicious, sweet smells Annie encountered nearly everywhere she went or the happy people who greeted her with genuine smiles and holiday cheer, something inside her was thawing. Her mildly cool heart? Perhaps. But the intoxicating sense of joy that radiated from every corner was nice. It was warm and peaceful, a tender landing place to rest awhile and recharge that something inside of her that she couldn't quite define.

"Still going strong, huh?" Nick asked with a knock, stepping into the room a little while later.

"How long have we been here?" Annie asked.

"I don't know, time is weird here. But rehearsal is over," Nick said, casually making his way around the costumes and admiring pieces that caught his eye.

"Already?" Annie asked. She was genuinely surprised that she had managed to busy herself with the faint sounds of children singing for the rehearsal's entire duration.

"Everyone is heading out. Apparently, it's nighttime," Nick said.

"Wait, what? I haven't eaten anything since the pancakes and I'm not even hungry . . . and I still haven't even seen Chris, let alone almost kiss him!" Annie moaned.

"Don't worry, it's the first night of the Christmas festival, we can make up time there," Nick assured her.

"So no almost kisses for you either?" Annie asked.

"No, I was consumed with putting set pieces together and painting a backdrop . . . and then Bailey asked if I'd help grab a few things for the bakery's booth and I realized rehearsal had ended."

"Maybe you can attempt your food fight idea," Annie suggested.

"Nick? Can we head over now?" Bailey asked, appearing at the door. "I can treat you to a warm cup of hot chocolate," she added with a wink. Bailey looped her arm through Nick's, and Nick turned to Annie with a raised eyebrow, suggesting his almost-kiss opportunity window might be opening.

"Okay, we'll meet you at the festival," Nick said reassuringly as Bailey led them off, and Annie nodded, ignoring the unwelcome knot in her stomach at the sight of Nick and Bailey leaving together.

Giving herself a moment to not immediately shadow Nick and Bailey, Annie double-checked everything had been neatly placed back on racks and turned off the lights in the costume shop. The school was eerily quiet and still as Annie navigated herself outside, where it was indeed dark, all signs pointing to an ambiguous evening hour. Within a few short steps, she was enveloped into a crowd all traversing the incredibly short distance to the Christmas festival in the town center square.

CHAPTER FOURTEEN

"Happy first night of the Annual Simsbury Tri-Night Yuletide Festival of Light and Holiday Merriment, Featuring Joy, Wonder, and Magic!" Noelle thundered.

Annie wasn't sure if it was the event's title or Noelle's very sudden appearance, popping out from behind a decorative inflatable reindeer alongside a deafening squeak from the plastic, but she jumped back before freezing abruptly in surprise.

"Noelle, hi, I didn't see you there," Annie muttered, giving her heartbeat a chance to return to normal speed.

"Sounds like someone needs to let loose and enjoy the real fun of the night." Noelle smiled broadly, reminding Annie of a jack-in-the-box still taunting the person it had just frightened. However, she was intrigued about what a woman who drove out of her way for oatmeal cookies considered "letting loose."

"There's nothing quite like the Annual Simsbury Tri-Night Yuletide Festival of Light and Holiday Merriment, Featuring Joy, Wonder, and Magic. I'm so happy it's here!" Noelle beamed. To Annie, three nights of celebration were three too many, and that title might be the most egregious one yet. However, if time passed as quickly as it had that day, perhaps it wouldn't be as traumatic as she imagined.

"And then, don't forget, it's the Christmas Ball," Noelle smiled again, her twinkling eyes landing on Felix, who was a few feet ahead. "This is the most magical week of the year," Noelle breathed, stopping in her tracks and closing her eyes to take it all in. When she didn't immediately open them again or attempt to move, Annie broke the moment.

"It really is," Annie said loudly, hoping Noelle would come out of her trance. She did not.

So Annie entered the festival alone. She was grateful to have the moment to herself as it forced her to slow down and better appreciate the sights, sounds, and scents flooding her senses. She stepped through a broad, lighted archway. The tiny white lights gave the illusion of walking among the stars and being blanketed in the power of their wishes, and even Annie had to admit the scene was beautiful, and she could feel a surge of endorphins dancing inside her brain. Once officially through, she was greeted by multiple small booths arranged in a row. Sellers were showcasing displays of cashmere scarves, leather bookmarks, and journals. A vendor immediately handed her a small, covered white cup of what she assumed was hot chocolate.

Annie took a sip from the cup and was surprised to find it completely empty. Huh, perhaps the prop person purposely hadn't filled it to keep the hot chocolate budget within its daily range? Or perhaps to-go hot chocolates were always served without actual contents in the made-for-television movie world. Either way, she was impressed that her lipstick hadn't left a trace of its rosy pink color on the lid. Around her, the jovial hum of voices circled.

"What am I supposed to do with this?" Annie asked no one in particular, and when no one answered her, she shrugged and continued to hold it as if it were a full cup of cocoa and it was warming her hands. When Annie turned back to the closest hot chocolate stall, she watched Grant and Perry collide. Though the "crash" was more of a choreographed dance of two committed actors hitting their respective marks.

"For someone who doesn't celebrate the season, I didn't think I'd see you here," Grant said cooly.

"Is this about the mistletoe? I told you, it was an accident. Corporate wanted shots of the lobby without all the holiday clutter. I didn't know it would be so fragile—" Perry explained.

"Are you talking about the mistletoe, the inn, or me?" Grant challenged, eyebrows arched. He masterfully pivoted on his loafered heel with a grand flourish and disappeared into a crowd. Perry's face fell, but just as quickly, he pulled himself together and exited in the opposite direction.

"Hi, Miss Annie," Holly said, suddenly appearing and snapping Annie out of her trance. "I'm ever so happy to see you again at the Annual Simsbury Tri-Night Yuletide Festival of Light and Holiday Merriment, Featuring Joy, Wonder, and Magic."

"You snuck up on me, Holly!" Annie said with a small laugh. "I almost dropped my cocoa," she joked.

"Oh no, I'm terribly sorry," Holly said.

"No need to apologize, I was caught up in my own thoughts and not paying attention. How are you enjoying the festival?" Annie asked.

"It's divine," Holly said. "This is the stuff of dreams."

"Wow, you're a little poet, aren't you?" Annie asked, and Holly smiled.

"Do you want to come see the Christmas tree lighting with me?" Holly asked hopefully.

"Sure." Annie shrugged, her eyes glancing around the crowd. "Where's your dad?"

"He's right near the tree!" Holly grinned, pointing at Chris. He looked taller than ever set against the green branches, and when he caught her eye, Annie gave him a small wave. She had to make him feel his heart was safe with hers and still hot enough to try and almost kiss.

Holly guided the way to a ginormous Christmas tree, covered in unlit lights and red round ornaments with "Simsbury" scripted in white writing. There was a small crowd already orbiting around it.

"Hello, stranger." Chris smiled at Annie, his teeth looking unnaturally white. "I'm sorry I didn't have the chance to visit the costume shop during rehearsal; the kids were really connecting with the material, and I didn't want to interrupt their creative flow. How are you finding the Annual Simsbury Tri-Night Yuletide Festival of Light and Holiday Merriment, Featuring Joy, Wonder, and Magic's first evening?"

"Oh, I'm okay," Annie said, already flustered. She realized that this might have been the first time Chris had ever asked her a genuine question and waited with care and attention for her to answer it. She felt butterflies unleash themselves through her body, and Annie cleared her throat, hoping it could also clear her head. "The costumes are great. Holly was a wonderful help in getting me all set up. I'm really enjoying her company," Annie continued, seeing Chris light up at her words. *Keep it up, Annie, and maybe you can flatter and flirt your way to this almost kiss,* she coached herself. "Oh, and the music is great. I didn't realize you were also the musical director; you're doing so much," Annie said, trying to match Bailey's tone and essence when she talked to Nick. Annie leaned closer and tried to make her eyes smolder before deliberately lightly biting her bottom lip in slow motion, hoping Chris's eyes would linger there. Instead, a ringing noise cut through their conversation.

"Sorry, Annie, looks like I'm needed, I'll be right back," Chris said, abruptly speed-walking to the podium where a small group of people were securing the microphone equipment. Annie sighed. *Guess I'll have to go harder next time*, Annie mused before turning back to Holly, who had been admiring the tree.

"Who lights this thing?" Annie asked, gazing upward at the massive spruce.

"Only the kindest, wisest, and best hot chocolate maker in the world! The mayor, of course," Holly answered proudly.

"We have a mayor?" Annie asked.

"My uncle!" Holly grinned.

"Felix is the mayor? Like there was an actual election with more than one candidate, and Felix won? What's his platform?" Annie asked, beyond fascinated to get a pulse on the political scene in town. But Holly only giggled, assuming Annie was making another one of her silly jokes. Before Annie could press for more information, the cluster of people parted, sparking action and making way for Felix to approach and officially welcome everyone to the Annual Simsbury Tri-Night Yuletide Festival of Light and Holiday Merriment, Featuring Joy, Wonder, and Magic. He didn't appear to be hurt or walking with a limp. "Wait. Didn't Felix injure himself this morning?" Annie asked, but her question was swallowed up in the applause and cheers for the mayor.

"Why, hello there," Felix began, his cheeks rosier than ever and glistening under the pale moonlight, his eyes already looking wistful and far away. "It fills me with great joy to be with you all tonight. This charming town and its charitable people are surrounded by the magic of Christmas. Every year we have together is special, but this one feels like it has a little extra something," Felix said, and Annie swore he directed that last bit to her. "This is a time for love and light. A season made for surprises and magic. So without further ado, let's bring our beloved tree some of our renowned Simsbury spirit!" Felix reached over to flick the large switch next to the podium, and everyone collectively drew in a breath of anticipation and looked expectantly to the tree. When the tree remained dim, Felix chuckled nervously. "Hmm, well, perhaps we'll try that again, shall we?" He switched the contraption again, but nothing happened. A faint disappointed and confused murmur grew among the crowd of people. Annie found herself moving a bit closer to the tree and noticed immediately that the main plug was out of place and dangling limply, making it impossible for any electricity to reach the myriad lights. From a few feet away, Annie found Nick.

"It's not plugged in," Annie mouthed to Nick. When he didn't understand her, she mouthed it again, miming accompanying hand gestures. Once Annie could see his mental light bulb illuminate in understanding, Nick lowered himself under the tree to plug it in.

"Try it now!" Nick called out. Annie saw him stand up from under the tree, adjust his wool beanie, and beam. Felix took a deep breath and pulled back his shoulders and for the third time, switched on the panel. With this attempt, the tree exploded to life with sparkly brilliance, Annie's mouth dropped open; it was blindingly beautiful. Her eyes widened, longing to take it all in. Voices around them erupted into celebration and cheer. Annie made her way closer to Nick, Holly at her heel, but before she could reach him, Annie watched Bailey plant a kiss on Nick's cheek, leaving a very bold red imprint where her lips had been.

"Oh, Nick, your quick thinking saved Christmas!" Bailey beamed.

"Give the man the credit. Typical," Annie muttered.

"It was nothing. And it was Annie who noticed it was unplugged in the first pl—" Nick smiled bashfully, realizing he was standing under a curiously placed bundle of mistletoe hanging off the tree.

"Should we? For old time's sake?" Bailey whispered, her eyes looking like two hearts targeted on the mistletoe. Annie held her breath, waiting for one of them to make a move. Nick glanced at Annie and she gave him a weak thumbs-up. Maybe Nick would full-on kiss Bailey and this would all go away so they'd be able to escape. Instead, though, Bailey grabbed Nick's face and planted another red-staining kiss on his other cheek. Annie let out a sigh, unsure if she was relieved or disappointed to find that nothing appeared to have changed.

"Wow, Annie, always such an eye. The hero of night one of the Annual Simsbury Tri-Night Yuletide Festival of Light and Holiday Merriment, Featuring Joy, Wonder, and Magic," Chris whispered in Annie's ear without even a shade of sarcasm. Instead, he stared at her fondly and with such warmth, opening his arms and offering a grateful hug. "Want to walk around a bit?" Chris asked and Annie nodded. Holly reached for Annie's open hand and Annie jumped, unaware the child had been so close, but after a moment they eased into a companionable quiet as they meandered through the wares of various stalls and traded their old empty small cups for new empty small cups.

Once Holly had joined a few school friends, Annie kept her eyes peeled for rogue mistletoe clusters she might be able to take advantage of; perhaps if she could time it just right, she could maneuver Chris under one and he would make a move. But she should have been looking down because it was on a piece of fallen mistletoe that Annie's foot caught and that spun her body into yet another classic clumsy moment. On cue, and without giving her a chance to fall, Chris wrapped his arms around Annie's body.

CHAPTER FIFTEEN

"Can't have you falling head over heels for mistletoe, even when it's clearly trying to sweep you off your feet," Chris smiled, the dimple in his cheek reappearing.

"I swear, I'm not normally this clumsy!" Annie told him, feeling ruffled.

"I like being around to catch you," Chris said. "Makes me feel useful . . . and also, down to earth and grounded," Chris joked with a small wink. Annie's face broke out into a surprised smile. His small joke had actually landed for her, and she couldn't help but feel charmed.

"Cute, very cute," Annie said, enjoying the way Chris was looking at her.

"Chris, do you think you could lend me a hand?" Felix asked, interrupting their eye contact. He was now dressed as Santa, and Annie wondered if it was the same costume Nick had been forced to put on that morning.

"Glad to see you seem to have made a full recovery, Felix," Annie said, eyeing his leg before shooting him a sigh of annoyance for interrupting her moment with Chris.

Felix let out a "ho ho ho" chuckle in response.

"How can I help?" Chris asked eagerly.

"I'm preparing the sleigh," Felix said, and Annie's eyes widened. "For the festival's complimentary sleigh rides," Felix explained to her.

"We're going to make sure everything is set with the horses, Annie. Why don't you come join us in a little bit?" Chris smiled, and Annie uncharacteristically lit up. Even if this place wasn't real and was otherwise absolutely absurd, the idea of getting to ride in a sleigh with Santa sounded downright delightful.

Once Annie was alone again, determined not to fall again today, she found Nick admiring a stall of homemade ornaments.

"Where's Bailey?" Annie asked.

"Baking emergency," Nick shrugged. "I think their stall ran out of cookies."

"You didn't go with her? That could have been a good almost-kiss opportunity," Annie scolded, though she didn't want to acknowledge that a part of her didn't want Nick to complete it.

"I tried, but she said she'd be right back . . ." Nick explained. Annie and Nick turned to see a line of people now waiting for sleigh rides. Felix had control over two beautifully adorned horses with green coats covered in small bells and was taking small groups around in a circle. Annie saw Chris, Holly, and Bailey in the sleigh now, and when Bailey saw Nick she gave him a huge wave.

"What the truck?" Annie groaned. "How and why are they now all on a ride together?"

"I'm sure there's a reason," Nick said so softly that Annie wasn't sure he had actually said it. He turned to her and asked, "Do you want to take a sleigh ride?"

"Duh," Annie answered immediately and moved to get them a place in line. "But I thought I was going to ride it with Chris," Annie muttered.

"Did you want to wait for him?" Nick asked.

"No, it's fine . . . Oh, unless you wanted to go with Bailey? We can wait in line if you want to ride with her . . . ?" Annie asked, trailing off.

"I'm okay to ride together if you are?" Nick asked hesitantly, and Annie couldn't tell if he felt bad for her or if he genuinely wanted to ride with her, and the unknowing made her uncomfortable. "I've always wanted to ride in a sleigh."

"Me too," Annie said as they stood quietly in line. Around them, kids were playing "pin the nose on Rudolph" by taking turns to cover their eyes and spinning around before attempting to place their red, round felt pieces on the reindeer. Annie was impressed that, even after spinning around in circles, the kids managed to maintain their accuracy and all of the noses landed somewhere on Rudolph's face.

"Hi, Miss Annie!" Holly said, running over to give Annie a squeeze.

"Hi there, how was the sleigh ride? Was it 'snow cool'?" Annie asked, immediately regretting her attempt to be punny when Chris let out a loud booming laugh.

"There she goes again," Chris laughed, wiping his eyes. "I'm sorry we missed the chance to ride together. Felix wanted to make sure the horses had been properly secured so we were testing it out. I didn't realize we were so close to Holly's bedtime," Chris said more softly to Annie.

"I understand." Annie nodded, noticing that Nick and Bailey were also currently involved in a hushed conversation of their own and turned away from it. "I'd love to take a sleigh ride with Santa while I have the chance," Annie admitted. Even if Nick wanted to ditch her here now, she had waited in line and was not about to lose the opportunity to be dragged around by Santa and two beautiful horses.

"Of course, you'll love it," Chris told Annie. He grabbed her hand to squeeze before trading it for Holly's mittened one.

"Have fun, I'll be at the bakery's booth," Bailey told Nick, batting her eyelashes up at him and heading off in the same direction as Chris and Holly.

"All aboard!" Felix said to Annie and Nick, his eyes twinkling with all the stars of the universe.

"That was fast," Annie said, turning to see that they had somehow moved up in line, and it was already their turn. Nick stepped in first and then turned to offer his hand to Annie to assist her in getting in.

"This has some magic carpet vibes," Annie marveled, taking Nick's hand.

"Do you trust me?" Nick asked, offering his best Aladdin impression.

"I do, actually," Annie admitted, settling into her seat. Throughout all of this, Nick had been just as trustworthy as he had been as a kid; it was so familiar and wonderfully comfortable to her.

"We have room for two more," Felix offered. "Grant! Come on up," he said after spotting him in line. "Chipperton!"

Felix hollered out, clocking the guy at a nearby hot chocolate stall. "Join us!"

"This guy's trying to be a matchmaker, huh?" Annie smirked at Nick, who was unexpectedly flustered at the suggestion.

"Take a seat," Felix smiled, tucking Nick and Annie into the same side. "I know how you city folk have a harder time with these cooler temperatures."

"Oh, um—" Annie said, about to say she didn't need a blanket, and she questioned how many people had used the thing and if it had ever been washed . . . even still, she wanted it. Grant and Perry reached the carriage and were stepping in when Felix turned his head to her and winked.

Grant and Perry avoided eye contact and both crossed their arms, turning as far as they could in a small carriage seat. Annie narrowed her eyes, curious to read the vibe unfolding here.

"Textbook forced proximity courtesy of lingering tension," Nick whispered in explanation.

"Is this the G-rated equivalent of the 'only one bed' trope?" Annie asked.

"I think so," Nick smiled approvingly, impressed with Annie's connection. "Classic unresolved feelings stuff . . ." Nick trailed off, lightly patting the blanket between them. "This blanket reminds me of the one my mom always brought for us to sit on during fireworks," Nick said, studying the item. His thigh pushed into Annie's, sending a wave of tingling heat she tried to extinguish. Rationally, she knew she should be strategizing her almost-kiss with Chris, but it seemed each time she tried to focus, she'd be distracted by Nick or yet another remembrance of her grandfather at Christmas. "I'm sure we used it for a Simsbury

Celebrates when we were growing up," Nick smiled, speaking of the yearly town event that actually did feel straight from a made-for-TV Christmas movie. Traditionally, crowds of people walked along Hopmeadow Street, securing their spot to watch the Simsbury Volunteer Fire Company showcase their decorated trucks, and kids would wait to catch candy tossed into their eager fingers. Afterward, there would be a fireworks spectacular launched from Simsbury Meadows Performing Arts Center. The event always heralded the holiday season and had been a treasured tradition for all the kids in their neighborhood to attend together. "You always made sure I got the same amount of candy as the older kids," Nick said fondly.

"I don't remember that," Annie laughed, craning her neck to Nick.

"You did, you were always in front and would pass candy back to me if I missed some."

"Are you sure I wasn't just giving you the non-chocolate pieces I didn't want?" Annie asked.

"I wouldn't have cared about that. You were always sharing with me, making me feel included. It meant a lot," Nick said, his cheeks rosy. "Did you go to Simsbury Celebrates this year?" Nick asked, finally making eye contact with Annie again.

"Um, no," Annie said with a laugh, though she was unable to remember what she had done the Saturday evening after Thanksgiving when Simsbury Celebrates was scheduled. Most likely, it had involved her couch and reality television.

"Maybe next year," Nick said, admiring the night sky. The wind whooshed at them as Felix took a turn, sending Annie closer to Nick and Perry closer to Grant.

"I'm sorry," Perry said.

"You keep saying that," Grant replied.

"What's going to resolve this?" Annie asked Nick, gesturing to Perry and Grant.

"A partridge and a Perry," Nick joked. When Annie ignored him, he went on, "Continued involvement in some sort of community activity?"

"Hey, Chipperton," Annie said, jumping on the chance.

"You can call me Perry," Perry said.

"Nah," Annie brushed him off. She knew she'd likely never have the chance to address a Chipperton again, and she wasn't going to waste it. "I wanted to say how nice it was that you volunteered to help with the play since you're snowed in here too and all."

Annie saw Grant take the bait and give Perry a kinder, quizzical look of interest.

"I wanted to lend a hand, or a foot really, with choreography," Perry started before turning to Grant and lowering his voice. "Maybe you'll see I don't hate the holidays after all . . . and that I can be more mindful of the more delicate items in town." Grant gave Perry a nod as they engaged in meaningful eye contact.

Annie grinned as a gust of wind made its way through her hair. She closed her eyes for a moment to fully appreciate the sound of the horse's hooves rhythmically meeting the road. When she opened them again, Nick was smiling back at her, equally enchanted by the wholesome experience. And with his warm frame beside her, it somehow blissfully silenced the thoughts in her head. Annie wanted to ask Felix to go around the path a few more times but knew better than to show Santa blatant naughtiness toward her neighbors; she eyed the older woman she had confronted outside the snow globe store, sending pointed stares her way.

When their ride concluded, way too soon for the four of them, Grant and Perry walked off together, and Chris greeted Annie to offer a warm side hug as a goodbye, already carrying a sleeping Holly in his arms. Not quite the almost-kiss she was looking for to check off her to-do list, that's for sure, and yet the evening had been surprisingly fulfilling in other ways.

Annie mentally twisted her brain, desperate to recall that intense desire to make out with Chris again. The stark clarity that she couldn't summon even a fraction of the passion she had felt wanting to bang Nick in that shed left her dizzy and breathless. Annie assumed she must be doing something wrong, allowing made-for-TV movie hormones to cloud her judgment. Wasn't she supposed to want to be engaged to this version of Chris?

All the way back home, Annie picked at the problem, unable to uncover what was standing in her way. Why wasn't the idea of being with Chris giving her any sense of hope or joy? What was missing here, considering he now had everything she had wanted before? Was this why Marsha had shown up on the scene? So she could be the "voice of reason" or whatever Nick had said?

When her thoughts couldn't provide relief, Annie decided to try and smooth out the spinning spirals in a bath. The beautiful tub was a singing siren she allowed to lull her to its depths. When she had relaxed, she toweled off and found a jar of body butter in the bathroom that smelled like orange and ginger. She generously applied it across her skin, imagining herself as the two-dimensional wife character "lotion acting" as she confronts her husband about some grave matter. It had been a private joke between Annie and Marsha since high school, both of them remarking on screenplays (almost always written by a man) with a punctuated emotional moment that also still prioritized female moisturization. Annie instinctively reached out for her phone to text her friend, only to find her fingers empty. Ah, Marsha. Or perhaps, Eve? Annie's heart ached, realizing that seeing her best friend without being recognized hurt more than she could have imagined.

Annie had now completed another day in this weird world, and she was no closer to getting out of it; if anything, she was more confused than ever. She needed answers. Or at least to vent out her frustrations, and the only person she had to meet the challenge was Nick. She glanced out her window and saw the Laurels' lights were all on, so before she could second-guess herself or overthink it, Annie grabbed a blanket for a coat and marched next door.

CHAPTER SIXTEEN

Nick had the door open before Annie could knock on it. "Hi!" he said, his eyes widening in surprise.

"Glasses," Annie sputtered, seeing Nick wearing a pair. *Slutty little glasses I want to lick off his face*, she thought.

"Oh, yeah, I usually wear them at night, but my vision seems to have improved here, I put them on more from habit—"

"Don't take them off," Annie ordered as Nick adjusted the glasses. "I mean, do what you want!" Annie tried to laugh her lust off.

"I was about to come knock on your door and ask if you'd walk around the house with me and turn off the lights," Nick admitted, and Annie was grateful for the subject change.

"Turn off the lights?" Annie asked and allowed herself to be ushered inside.

"Yeah, like when Judy Garland asks the boy next door to accompany her around the house . . . ?" Nick continued heartily.

"What are you talking about?"

"Annie Meyers. You've never seen *Meet Me in St. Louis*?" Nick asked, putting his hand on his heart in mock disbelief.

"I don't think so. I don't remember."

"Oh. This is not a film one forgets," Nick told her. "We are watching it immediately. Or, fine, I will restart it because I watched some last night . . ."

"I thought we didn't have access to TV!" Annie yelled, whacking his arm.

"We don't. This is on VHS." Nick winced, rubbing the area.

"VHS," Annie exhaled in wonderment.

"A relic, that's for sure," Nick nodded.

"Wow, well, okay. Sounds better than talking to Arthur . . . but at some point, we need to talk strategy and reevaluate our circumstances. Today was a bust," Annie sighed. "Any luck on your end?"

"I wouldn't call today a bust. We did a ton of stuff. But if you're asking if I won an iced coffee tonight, no, I did not."

"Oh, hey, do you have any snacks? And if you offer me hot chocolate or a sugar cookie, I will light the street on fire," Annie cautioned, and Nick laughed. She still didn't feel an urgency to eat or any pangs of true hunger, but she liked the idea of keeping her mouth occupied and the sense of normalcy only a snack could offer.

"We can raid the kitchen, but I'm afraid there may not be much," Nick said, leading the familiar walk to the kitchen, his own matching pajama set crisply swishing each time he tried a cabinet.

"I found popcorn!" Nick cried out. Annie gasped in excitement. "Looks like we can heat it on the stovetop."

"Let's pretend we're Drew Barrymore in *Scream*," Annie prompted before clearing her throat and doing her best impression of Casey Becker. "I'm getting ready to watch a video!"

"I don't think I've seen *Scream*. Or any of the *Screams*, actually," Nick admitted.

"Are you serious? What were you doing in high school?"

"Probably singing along to old movie musicals. Scary movies are scary!" Nick said, and Annie laughed. It struck her that she and Nick had laughed together more in just a few minutes than she had ever laughed with Chris.

"Well, you need to watch *Scream*. It's iconic and surprisingly funny," Annie told him as Nick turned the stove on.

"I'll see if it's in our VHS collection," Nick said.

Suddenly, a kind of nervous energy jolted through Annie. "This is kind of weird," she confessed.

"What part?" Nick asked, turning to her with a look of, what, exactly? Sadness, maybe? Whatever it was, it crept into his soft eyes and settled there.

"I mean, like, um, the two of us here hanging out without the rest of the neighborhood kids," Annie trailed off, the strange flush of butterflies returning. A particularly loud kernel burst nearby, making her jump. She was now much closer to Nick and her heart raced. She cleared her throat and stepped back. "You're also so much calmer about this whole 'we're stuck in a made-for-TV Christmas movie' scenario."

"I've always been a go-with-the-flow kind of guy," Nick said, looking away and shrugging. "Oh, I also came home and took a bath," he gushed like a child telling his friends about all his surprise birthday gifts.

"Me too! It was really nice."

Nick stepped a little closer to Annie and she involuntarily shivered. "I thought so," Nick said.

"Yeah?" Annie asked softly.

"You smell—" Nick started.

"I smell?" Annie frowned and moved back.

"No, no, it's nice!" Nick smiled. "You smell very nice."

"Oh. Okay. Thank you," Annie flushed.

"Smell me," Nick said, throwing his body closer to Annie's nose. She laughed and pushed him away. "C'mon, Annie, do it!" Nick continued.

"Do you think the movie gods would allow it?" Annie asked. "You know, since they wouldn't let us . . ." Annie trailed off, heat rising in her body, unable to stop admiring how broad his chest looked in his pajama top, her fingers desperate to unbutton it and get a look underneath. When she looked up, Nick's face carried its own intensity, and Annie wondered if he was playing out similar scenarios in his head.

Stop it, Annie, she scolded herself. Time to change the subject.

"Before we got here, did you ever wonder if you and Bailey would get back together?" Annie asked.

"Huh . . . um, honestly, no, not really. I'm not sure I'd say we're 'together' now either . . . She was my high school girlfriend, and that was a long time ago," Nick explained before laughing at a realization. "We met thanks to Simsbury's summer theater program, and the show we did was *Annie*. Bailey played the title role."

"Of course she did," Annie said, rolling her eyes. "Were you in that show? I can't remember."

"I wanted to do backstage stuff, but they were down teenage boys who willingly wanted to wake up and work on a musical all summer, so I had to play a few different parts like the trash guy and the chauffeur. Bailey and I hung out so much we ended up a couple." Nick shrugged. Annie assessed his demeanor, trying to gain a better understanding of their relationship, but was unable to truly discern anything. "Anyway, it's hard to be here and consider what's next. Like, is this our new reality now or do our old lives still exist outside of whatever this is?" Nick asked, gesturing at everything around them.

"Please don't say that. I can't commit myself to the idea that this is now our life," Annie said, shaking her head. "Does this place even exist after Christmas? And when is the made-for-TV Christmas time frame anyway?"

"That's a complicated question," Nick started.

"It shouldn't be," Annie countered, already uncomfortable with an involved answer.

"Well, there's been a whole new push of Christmas movies in July now, but traditionally, it's around mid-October running into the first week of January," Nick said.

"January sucks on its own, no way it'd survive here," Annie mused, biting her lip.

"January sucks, huh?" Nick asked, curious about her meaning.

"Duh. We're left with lights to take down in the dark. It's cold, the snow has certainly lost its charm, and what are we all supposed to look forward to? Freaking Valentine's

Day?" Annie asked. "January lurks outside the holiday snow globe, and it's gloomy and frigid. No more bells and whistles, no decorative coffee cups, once beautiful trees are sent to the garbage to be hauled away. What if this is just another thing that gets packed up and put into storage too?" Annie asked, fearful of their future.

"Is this better than spending the holiday alone?" Nick asked.

Annie wasn't sure how to respond. Her instinct was to deflect and deny, but she was more aware of that behavior being something "Past Annie" would do, and despite the odds, she wanted to be better than that. She swallowed the sassy remark she would normally have made. Nick seemed to sense she was censoring something and met her eye, ready to backtrack.

"I just mean, maybe there's something we're supposed to take away from our time here," Nick said.

"How do you know so much about these movies, anyway?" Annie asked, looking his way with a sudden, critical gaze. Nick's face flushed, and he broke their eye contact again, curling back into himself.

"I watched a lot of Christmas movies my junior year of high school," Nick said after a moment staring at the floor.

"Oh," Annie said, trying to soften her approach. Nick's demeanor clued her in that he was suddenly more exposed than she had ever seen him, displaying a seriousness that was somehow foreign. "You don't have to—" Annie started, but Nick cut her off.

"My aunt and I would watch them together when she was doing her chemotherapy," Nick said through a weighty sigh, like bringing back memories that were heavier than he realized.

"Oh, wow, Nick, I had no idea," Annie said. "I'm so sorry." Annie's stomach turned into strings of knotted Christmas lights. She had thoughtlessly teased him, assuming him to be a sentimental nerd, as if that were even a negative notion. It made her sick and disappointed in herself for not seeing him for more.

"She's been doing a lot better now," Nick said, finally allowing his face to fall back into a weak smile. "But it was a longer road than the family expected. At the time, both of my parents were working and my siblings had already finished college and were living out west, so I volunteered to sit with her once a week. It was around the holidays, and she found the movies to be a comforting distraction, and I guess I did too." Nick shrugged.

Annie's heart tried desperately to escape her chest to try and comfort Nick. She opened her mouth, trying to formulate a coherent thought, and had to close it when she couldn't quite articulate the feeling.

"You're a good person, Nick," she finally said.

"Eh," Nick shrugged. "I'm sure anyone would have done the same thing."

Annie doubted that. In any case, she didn't trust her own family to have the same faith in her, given they all thought she needed to grow up and become the adult they assumed would have shown up already.

"I'm serious. Your family is so lucky to have you in it," Annie insisted. "And I'm really glad your aunt is doing better. Does she live nearby?"

"She's become a bit of a nomad, actually," Nick said warmly. "She takes any opportunity now to travel and try new things. She's been working at an animal shelter in Hawaii for the past few months."

"I love that," Annie smiled. "That sounds like an ideal way to spend any season to me." Annie noticed the sound of popping had stopped and turned to the stove. "Do you think the popcorn is done?"

"Honestly, I don't know. I've never actually made one of these before . . ." Nick studied the aluminum tin and its foil cover. "But let's go for it." He put on an oven mitt featuring a Santa print, balancing the container in his gloved hand. Slowly, he pulled back the foil to release the steam and tipped the popped kernels into a bowl.

"Whoa, where are you taking my popcorn?" Annie asked as Nick started to move.

"Oh, the VCR is in my room," Nick said, looking slightly shy. "Is that too weird? I could try to move it?"

"No, no, that's okay, I think we're past anything being that weird here. Lead the way," Annie said, hoping he'd stop looking at her long enough that she could blush without him seeing. She had to steady herself; a bed seemed like potentially dangerous territory.

When they got to the top of the stairs, Annie admired the elaborate decorations filling the hallway. The design of the room looked similar to the one she had woken up in, a big bed covered in a red quilt and way too many decorative pillows with snowflakes on them. There was also a Christmas tree in the corner and garlands wrapped around the headboard. In the corner, Nick had his own magical suitcase, and Annie moved closer to examine it and the ornament at the handle. Sure enough, 'You mean snow much to me' was scripted across a red scarf being shared by two cartoon snow people.

"I don't get these. Why did I get the stupid math one?" Annie asked. There was something vaguely familiar about

Nick's ornament now that Annie could see it with her own eyes, but she couldn't quite place it.

"Not all math puns are bad," Nick said, watching Annie trying to recall when and why she had seen that decoration before. "Just sum," Nick smiled, watching her for a reaction. "Get it? S-U-M?"

As Annie was rolling her eyes in response, she noticed that at the edge of Nick's bed was a tiny TV with an attached VCR compartment at the bottom.

"Nick, that screen is smaller than my laptop," Annie laughed.

"Judy Garland can fill any space." Nick smiled.

"I can't believe you're making me watch a movie on that," Annie said.

"Quiet, she'll hear you," Nick said, giving the TV an affectionate tap. He then handed Annie the bowl of popcorn and grabbed a few pillows. Within moments, he had set them up so they could both lie comfortably on their stomachs and watch the screen, with a pillow for the popcorn to rest on between them. "Should I see if I can find us anything to drink? And keep your expectations realistic, okay, I may only be able to offer fake Folgers coffee," Nick warned.

"Yeah, sure," Annie shrugged, taking her first handful of popcorn. "Oh, wow, it's so dry and plain! I feel like I'm eating sand," Annie cried, and Nick laughed while taking his own handful.

"Oh yeah, that's bad," Nick agreed, trying to remove the bowl.

"Don't take it! I mean, I'm still obviously going to eat it. I'm just going to loudly complain about it the whole time," Annie told him.

"Okay. Let me see if I can find anything else downstairs. Don't start the movie without me."

"You've seen it before!"

"Yeah, but I've never seen you watch it before!" Nick called, racing out of the room as if he were being timed. Annie's stomach did that annoying thing where the butterflies cartwheeled and somersaulted. *No, no, stop it*, she begged herself.

She heard Nick cheer from downstairs, and her face broke into a smile

"What did you find?" Annie asked, standing in between the doorframe and calling out.

"Sleepytime tea!" Nick hollered back.

"I don't know if anyone has ever been that pumped for Sleepytime tea in the history of humankind," Annie said to the room, moving back toward the bed and trying to find a comfortable place to sit that didn't make her think of other activities they could get up to instead.

"I also found ice cream!" Nick grinned, slightly out of breath, reentering the room.

"Oh, way to bury the lede!" Annie exclaimed.

"It's vanilla," Nick told her. Annie took a pillow and screamed into it. "But I did find some semi-sweet morsels in the baking cabinet. I guess my family now has a baking cabinet."

Annie stared up at him. "I love you!" she gushed, looking over the tray.

"I know you're talking to the chocolate, but you're welcome," Nick told her. Annie grabbed the bag and pulled out a handful of chocolate chips, dumping them in her mouth.

"Chocolate anything is the answer to everything!" Annie said with her mouth full. "Well, chocolate you can chew, I mean."

"Scoot over so I can introduce you to a magical place called St. Louis," Nick implored, and Annie quickly settled back, holding a pillow in her lap and permitting a content sigh to escape. She didn't even think about missing her regular evening lineup of Bravo and booze as she took the bag of chocolate chips and dumped more into her open mouth.

She had a snack, a movie, and absolute control over her raging holiday hormones . . . sort of.

CHAPTER SEVENTEEN

An hour and fifty-three minutes later, Annie was bawling, tears falling down her face, leaving wet imprints on the embroidered snowflake-designed pillow in her lap.

"Okay, wow, you're still crying, huh?" Nick asked, awkwardly handing her another tissue. "But this movie has a happy ending. Apparently, in real life, the family did actually move to New York."

"I don't want to know that!" Annie yelled, throwing another decorative pillow in Nick's general direction.

"Good movie, right?" Nick asked when he was safely out of Annie's direct aim.

"It was amaziiing," Annie languished, using her palms to trap the last of her tears. But then she paused in thought and turned to Nick. "Why do you think we were allowed to watch it? Nothing here works the way it should; we can't access TV or the internet or use our phones . . . It's not even an exclusively Christmasy movie . . . but there has to be some reason we could watch it here, right?" Annie asked Nick. His face clouded in contemplation.

"Maybe." Nick nodded after a moment. "Well, let's see. It's also set in a smallish town community, and made-for-TV Christmas movies usually place a lot of value in strong family relationships, so there could be some insight there? Both also have romantic storylines occurring within the hometowns, and both have a Christmas ball? Could that be something?" Nick shrugged.

"Could be. It feels like there should be more than that, though," Annie considered.

"Let's consider the structure of the movies' happy endings," Nick started, and Annie turned to fully take in his words. "Okay, one possible common denominator with *Meet Me in St. Louis* and your traditional made-for-TV Christmas movie is that the path to a happy ending opens up once the characters embrace their true, deep-down, honest feelings."

The words "happy ending" and "honest" made Annie's body break out into goosebumps, plucking on some sort of emotional string. She shivered and stood up, rubbing her arms and pacing the space, needing to move some of the restless energy swirling inside her. Annie noticed a stack of high school yearbooks on a bedside table and moved closer to examine them.

"The yearbooks?" Nick asked, reading her thoughts. "Yeah, they were stacked like that when we arrived here."

"Yeah, it's funny, I have a similar stack in my room too," Annie said, taking a closer look at the yearbook on top of the stack. "Can I see what I wrote in your freshman yearbook? I signed it, right?" Annie asked.

"Um, yeah, you did . . ." Nick said, and Annie caught his eye. "You're on the last page crammed in the right corner," Nick said.

"Nick, how on earth do you remember that?" Annie laughed. She picked up the hefty tome, flipping through the glossy pages. Annie saw handwritten notes in all different colors decorating the inside. A long passage in purple script handwriting, enclosed in its own giant heart made her stop. She skimmed to the signature and rolled her eyes when Bailey's big, bold "B" came into view. Annie quickly turned to the back of the book. Before she could find her inscription, a small piece of greenery tied with a red ribbon slipped loose onto the carpet. Nick's eyes grew into saucers, and he made a dive to catch it. "What is this?" Annie asked, grabbing the item first. She held it carefully in her palm, looking at it before she realized what she was holding. "Is this mistletoe?" Annie asked, knowing already that it must be, but she looked at Nick, who had gone crimson and seized with embarrassment.

"Um, yeah, it's mistletoe, I forgot I kept it," Nick muttered, offering his hand and hoping that Annie would give it back. But Annie held on to it a moment longer.

"Is this the mistletoe of our, um, moment?" Annie asked him, her own face flushing with color. Nick nodded slowly.

"It's nothing," Nick said, clearing his throat and gathering the courage he didn't quite seem to feel. "I was fourteen and very sentimental." Nick used his thumb and forefinger to pluck the mistletoe from Annie and put it on his dresser behind a seasonal candle, momentarily out of sight.

"Oh my. That's . . ." Annie started, unsure how to put words to her feelings. "Well, it's really sweet. If I had known any boy would be sentimental over something I had been a part of . . ." Annie swallowed, shaking her head and trailing off. "It's really sweet," Annie repeated, and Nick shrugged, clearly wanting the moment to pass without further acknowledgment of the kid he was in high school. Annie found her inscription and read it aloud.

"'Only three more years to go and then you're out of here. LYLAB (Love you like a brother!) TTFN! ♥ Annie.' Oh, yikes, that's so bad, Nick. You should have taken some Wite-Out to that," Annie said, shaking her head. "Ha, remember when Marsha and I dared you to let us paint your nails with Wite-Out?"

"Um, yeah, you guys were ruthless," Nick said. "That Wite-Out nail thing was one of your nicer schemes."

"I don't think you're in danger of any of Princess Eve's pranks," Annie continued, trying to lighten the mood. She felt like a walking kaleidoscope of idiosyncrasies, unable to pinpoint a specific emotion but rather a myriad of too many of them, and it was giving her mental whiplash.

Annie burned to talk to Marsha and make sense of the fact that she might want to jump Nick when she was supposed to be wooing Chris. Did she have an actual, legit crush on Nick? The deep wanting to kiss him earlier in the day had been all-consuming, sure, but was that because she was unsure if she even wanted to kiss Chris again? Or maybe it was knowing that real-world Annie disliked herself every time she followed Chris back to his apartment, allowing herself to believe that maybe that was all the romance she deserved and she didn't really want to go back to that.

"I should get home and try and sleep?" Annie said, almost as if it were a question. She wasn't tired, exactly; she just wasn't sure how much longer she could hold on to all these racing feelings without them spilling out in ways she couldn't control.

"Oh, okay, right," Nick said, not meeting her eye. Annie thought she picked up the slightest note of disappointment. "I'm glad you liked the movie," he said earnestly.

"The soundtrack! So many bangers," Annie said appreciatively. She could handle conversations about the movie and its music. Easy-peasy.

"So many!" Nick nodded. "I'll have to make you a mix tape."

"Oh, yes, please. I'll play it in my cassette player," Annie said, and before she could stop herself, she blurted out. "Thanks, Nick. This weird alternate reality is more fun with you."

"Likewise," Nick said with the slightest bit of grit in his voice. It caught in Annie's ear, and she dared herself to make eye contact with him. His eyes looked serious and focused. She didn't trust herself to stay a moment longer and risk doing something very stupid and reckless; she wouldn't be able to blame it on one too many boozy seltzers. Without another word, Annie made a move to go downstairs, Nick a step behind her.

We're both probably breathing in crazy Christmas pheromones, Annie thought. *I'm carrying some pent-up sexual frustration that has absolutely nothing to do with Nick, but he's the only normal human nearby, so that's why I want to hump him*, Annie mused before letting out a tiny huff as she hurried down the stairs and internally berated herself. But the more she wanted to stop thinking about anything remotely sexual, the more she wanted to keep considering it, and her body sparked with heat.

When Annie stepped outside again, Nick still just behind her, a sudden burst of snowflakes landed atop their heads. Nick jumped out and looked toward the sky, more snow falling on his face.

"Real snow!" Nick laughed. "And it actually feels somewhat cold," he marveled before opening his mouth to try and catch a flake.

Annie moved more cautiously and slowly held out an open palm, allowing a series of snowflakes to land and melt against her hand. The beautiful, Instagram-worthy moment was not lost on her, but it brought to mind those hours before she had ended up here, stalking Chris's page and seeing pictures of his assumed girlfriend enjoying similar scenes. Already, it felt like forever ago and like it had happened to a completely different person. If they were trapped in a time outside of their reality, why were they stuck here in this Christmas movie set? What was she missing?

Nick was doing figure eights around the front yard, careful to give the inflatables their space as he sought out more fresh snow to fawn over. Annie took a few timid steps, not trusting her recent proclivity for falling to take advantage of these slippery conditions, but the LED blinking nose of an eight-foot giant Rudolph summoned her close. The snow kept falling, the flakes fluffy and picturesque, landing on the ground freshly covered in a smooth layer of white. Annie closed her eyes for a moment, taking in the stillness and riding waves of calm.

"Don't move," Nick said, closing in on her. Annie's eyes blinked wide open. Nick's breath warm against her neck, his eyes focused on her mouth.

Annie's pulse quickened, and she gulped as Nick got closer. From Annie's perspective, time itself seemed to slow as if trapped in a beautiful, languid fog; even the snowflakes lingered longer, catching on Nick's eyelashes as his flushed face moved closer, and Annie's anticipation rose with each one.

"There's a little something," Nick said, his thumb making contact with the corner of her mouth. His hand hovered a moment, hot against her cheek. "Chocolate mixed with snow," Nick continued, his voice heavy and husky.

Annie's breath hitched, her heart now speeding up time. She yearned to lean her face a little closer to Nick's, to test their boundaries, when a sharp sound erupted behind them, followed by a loud, piercing "pfft" noise, reminiscent of a whale experiencing full-fledged, fervent flatulence.

The gigantic inflatable reindeer was rapidly deflating, its limbs tangling themselves in between a stunned Annie and Nick. They yelped in surprise, trying to free themselves as the blinking nose threatened to find and flatten them until, finally, the beast stopped writhing and surrendered in a heap of snow, the red light slowly blinking until it stopped completely.

Annie and Nick finally made eye contact, and all they could do was crack up at the absurdity of witnessing the dramatic death of Rudolph. They both stepped back mid-laugh, trying to center themselves until they could look at each other without immediately breaking.

"I wish I could say that was my only run-in with an inflatable," Nick chuckled, shaking his head at the adornment's remains.

"Honestly, that doesn't surprise me," Annie teased. "Was it another yard decoration?"

"Actually, it was my senior year when we did *Wizard of Oz*. The tech team designed the bulk of our hot-air balloon using a series of inflatable pool toys glued and shaped together. We had to pump up each one before every performance. But on closing night, a series of them deflated when the kid playing the Wizard stepped into the basket."

"Yikes," Annie said. "Did the show go on?"

"Oh, yeah. Bailey was Dorothy, and she made it seem like the whole thing had been scripted," Nick recalled fondly.

Annie's stomach sank. Nick's eyes were twinkling at the memory.

"She improvised some lines about the best adventures and life lessons happening when things don't go exactly as planned, and that while there's no place like home, home is where the heart is, which was where they were in that moment, together among friends."

"Wow," Annie murmured, unable to articulate another sound or sentiment.

"She took what should have been an awkward and embarrassing moment and turned it into something lovely; I guess that's always been Bailey's charm," Nick mused.

The way he said Bailey's name with such earnest admiration was a gut punch; the sharp realization that he was rekindling his relationship with her a slap to Annie's face. She had been about to kiss Nick only moments before. Thank goodness for Rudolph's death scene because she would have pointlessly humiliated herself and likely made Nick uncomfortable. It had felt mutually charged, but obviously Annie's feelings were not reciprocated; Nick still pined for Bailey. Her heart ached, tears threatening. She knew with urgency that she had to get out of the snow and away from the boy next door.

CHAPTER EIGHTEEN

Annie woke up the next morning, curious to see what the magic suitcase had planned for the day. She remembered hearing whispers of an event with "ugly sweaters," but when Annie pulled out the cheery, cherry-red sweater with intricate gold bells woven with cream-colored pearls, she was underwhelmed. It wasn't so much ugly as it was uninteresting.

Annie thought fondly of the "All I Want for Christmas" sweater that she had worn to a SantaCon bar crawl a few years back. It had presented a scantily clad Santa perched on a sleigh, but instead of reindeer, there were nine, diverse cartoon penises dressed in holiday wrapping paper of various colors and shapes. Annie made out with two random Santas and an elf that night. She also recalled dry heaving into his hat. Aw, the memories of youth.

When Annie arrived back at the school, Nick was waiting near the entrance, wearing a green, ferociously furry sweater. It took Annie a moment to realize that he was meant to look like a Christmas tree.

"Don't you look like a perfect Christmas present, Nicholas Laurel," Bailey giggled, approaching Nick in a form-fitting dark green knit sweater dress. Small bows adorned the bottom half, and she wore nude, iridescent tights that sparkled with tiny red and green sparkles. She wore tall Mary Jane shoes, which gave her some added height, and she looked like the true and rightful Queen of Christmas.

That's the kind of woman Nick should be with, Annie thought, trying to ignore the swelling of emotion in her chest. *A beautiful, holiday-loving, family-driven gal who adores him, that's what he deserves.* Yes, the best tactic for both of them would be to give Nick some space so he could focus on Bailey and she could get back on track with Chris.

"It lights up!" Nick grinned, pushing the buttons of the remote attached to the sweater and changing the colors and blinking speed. Bailey giggled in delight, and Annie deliberately took a step back, allowing Nick and Bailey their moment.

The cafeteria space had transformed into a gingerbread palace. The scent alone was the stuff of holiday fantasies. Long tables had been moved to create a large square, and each had a bright red and green striped tablecloth. On top were bowls of various decoration options, including glittery snowflakes, marshmallows of every size and color, and bags of frosting ready to pipe. On a center table were plates of gingerbread cutouts in different shapes that could be used to structure the homes.

"The bakery supplied the gingerbread," Bailey purred to Nick. She looked up at him, batting her eyelashes in mockingly bashful blinks.

"They look and smell incredible," Nick smiled back.

"I'm sure you two will win this contest," Annie said by way of a greeting.

"Aw, Annie, you're so cute," Bailey laughed.

"And funny," Annie returned.

"Unfortunately, I'm not allowed to be on a team, it wouldn't be fair to the rest of the town participants. But I will be on the judging panel, of course!" Bailey told them. "This event is done in teams of two—"

"Well, I better find Chris!" Annie said; she didn't trust herself to abstain from volunteering to partner with Nick.

"Hi, Annie," Chris said loudly, jumping up from a nearby table upon hearing his name. Annie involuntarily stumbled back in surprise at his sudden appearance, but Chris didn't seem to notice. "Actually, my little reindeer and I will be teaming up," Chris said, and as if he had summoned her, Holly hopped past Annie, causing her to then stumble forward again. As Annie steadied her heartbeat, Holly snuggled into Chris's open arms. The two were dressed in matching reindeer sweaters with scarves that looked like candy canes.

"That's right, Rudolph! You light up my life!" Holly said in what sounded like a practiced routine between them. Chris's eyes misted over, and he put his hand over his heart.

"Oh, I love you deer-ly," Chris told her.

"Let's make it rein with holiday cheer!" Holly answered, and Chris let out a loud booming laugh.

"Isn't she so wonderfully precocious?" Chris asked, his eyes still fondly on Holly.

"The most precocious!" Annie replied. "But surely, I can join your team, right?"

"That's against the rules, Annie," Bailey said coolly.

"Then I'll sit this one out," Annie tried.

"Aw, Annie, I hope not," Chris said, his eyes looking full and disappointed.

"Fine, Felix can be my partner," Annie said, searching the room. She found him standing next to a very protective Noelle. Noelle's sweater read "The Twelve Cats of Christmas," and Annie counted an even twelve cats adorning every angle. Annie couldn't help but be charmed by the thing and by the woman wearing it, and she had no intention of cock-blocking her.

"Good morning, Annie," a voice said. Annie whipped around to identify the speaker.

"Marsh—I mean, Eve, hi!" Annie said, her eyes glimmering with hope. Eve was wearing a delicate satin skirt in a deep pink with three tapered tiers, with a light pink sweater with tiny candy canes embroidered on its collar. "Great outfit," Annie said admiringly. Marsha would actually love that look.

"I have been brought in as a judge for today's competition," Eve said bashfully before Annie could beg for her partnership. "I so look forward to your entry." Eve gave Annie's arm a small squeeze of encouragement and walked to what looked to be a judge's table with leather-bound notebooks atop the red cloth and three chairs facing a series of smaller tables ready for teams of two to use as workstations.

"Hmm, I wonder if Ferguson can compete," Annie considered.

"He's partnered with Perry," Bailey explained.

"Oh, c'mon!" Annie muttered.

"Annie, why don't you partner with Nick?" Chris asked.

"Oh, I'm sure Nick has someone else in mind—" Annie started, still unable to look Nick in the eye.

"I don't actually. My only plan is to sleigh it," Nick said, attempting a joke. Annie looked up at him and could swear she recognized him trying to cover hurt feelings. Ugh, Annie didn't want him to feel rejected or like some consolation prize; that wasn't her intent.

"Yeah, okay, if you want to," Annie conceded, chewing nervously on the inside of her cheek.

"Let's go get your aprons," Bailey directed. She seemed resigned to Nick pairing with Annie, though not exactly happy about it.

"What aprons?" Annie asked.

'Oh, Annie, honestly, you're acting like you've never attended the Annual Simsbury Grand Gingerbread Jubilee, Featuring a Creative Confectionery Construction Challenge with Extravagant Adorned Apparel Encouraged Competition before. The pairs need to wear matching holiday aprons. How else will the judges keep track of who is partnered together?" Bailey asked, a hint of annoyance in her voice. "I'll see if I can find the snowman and plaid print for you, it's my favorite," Bailey said, smiling at Nick.

"Okay, partner," Nick began. "What are you thinking about our design?"

"Oh, whatever you think, I don't care," Annie mumbled, making her way to an empty table for them to work.

"Annie," Nick said softly. "Are you okay? Did I do something?" Nick asked, his voice breaking ever so slightly. It felt like a direct punch to the gut.

"What?" Annie asked breathlessly. "No, no, I'm fine, sorry, I'm, um, trying to figure out how to get time in with Chris," Annie trailed off. Her face flushed, and she was scared Nick could see right through her, that he would be able to read her thoughts spelled out across her body language. "Why don't we make the Smiths' family house?" Annie suggested, thankful for the burst of inspiration.

"The turn of the century Victorian on Kensington Avenue?" Nick perked up.

"I mean, let's be real, you'll absolutely be doing most of the construction, and I'll mostly be snacking on the supplies, but if you think it's possible?"

Nick nodded enthusiastically. Annie could see him mentally making notes of which items they would need first.

"Welcome to the Annual Simsbury Grand Gingerbread Jubilee, Featuring a Creative Confectionery Construction Challenge with Extravagant Adorned Apparel Encouraged Competition!" Grant's voice rang out across the space. He was wearing a bright green headset that was the same color as his blinding, sequin-covered suit, bedazzled with candy canes.

"It burns," Annie hissed, covering her eyes.

"We'll ring the bell to start the festivities in one minute! Judges, please take your places," Grant summoned, and Bailey and Eve joined Grant in front of the large table. Perry sent Grant a small wave and it lit them both. Eve was waving like the princess she apparently was, her hand cupped and elbow gracefully bent. Bailey had a big smile, but she focused it solely on Nick. "You and your partner will have one hour to complete your gingerbread entry, and a winner will be crowned. So put those creative hats on." Grant paused to reveal a green sequin hat and tossed it on top of his gelled head. The hat sat with a slight tilt but looked like it was now permanently fixed and unmoving. "The real recipe today is a hundred cups of holiday cheer, a generous helping of fun, and sure, maybe a pinch of allspice," Grant grinned. "Now get ready, get set, go decorate!"

Nick raced to the supply tables first, dropping items off before returning for more. Annie did her best to keep the space organized and when Nick had finished his final trip, he found Annie popping another tasteless gumdrop in her mouth and chewing in thought, gathering her own pieces of the allotted tools.

"What are you up to over there, partner?" Nick asked.

"I'm going to make the snowmen," Annie told him matter-of-factly. "Before Tootie iconically destroys them, I mean."

"That's a great idea," Nick said, stopping to look at her. Annie blushed slightly and simply shrugged back. "Some of those faces are kind of creepy though . . ."

"Oh, yeah, they're unearthly. That's the best part. Those scary faces under a gorgeous hat collection? I'm going to recreate that whole scene," Annie answered, gathering a stash of marshmallows and toothpicks.

"You know, the snow people in the movie were made of Styrofoam, not actual snow, so I think you're on to something, but if you need help ensuring their sturdiness—" Nick started.

"Shh," Annie told him, holding up a finger. "I need to take advantage of my creative daze abilities while I can."

Nick swallowed back a smile and returned back to his own task at hand, allowing Annie to turn off everything around her and slip away into her Tootie tunnel.

Her hands were possessed by some sort of divine, creative Christmas genius, and her fingers moved quickly to stack marshmallows on toothpicks, lightly pulling the sweet confections to create the snowmen mounds and the snow jackets they appeared to be wearing in the movie. She used white icing on top and sprinkled edible iridescent glitter over their bodies. Thankfully, Nick had also secured her some edible markers to hand design some of the smaller details, like glasses and their strange, eerie faces. With small strings of licorice and some fondant, Annie formed the additional accessories for her creations, giving them hats, and even a purse. Her favorite touch came from using some shredded coconut and icing to make a small fur-like cover for a snowman's shoulders.

Somehow, an hour passed in a blink, and when she heard Bailey ringing the large golden bell to signal the contestants to stop, she looked down to admire her tiny creatures, and she was proud of the weird little family of snow people she had formed. Each one was so purposefully strange and uniquely adorable.

Nick had done a tremendous job on his construction of the house; of course, he managed to capture the Victorian architectural features with intricate piping along the window frames and decorative trims, using tiny candies to define the roofing tiles and using some of the edible glitter to look like snow dusting the home and its surroundings.

The snow people certainly added an additional element of festivity and playfulness. The only thing missing was a soulful Judy Garland singing "Have Yourself a Merry Little Christmas" to complete the winter wonderland in its entirety. Unfortunately, though, their gingerbread house did not win.

"This is bullsh—" Annie moaned miserably once the judges had reached a decision. A cookie sheet loudly clanged to the floor, cutting her off. "I can't even properly express my rage with profanity," Annie hissed.

Chris and Holly had earned the grand prize of the Annual Simsbury Grand Gingerbread Jubilee, Featuring a Creative Confectionery Construction Challenge with Extravagant Adorned Apparel Encouraged Competition, and Annie was furious.

"Our design was gorgeous. I'm proud of what we made," Nick told her gently.

"Nick, we were robbed. Again! You should be more mad about this," Annie wailed.

"Annie, they made a super solid rendition of the Nutmeg Nest. You know, the inn this town apparently now treasures above almost anything else. We didn't have a chance once they pulled the hometown Simsbury spirit card into their design. I'm happy we got an honorable mention, honestly," Nick said.

"We only got that because one of the judges is obsessed with you," Annie muttered, crossing her arms across her chest, causing her sweater to emit a few jolly jingles in the process.

"Hi, Annie," Chris said, approaching her, Holly's hand in his. Annie did her best to plaster on a gracious, congratulatory smile, even though they had been robbed of their rightful win.

"Chris, Holly, congratulations," Annie said stiffly.

"Annie, my precocious daughter here has a question for you," Chris grinned conspiratorially with Holly who let out a little giggle and hugged Chris's arm.

"Miss Annie, would you come to our house for dinner tonight?" Holly asked hopefully.

"Felix is making his famous spaghetti and meatballs," Chris explained. "We'd love to have you as our guest,"

Chris said, his voice full of pure sentiment. "I thought we could walk home together after rehearsal."

"Oh, I hope you say yes, Annie," Bailey encouraged, moving to stand closer to Nick. "Nick and I were invited to meet Eve at the inn for dinner," she continued.

"You're having dinner with Eve?" Annie asked, a pang of hurt ping-ponging across her chest.

"We really bonded as judges," Bailey explained. Annie flushed with more feeling. Wait, was Eve here to be Bailey's best friend? Maybe she wasn't here for Annie at all. The idea brought a prick of tears to Annie's eyes. "A chance to have dinner with a real princess, I'm so excited!" Bailey squealed, completely unaware of the pain her words were causing Annie.

"Right," Annie said, trying to get herself back on track. She blinked away the emotion and brought her eyes back to Chris. "Well, I would love to try some of Felix's famous spaghetti and meatballs, that sounds like something that can't be missed! Made even better if I can sit next to Holly, of course."

If she was ever going to get out of here, she had to take advantage of this opportunity with Chris. At this point, she worried that if she didn't escape soon, the confusion might knot around her like a string of lights she'd never untangle.

CHAPTER NINETEEN

That day's rehearsal gave the kids the opportunity to practice in their costumes and ensure everything was in its proper place for the show. Chipperton had been welcomed into the fold and had added a few unexpected dance moments that were quite moving, and Annie had clocked Grant's visits and growing support. Having front row seats to their unfolding love story was quite charming, and despite this Grant not encompassing all the color and vibrance of her friend from the real world, she was still rooting for his happy ending.

Annie easily solved two "major disasters" when two kids accidentally switched costumes and another kid put her dress on backward. In both instances, once again, she had been showered with praise by Chris and the cast thanks to her "quick thinking" skills. Annie couldn't help but admit this time, though, that it felt nice to be so thoroughly appreciated, even if she didn't feel it matched what she deserved.

When it was time to leave, Annie helped Holly into her coat, and the trio quickly covered the distance to Chris's house. Traveling within this contained block continued to be delightfully easy. Annie knew once she was back in the real world, relying on her car again would be a lot less fun, though at least she could return to her murder podcasts without the threat of mindless small talk from someone in town. As they approached the large, circular driveway, the entire house glowed with the volume of lights strung across every available surface and ledge. Annie had to squint and avert her eyes to avoid going blind.

"We're still working on our decorations," Holly explained, and Chris eagerly nodded.

"I think you have all of them," Annie said, which made Holly and Chris chuckle heartily. The exterior of the house itself was also wallpapered in wreaths of every size. All the interior lights of the midsize brick home appeared to be on the highest wattage, and fake candles were flickering away in every visible window. Annie desperately wanted to ask about their electric bill.

"Felix is in the kitchen preparing supper," Chris said, escorting Annie through the front door. The inside of their house was as bright as the outside; where there wasn't a literal light, there were Christmas decorations, even some of the weird ones that Annie had never understood, including those large glass cylinders filled with red and green balls. Who were those meant to appeal to besides Nick, circus camp juggling star? *No, why are you thinking of Nick, or juggling, or circus camp, gross*, Annie scolded herself. She was here to get closer to Chris.

Annie spotted Felix in the kitchen wearing an apron decorated with cartoon hot chocolates in various holiday-inspired mugs. He hummed softly while stirring a large pot. "Annie, can I interest you in a seasonal beverage?" Chris asked.

"Anything but hot chocolate," Annie said, and everyone turned to look at her with concern. "I'm planning to have another cup at the festival," she explained nervously. "But anything should be fine! What's good here? You seem like you'd have an eggnog tap at the ready," Annie joked. Felix dropped the large, decorative serving spoon he was holding, Holly whimpered, and Chris silently picked up the utensil, which had luckily only landed on a rug and remained completely intact. He held it firmly in his hand and cleared his throat before summoning the courage to speak.

"We don't have eggnog in this house," Chris said somberly.

"Oh, okay," Annie said softly. When no one spoke, she asked, "Is it, like, because of the high-fat content or something?"

"No, no, dear," Felix said, his eyes still twinkly but drenched in sorrow now too. "My sweet Caroline passed away almost twenty years ago. She accidentally consumed some expired eggnog, and it made her quite ill," Felix said sadly.

"She died from eggnog poisoning?" Annie asked, secretly making a mental note to look up holiday-related deaths once she had easy internet access, because that would be a fascinating rabbit hole to fall into.

"She did. Instantly," Felix said matter-of-factly. "The eggnog debacle was a traumatic ordeal for our family."

Chris rubbed Felix's back in small, loving circles. Annie was now both dying to know how Chris had lost his wife in this universe and terrified of the answer, as it would surely be another bewildering tale, and it would surely come out soon.

"I'm so sorry for your loss, Felix," Annie said instead. She hated to see this adorable old man sad or in mourning; he was Santa for goodness' sake. "I'm sure she was a wonderful woman." Felix gave Annie a small smile and turned back to his cooking duties. "Do you need any help with dinner?" Annie asked, hoping to reset the mood and also to get this part of the evening over and done with already. She would take their bland food over listening to these sappy, sad stories any day.

"I'll assist Felix," Chris assured her. "Please make yourself at home in the meantime." Chris smiled at her warmly, and she returned a nod. Annie walked closer to the Christmas tree in the living room, admiring the many handmade ornaments decorating it.

"My mom made this," Holly's small voice said as she stood next to Annie. Her hand cupped a handmade tree that had been constructed with cinnamon sticks.

"Very cool. And it smells good," Annie told her, hoping this wasn't going to be the moment she got another big death reveal story, but already sensing that's exactly what was about to happen.

"Want to hear a joke?" Holly asked in a small voice.

"I really do," Annie told her. Huh, maybe they could share jokes until dinner was over.

"What is a Christmas tree's favorite candy?" Holly asked, still looking straight at the tree.

"What?" Annie asked, slightly afraid of the answer given by Holly's somber tone.

"Orna-mints," Holly finished.

"That's a good one—" Annie began, but Holly cut her off.

"My mom taught me that," Holly said.

"It's very solid—" Annie said.

"Why did she have to die?" Holly's voice cracked. *Oh, man, Mamma Mia, here we go again*, Annie groaned internally, her muscles immediately tensing up.

"Oh, Holly, I'm sorry. Do you, um, have any other jokes?" Annie attempted as Holly continued to cry. Ugh, she didn't want to be here for this, but maybe Nick had been right, maybe the only way out was through. If they got it all out now, it'd be like ripping off a figurative Band-Aid in one quick swoop.

"Why couldn't she have chewed through that cursed chestnut?" Holly wailed. Her hands questioned the ceiling fan for an answer that would never come.

"I'm sorry, what? What do you mean?" Annie asked in a confused, hushed voice. "Did you say chestnut?" Holly let out another choked sob.

"Yes," Holly said after a moment. "We were enjoying some warm chestnuts, roasting on our open fire, and she took a large one . . . it was too hot, too hot for her to handle, Annie! She choked on it. I can still see the flames," Holly whimpered, staring at the empty fireplace in the corner.

"Oh, Holly. That must have been so hard on you," Annie said.

"Could I have a hug?" Holly asked, surprising Annie into action, bringing her body to embrace Holly's small frame.

"You know, I actually lost someone at Christmastime too," Annie shared, surprising herself. She never talked about this. Holly looked up at her, her eyes desperately searching.

"How do you keep your spirits up every year?" Holly asked. Annie had to swallow down the urge to cry. The truth was, her Christmas spirit died when her grandfather had, and she had never tried to revive it.

"It's hard, isn't it? Annie returned. "What do you do?" Annie turned the question around. Holly gave the question some consideration before answering.

"I try to remember the good holiday memories. And then I try to keep making more of them because I know that would make my mom happiest," Holly said sagely. It was so simple and her words so pure, they pierced right through Annie's heart. Her grandfather would hate how she had been celebrating his favorite holiday.

"Hey, you two, are you ready to get washed up for supper?" Chris's voice rang out from the kitchen. Annie let Holly release her and turned to catch her eye.

"Do you want another minute?" Annie asked her. Holly shook her head no.

"I'm starving," Holly giggled, switched back to her precocious child self, and Annie let out a big breath, grateful they could now eat and fill their mouths with something other than sadness.

"Me too," Annie winked at her, and Holly offered her hand.

The dinner portion of the evening was as strange as Annie could have predicted. The food had been artfully plated, each meatball garnished with a sprinkle of parmesan cheese, and the spaghetti had been covered generously in bright marinara sauce. There was also a basket of garlic bread and a pitcher of hot chocolate. The weirdest thing, though, is that Annie couldn't recall eating anything. One moment the food was there, looking as appetizing as a chain

Italian restaurant's attempt at authentic cuisine straight from Italy, and the next the plates were empty with only the smallest impression that the food had once been there. Her clothing was also devoid of marinara stains, which was suspicious given her usual proclivity to make a mess.

Felix and Chris were dramatically dabbing their mouths with cloth napkins, and Holly was letting out a contented sigh.

"Well, I can't imagine eating another bite!" Chris beamed at Felix.

"Daddy, you have to save room for hot chocolate," Holly encouraged him.

"I think a walk through the festival tonight will do the trick," Chris winked back. "Did you get enough, Annie?" Chris asked. Annie stared down at the table, now free of all food.

"Apparently!" Annie shrugged. Luckily, her real-world appetite had yet to make an appearance in the made-for-TV Christmas movie world. Annie wondered about how Nick's dinner must be going, but thinking of him with Bailey and Eve made her stomach squirm. "Can I help with any of the cleanup?" Annie offered. She hoped moving her body might shut off her brain. Felix agreed, and the pair moved into the kitchen to mindlessly wash dishes in comfortable silence, Annie drying each piece as Felix smoothly handed them to her. As the sink emptied, Felix slowed and gave Annie a look, turning to meet her eyes before gazing out the nearby window.

"There's nothing better than a starry night in Simsbury, don't you think, Annie?" Felix asked with his eyes sparkling. Annie studied his twinkly face. "The sky is full of magic and wishes."

"Felix," Annie said in a whisper. "Are you, like, in on this? Do you know what's going on here?" Annie watched Felix's cheeks bloom into peach roses. His answer came as a small laugh that sounded a lot like a happy "ho ho ho." Annie would even go so far as to declare it merry. Her eyes narrowed in on him urgently, needing Felix to offer a shred of understanding.

"What's your Christmas wish, Annie?" Felix finally asked, his voice soft. Annie shook her head in annoyance. What was this? Some sort of game? "What's your happily ever after?" Felix continued, his eyes full of fantastical radiance.

Annie stared back, momentarily dumbfounded. It was a question Annie often didn't allow herself to answer because too often her thoughts were clouded by negative memories and fear. If she didn't hope to be happy, then maybe she could save herself from feeling hurt when it never came.

But, okay, fine, if Felix wanted an honest answer, maybe Annie should try and give one. She wanted to fall in love, to finally, fully take the plunge. Stop the lazy stumbling and catching herself right before the leap and let go. She wanted to build a family like her grandparents had, full of tradition and celebration and shared meals and laughter and love. She wanted—

"Are you ready? I can't wait for you to see the maze!" Chris boomed in excitement, interrupting Annie's thoughts. Chris and Holly skipped into the kitchen, holding coats, and Felix winked at Annie.

Chris escorted them all out of the house and straight to the festival, specifically to the entrance of the maze. As Annie was trying to take it in, Holly clapped in delight and looked at Chris.

"Beat you to the giant tree inside!" she squealed and hurled herself into the opening. Felix emitted his "ho ho ho" chuckle and waved to Noelle, who was holding a cup of cocoa for him. Chris looked at Annie with a grin, his eyes asking if she would race with him through the maze in search of Holly.

"Annie!" Eve called as she approached them. Annie looked up in surprise and felt immediately calmed by her familiar Marsha-like presence. "Please say you'll be my escort through the maze. I've been hoping to become better acquainted," Eve said, her eyes seeming to beg with each blink of her long lashes, and Annie's heart tried to blossom within the winter's snow. She needed Marsha, but she'd rather have her in an Eve costume than not at all. Annie looked at Chris to get his thoughts; she didn't want to keep him from racing his daughter through their family creation.

"You two enjoy it and go at your own pace, we'll meet somewhere in the maze, I'm sure," Chris reassured her. "Wish me luck, Holly's so precocious, she may have already won," Chris added as he trotted off.

The Christmas Tree Maze was not only in the shape of a large Christmas tree, but it had been constructed using beautifully lit trees, as well. Around corners, you could see various light displays, some more ornate than others, creating additional spectacles everywhere you turned. Around one bend lights had been shaped into presents, and around another a waving Santa Claus. There was truly no end to what else was hidden here, but Annie allowed herself to walk slowly, Eve's arm still trapping hers as Eve spoke in hushed urgency, Ferguson's shadow at their heels.

"Annie, may I confide in you?" Eve asked.

"Yes!" Annie encouraged. "Please confide in me." Apparently, Eve, this beautiful princess from a completely fictional country, also carried around Marsha's signature flair for the dramatic. And considering Annie had been away from her beloved bestie and Bravo for a few days, she was thirsty for theatrics.

"Well, the truth is, I've been matched with Nigel," Eve began in a somber tone.

"Nigel?" Annie asked, her mouth twitching as it waited for her to add some variation of "that must be Nigel with the brie." When Eve didn't say anything, Annie tried to prompt her. "With the brie?" Annie asked hopefully.

"Sorry?" Eve asked.

"Oh, just making sure I had his name correct. Nigel, you say?" Annie asked, knowing it was unlikely Eve would understand the *Ten Things I Hate About You* reference, but it still stung, reinforcing that this person was not her beloved bestie.

"Yes, Nigel. It's been our destiny since before we were even born. Our parents arranged it, you see, and for years we've been expected to make the grand announcement, but I've managed to put it off, for one reason or another. Until now. This year, our engagement was planned to be shared with the kingdom of Wintermore during the annual palace gala on Christmas Day," Eve explained. "When my plane was forced to land in an abandoned field due to a massive snowstorm, who would've known that Grant would be driving past, at that very moment, on his way to take over the ownership of his great-aunt's inn?"

"Literally no one could have known any of that," Annie assured her.

"But since I've been here, I've seen Ferguson in a new light," Eve whispered close to Annie's ear. "Since my father's death, the royal family legacy lies on my beautiful, delicate, and small shoulders. It's sometimes heavier than even I can bear," Eve admitted.

"I'm sure," Annie nodded, not having any idea what it would be like, but knowing that Marsha had also lost her father at a very young age and how it had impacted her. "I'm sorry to hear about your father. You must really miss him during the holidays."

Eve glanced at Annie and nodded her head somberly. "I do miss him," Eve said softly. "Every day. He passed away when I was only three."

"That sounds so hard. Was he ill?" Annie asked, curious if Eve's father had also been involved in a fatal car accident.

"No, he had a rather unexpected and traumatic encounter with a nutcracker," Eve shared.

"Oh, wow, okay," Annie said, trying not to ask the thousands of questions swirling through her head about what that death must have actually looked like, but thankfully for both their sakes, Eve spoke again.

"I still miss the memories we had together and all the ones we'll never share." Eve used her gloved hand to dab a dry eye.

"I know your dad would be so proud of you," Annie said, and Eve squeezed her arm back in thanks. It had been something Annie had said to Marsha countless times before, but she hoped it would resonate with Eve.

"But I am to be the queen, and I must consider my loyal subjects," Eve said, clearing her throat, her face a shade of mild anguish, but still quite lovely.

"Well, what's Nigel like? Be honest, is Ferguson the one you really want to, bone, er, be with?"

"Nigel's a dear friend, but, oh, Annie, he's such a bore!" Eve gushed.

"But is he hot?" Annie asked. "He's clearly pretty well off if he's been promised to a princess, right?" Eve shook her head. "Do you have a pic?" Eve thought for a moment before pulling out a small black leather wallet and finding a tiny image tucked away in a small sleeve. She looked at the picture and sighed before giving it to Annie. Annie took it and let out a puff of air, nearly choking. "Woof," Annie sputtered in response, and Eve nodded. Nigel looked like a real dweeb. And not the secretly sexy kind. This Nigel looked much older than Eve, and his crooked grin was full of thick metal braces. His hair was shoulder-length and gave off an appearance of being wet with grease, framing his unfortunately acne-ridden cheeks. "Wait, is this a painting?" Annie asked, bringing it closer to analyze.

"Yes, it's his royal portrait, so they've enhanced his features a bit. I'm afraid he doesn't quite look like this in person," Eve admitted.

"Ah, I see," Annie said, trying to imagine a rougher version of this already very rough painting.

"I don't want to marry him, Annie," Eve said, stopping abruptly in the middle of the path, allowing Ferguson to get much closer to the linked duo before he silently stepped backward, always keeping his sights on Eve. Annie thought Eve's eyes actually now looked wet with real, human tears.

"Then you won't," Annie told her, giving her arm an affectionate and supportive squeeze. "It's your story, Eve. You need to follow your bliss and all that. Your country is rooting for you to be happy, like genuinely happy. The kingdom of

Wintermore needs a queen who is living her best life so they can too. If you want to marry someone other than Nigel—Ferguson, even—I'm sure everyone in your country would support you. And I bet your dad would say the same thing."

Overcome by the moment, Eve let out a small sob before wrapping Annie in a huge hug.

"Thank you, Annie," she whispered, refusing to let go. "You don't know how much I needed to hear that."

"Eve, you're a real babe. I couldn't dislike you if I tried. You remind me of the best person I know, and that's the highest compliment I could give someone," Annie smiled. "You deserve your happy ending."

"That's so kind," Eve said, swabbing her eyes until they looked dry again. "Oh, I must sound like such a silly schoolgirl to a big-city professional like you, but I believe my feelings for Fergie represent the purest love I've ever known."

"It's not silly," Annie said kindly. "Allowing yourself to fall in love fully like that seems like the ultimate act of bravery to me. Does Ferguson know how you feel?"

"I don't think so," Eve said, shaking her head. "It's so very complicated with the storm and being unable to talk to anyone back home. I don't want to hurt Nigel either. I should confront him in person," Eve continued, nibbling a tiny corner of her pink lip in thought.

"It will work out," Annie reassured her. "It has to."

Eve gave her an appreciative squeeze. "Now that you've offered such loving advice, please tell me more about your beau," Eve said, batting her eyelashes playfully in Annie's direction, making her laugh.

"My beau?" Annie asked. "I don't believe I have one of those at the moment." Annie reddened, thinking that the last guy Annie had kissed now had a Christmas maze, the grief from his dead wife, and a precocious child to manage. And she still couldn't get him to almost kiss her.

"You're blushing!" Eve squealed.

"Am not!" Annie laughed.

"You say you don't have a beau, but there's clearly a man who thinks of you as his sweetheart; it's so obvious," Eve said.

"Chris?" Annie asked, and Eve's face clouded in confusion. "The widower dad who's directing the annual Christmas play but also volunteers at his family's Christmas tree farm?" Annie added in a rush.

"No, no, Santa Claus!" Eve laughed.

"Felix?!" Annie cried, a look of momentary horror followed by careful consideration playing across her face.

"No, silly, *your* Santa. From the rink! Nick," Eve explained.

"What? Nick? No, I'm just his neighbor," Annie muttered, her face growing hotter by the second.

"He looks at you like you're a prized jewel from the royal family's collection." Eve smiled.

"I think he's sort of with Bailey," Annie said, chewing the inside corner of her mouth.

"The little bakery shop girl? No, she's not right for him at all," Eve decided, making Annie laugh again.

"Why do you say that?" Annie asked. Eve stopped Annie and looked deeply into her eyes.

"We shared supper tonight at the inn," Eve disclosed. "I thought Grant should discuss a potential partnership with the bakery moving forward, to expand the culinary offerings and cross-promote within the town."

"Oh," Annie said. "That's why you wanted to have dinner together?"

"Of course. I know profits have been down for both of them, and I simply saw a timely business opportunity and wanted to bring it forward," Eve said simply. "Back home, we have a Michelin-star chef who creates all of our culinary Christmas cookies, but I thought here in Simsbury, perhaps this could be the beginning of providing more opportunities for the bakery."

"Huh," Annie said, processing her thoughts out loud. "That's a smart idea. I hope the meeting went well," Annie said, impressed to see Marsha's business brain shining through.

"Thank you." Eve beamed. "Economics was one of my many higher learning degrees," she said with a smile of humility. "Bailey arrived with Nick, but they certainly did not appear to be together in any kind of romantic sense, and I'm very good at spotting such things. Bailey isn't his rightful match." Eve finished matter-of-factly. "Because you're his match, Annie. You two make magic," Eve finished strongly.

"Whoa," Annie said slowly. "You gave me goosebumps with that one."

Eve laughed.

"Magic?" Annie asked, her voice thin and wavering.

"Magic," Eve confirmed. "Look," Eve whispered, pointing to someone behind the Christmas tree corner. "You summoned him." Eve gave Annie a conspiratorial wink before nudging her forward.

CHAPTER TWENTY

Annie saw Nick up ahead, in a discussion with someone hidden by a hedge.

"I'll leave you to it," Eve told Annie, eyeing Ferguson, who was walking right behind them. "Let's depart in pursuit of love."

And before Annie could utter a response, Eve and Ferguson slipped away behind a corner, rerouting their maze journey. Nick was in a hushed conversation with Felix, and as she approached, neither seemed to notice her. She crept closer, curious to hear what they could be discussing.

"This isn't what I wanted," Nick murmured. "Can't you help?"

"I just rang the bell, the rest is in your hands," Felix answered.

"Tell me what I'm supposed to do. Please," Nick begged.

Felix turned to catch Annie's approach and let out his infamous "ho ho ho." Nick turned to see Annie, and his face morphed from one of surprise to one of forced calm. Felix took the opportunity to leave by soundlessly easing himself between a hedge, disappearing à la Homer Simpson into the bushes.

"All okay?" Annie asked Nick after Felix had disappeared completely from view, curious what discussion she had walked in on. "What were you two talking about?"

"Oh, just Felix being Felix," Nick dismissed before explaining, "I lost Bailey somewhere a few turns back because I kept stopping to admire the artistry. Isn't this incredible?" Nick marveled, and Annie couldn't help but laugh at his childlike wonder, though he had good reason; their surroundings were indeed incredible.

"Did you get alone time with Chris?" Nick asked as Annie said, "How was dinner?" and then they both stopped to laugh before saying, "You go" at the same time, followed by both saying, "Jinx" at the same time. Annie gave Nick a playful push and laughed. "Seriously, you go first. How was your dinner date?" Annie asked.

"I'm not sure we'd call it a date," Nick began.

"No almost kiss, then?" Annie asked, and Nick shook his head no. "Did you at least get a good meal?"

"Actually, I don't know how to answer that. The weirdest thing happened—" Nick started.

"Did your meal disappear?" Annie gasped.

"I don't even remember getting it," Nick explained. "It was like we were waiting, I blinked, and then our empty plates were being taken away."

"Same!" Annie told him. "Oh, my gosh, I'm so glad it wasn't just me." Annie turned left and realized they were at the end of the maze, an enormous Christmas tree waiting for them. Next to it was a basket with a sign reading, "We were rooting for you—what a tree-mendous job!"

The tree was classically adorned with countless small white snowflake lights, and Annie thought it was spectacular, admiring the delicate lace snowflake ornaments placed thoughtfully around the branches, made even more pleasant by the distinct pine scent.

"Chris is talented," Nick said, doing his own appreciative loop around the tree.

"Do you think he did all this?" Annie asked. "How could one man who has a teaching job and a child do everything? Do people sleep here? How does it work? Oh, and Felix was definitely giving off some vibes tonight. His eyes were extra twinkly and Santa-like . . . and he mentioned something about the sky being full of wishes and asking what I wanted for Christmas . . ."

"That doesn't seem *that* out of character," Nick answered, avoiding eye contact.

"It was a vibe, Nick. We need to trust the vibe. What were you guys talking about over there anyway?" Annie asked again.

"Oh, the same, we were discussing Christmas stuff, he was vague and unhelpful . . . Wait, what do you want for Christmas? Maybe he was trying to offer you some kind of hint," Nick said.

"Maybe," Annie pondered. "I didn't exactly have a Christmas list this year. I was going to spend the day in a consistent, comfortable buzzed haze on my parents' couch. What did you have planned for Christmas? Other than that bloody Santa chair thing," Annie asked.

"I wasn't finished with that!" Nick huffed.

"So do you have a Christmas wish?" Annie asked, needing to reroute their conversation back to decoding the Felix mystery.

"Well," Nick said, a tangle of red growing up his neck like roots in undergrowth.

"Nick." Annie's voice was sharper now and full of warning. "Why do I now get the sense you made some kind of wish that got us stuck here?"

"I just, um . . ." Nick trailed off, searching for the right words.

"Nick!" Annie yelled.

"I didn't want to spend the holiday alone," Nick said, looking Annie right in her eyes, freezing them both in place. Before Annie could ask follow-up questions, Bailey sprang out of nowhere (though likely it was through a hedge), like a tiny firework.

"Nick!" she exclaimed. "Thank goodness I found you! There's been an emergency with the set! Some volunteers borrowed one of the show's backdrops for a booth display, and the snow destroyed it."

"Which one?" Nick asked, more quizzical than concerned.

"The canvas with the night sky. I'd go myself, but the bakery is in crisis; we ran out of red and green sprinkles. The snowflake ones don't stand out next to the marshmallows! Chris is wrapped up with Christmas tree sales, so he can't go either."

"I'll go," Nick assured her. "It's 'snow' problem," He finished with a smile, and Annie rolled her eyes, wondering if anyone had ever died from a pun overdose (may they rest in wreaths).

"Thank you, Nick," Bailey said, finally letting out a loud, relieved breath and hugging him with grateful arms.

"You're the best. I'll make it up to you, okay? Hot chocolate with extra marshmallows and sprinkles."

"Happy to do it," Nick said as Bailey fluttered back to the bakery booth.

"I don't think she noticed I was here," Annie remarked.

"Let's go. And before you say no, what else are you going to do?" Nick gave her shoulder a gentle nudge, and it sent an unexpected zing down Annie's arm. She knew what she should do: she should wait for Chris to finish whatever tree business he had and get the man to try and kiss her already. "It won't take long, we'll be right back," Nick added as if reading her thoughts. Annie gave him a shrug and wordlessly followed him across the street to the doors of the school.

"They don't bother to lock up the place?" Annie asked as they easily breezed their way inside through the dim hallway to the auditorium. The building was still, and there was something rather thrilling about being left to their own devices in such a large space usually filled to the brim with children and community events.

Nick switched the work lights on backstage and swiftly pulled out a partially decorated canvas backdrop. There was already some semblance of the night sky and a sketch of Victorian-era London-aged brick buildings, standing tall and narrow, atop a cobblestone street. It was almost as if someone had prepared a backup backdrop that only needed minimal effort to complete. Annie had a sneaking suspicion that the made-for-TV Christmas movie gods had orchestrated this whole debacle, though she didn't know why.

Nick taped a large blue tarp to the floor and draped the canvas over it alongside an arrangement of paints and brushes. Annie watched in curiosity, unable to keep her eyes off his skilled hands that moved with gentle confidence as he filled the canvas with a dark blue sky in swirls of color. The action was hypnotizing, and Annie reveled in observing Nick in his true comfort zone.

"You can help me with the stars," Nick said, looking up at her from the floor.

"Is that a good idea? I'm not great with art, and you seem to have it all under control," Annie said, though she did secretly yearn to paint next to him. It looked fun, and maybe if she distracted her hands, she'd have better control of her thoughts.

Nick handed her a wooden brush and motioned for her to kneel next to him. He demonstrated a simple series of yellow strokes and then used a lighter shade to mark a halo light around the shape, completing the first star.

"You try," Nick encouraged, and Annie hesitantly dipped into the paint, taking a tentative first brushstroke. "Don't be scared, you're doing great," Nick said, and Annie tried to channel her inner artist. "Be honest, working on the show has been kind of fun, don't you think?" Nick asked after a few stars had been marked.

"For you, maybe, this is your career! Your passion," Annie smiled.

"Ah, I see it making a little home in your heart too, you can't hide it," Nick told her, sneaking small peeks her way as they continued to paint.

"Sure, maybe. You could say I don't despise *A Christmas Carol* like I thought I did, and working on the play hasn't been the total torture I assumed it would be," Annie relented, focusing on the halo portion of her latest star.

"The theater is a welcoming place; I'm glad you've found a way to us," Nick said.

"Let's not go that far, buddy. I only admitted that this experience hasn't been all agony," Annie said. "Why didn't you want to do more acting onstage? Don't you want to work that money maker?" Annie asked, gesturing to Nick's face.

"My money maker likes the behind-the-scenes work most of all," Nick said with a laugh. "I love how all the little parts come together into something greater than all of us. It's magic. Plus, I was roped into a bunch of roles back in high school because we only had a handful of guys who consistently did shows, especially during crew or lacrosse season. I think you may have missed out on a lot of cool theater kids," Nick said.

"Cool?" Annie laughed. "Aw, you sweet, delusional nerds . . . but, honestly, I probably did, I could have used more sweetness back then, I was a tad sour."

"I don't remember you like that," Nick admitted, and Annie turned to take him in. This kind boy who had grown up into such a kind man. She wondered how in the world a person like this managed to live in an actual "big city" and remain so pure and down to earth, as he showed no signs of hardness and was earnestly soft and inviting.

"Oh, Nick, you've seen sides of me that I should probably feel embarrassed about, and I appreciate you not bringing any of them up," Annie deflected. "But I am trying to be a better person," Annie continued, putting the words out into the world and willing them to stick. She could admit that now, she truly wanted to be the person everyone in this fictional town thought she was, the person with an important job who took time to volunteer for the school play and dress up like Mrs. Claus and simply be a piece in this bright puzzle. It had all felt so strange, sure, but it had been nice and lovely too.

"Well, for the record, I've always found you to be a pretty solid person," Nick said, softly brushing his shoulder against Annie's. Another heated zing.

"You've always been such a charmer. No wonder Bailey wants to bone you so badly," Annie said before she could stop herself.

"I don't know about that," Nick said, brushing off the idea.

"Oh, I do," Annie answered, ignoring the incessant pulse of her honest interest in also boning Nick.

"How about you and Chris? Was he the last guy you were with?" Nick asked shyly.

"If you could call it that, I guess," Annie snorted. "I was lonely and he was there, until he wasn't."

"My last serious relationship ended a few months ago because she was picked to be on *The Bachelor*," Nick said nonchalantly.

"Really? How far did she get?" Annie asked.

"I don't know, she signed an NDA," Nick shrugged. "But we're still good friends. She asks me to pet sit while she was gone. I love her dog."

Annie stared in disbelief until she couldn't help but laugh. Nick and all of his multitudes felt more unreal than the very universe they were currently sharing.

"You're probably friends with all of your exes, huh?" Annie asked, and Nick mulled it over before answering.

"Yeah, I guess so. I never had to deal with a dramatic breakup scene or any tragic end to a relationship. Usually, things simply fizzled and we mutually agreed we'd be better off as friends."

"Okay, but most people don't actually stay friends," Annie responded.

"Really?" Nick asked, sounding doubtful.

"You're a more evolved and kinder person than the rest of us," Annie admitted, and Nick let out a small chuckle. "I'm serious. You're the kind of person who probably buys razors marketed to women because you feel bad about the pink tax," Annie joked before seeing Nick's serious expression.

"Well, yeah, I do find the price differences ridiculous. But the women's products tend to mean it when they say 'sensitive' and a lot of the products geared for men irritate my skin," Nick explained as Annie stared back, dumbfounded. "Well, thank you for the rave review. Want to be my reference for my upcoming job interview?"

"What interview?" Annie asked.

"I haven't told anyone," Nick admitted. "I get a little superstitious and didn't want to jinx it. I'm being considered for a position in Hartford, at the Bushnell, right after the New Year. With my siblings both in the Bay Area these days and since our parents don't get back until after my interview, I didn't want to mention it to my family unless I had good news . . ."

"Moving back to Connecticut would be good news then?" Annie asked. "You wouldn't miss all that big-city living? What will the bagels think about this blatant betrayal?" Annie said.

"Oh, I love big-city living, for sure. The food options, the people-watching, plus all the theater—"

"Nerd alert," Annie fake-coughed.

"But I feel like I'm Peter Pan-ing there. I still have three roommates because moving to a studio at this point would deplete all of my savings, and for what? So I can cram into a tiny place alone every night? I'm ready to try something else.

Set my roots and all that," Nick started as the lights of the theater flickered, and Annie and Nick looked up in unison. Something about Nick wanting to "set roots" also flickered in Annie—hadn't she thought something similar?

"We should probably finish this up in case the power goes out, I don't want us to get stuck in the dark," Nick said, standing up to review their work and spraying it with a sealant as Annie quickly washed their brushes.

They switched the lights off and made their way back through the quiet corridors as the automatic lights continued to flicker. Once they were back outside the school, the festival across the way had been closed and completely put away for the night; it was dark and devoid of movement. Not a single person was anywhere to be seen. It started snowing again, though the flakes didn't feel cold or bothersome. But it seemed they were still no closer to escaping this made-for-TV Christmas movie.

CHAPTER TWENTY-ONE

It was another dreamless sleep before the daylight woke her. Annie's suitcase had provided a sweater dress in a blush pink color today; it was still closer to white than to pink, but it brought out the rosy color in Annie's cheeks and lips without her having to apply makeup. Annie was also thrilled to see a new pair of rose-gold, sequined Ugg-like booties in her suitcase and a pair of sheer tights.

"A break from heels? Well done, suitcase," Annie said approvingly, wondering if perhaps her wardrobe keeper had similar power to the characters in the Beast's castle from *Beauty and the Beast* and would eventually sing out, teaching her an important lesson through song. Annie took one last look at herself and walked downstairs to see Chris waiting on her doorstep. He looked clean-shaven and was holding a midsized basket with a tiny green wreath hanging off the handle. She opened the door to greet him.

"Hello there, my good sir, I wasn't aware I had ordered anything to be delivered," Annie smiled.

"Good morning, Annie," Chris beamed. "I came to see if you wanted to walk to the town brunch together. I didn't have the chance to say goodbye last night and wanted to apologize. I had to cut down over twenty trees and deliver them. It's such a blessing for my family. It may save the business, if you can believe it."

"Congratulations," Annie smiled, still beyond confused about how their entire business model operated. "Thanks for taking the time to pick me up, I'm ready when you are," Annie said, boldly linking her arm through Chris's until they had reached the gazebo. She hoped that Chris showing up for her this morning was enough to get more momentum between them. If she was going to almost kiss him, she needed to push things in the right direction once and for all.

Annie's eyes were immediately lasered in on Grant, and she let out a small gasp, trying to take in him and his ensemble. He looked like Santa and a cowboy stripper had come together to make a masterpiece and plaster it over his body, wearing a red bedazzled cowboy hat and boots over form-fitting black leather pants. On top was a red and white jacket with black buttons covered in sparkly embellishments, and cutting the look in half was a black leather belt with a gemstone-shaped outline of the state of Connecticut. Only a few feet away, Annie could see Perry gazing toward Grant with genuine affection.

"Howdy, y'all!" Grant said, his face lit up into a full smile that seemed to extend past the tall hat. "Welcome to the annual A Very Merry Munch and Mingle Till You Jingle Basket Brunch Auction Social!" Grant gushed, his cheeks turning rosier with each word. "Fellas, if you want to place your baskets on our table, you can do so now. I promise I won't tell if you want to slip your lady a sneak peek so she can plan her bid accordingly," Grant winked.

Annie saw Nick and Bailey walk by together, and she gave them a small wave. Nick was holding a small basket. After Nick had dropped his own basket with Grant, he made his way closer to Annie, as Bailey said hello to Chris.

"This is like that scene in *Oklahoma!*, right? But with switched gender expectations?" Annie asked him.

"I think so," Nick nodded.

"So feminist," Annie sighed, grabbing a complimentary candy cane and ripping it open with her teeth before loudly chomping off the hook.

"Take it easy there, Ado Annie," Nick advised. Noelle caught sight of Annie and gave her two enthusiastic thumbs-up, and Annie returned them.

"Why, I'm only getting prepared, I'm jist a girl who 'cain't say no' after all," Annie said with a western twang. "In case I end up under some mistletoe with my basket boy."

"Basket boy?" Nick asked, the corners of his mouth perking into a smile, and Annie shrugged.

"Yeah, it sounds pretty gross out loud, never mind. So you put together a basket this morning?" Annie asked.

"Well, I tried. There were things around the kitchen I assumed were meant to go in there," Nick explained.

"Here are your Simsbury Bucks!" Grant sang out, handing Annie her bunch. In the middle of each bill was Felix's friendly face. "Blessed by Mayor Felix," Grant explained.

"Obviously," Annie said. There was no end to what Felix could do, and why shouldn't the man have his own currency? "What can I get with these?" Annie asked Grant.

"Oh, Annie," Grant laughed. "She's hilarious!" Grant said to Nick, shaking his head.

"I don't get it. Why don't they raise money for the businesses that are all clamoring for the play's proceeds instead of spending it on printing currency? All it gets me is Chris's basket of nonsense," Annie complained.

"You're not planning to bid on my basket?" Nick asked her.

"Um, no, I assumed Bailey had it in the bag. Or in the basket, I guess," Annie answered. When Nick didn't say anything, she asked, "Wait. Do you want me to bid on your basket?" But why wouldn't he want Bailey to get it?

Before she could ask him to clarify, Grant's voice sang out again. "Please follow me to the gazebo, the festivities are about to begin!" he exclaimed, shimmying his shoulders in excitement.

It all started easy enough, without a lot of fanfare. The first few baskets were auctioned off to rosy-cheeked women, happy to support their classically burly man's creation. Perry seemed to serve as Grant's personal hype man, and Grant's shimmy somehow grew as the auction unfolded.

"Hopefully, you gals still have some appetite left! Next up, we have this beauty! Though she be but little, she is fierce," Grant's voice sang out, waving around a modest basket with a simple red bow on its handle. Annie saw Nick scratch the back of his neck and run a hand through his hair. It looked voluminous in the morning light of the gazebo. Annie tugged on his jacket and gave him an inquiring look with her eyebrows. Nick gave the slightest nod, and Annie made a production of counting her Simsbury Bucks. Maybe Nick was worried Bailey wouldn't know to bid or that he'd get a low bid, and perhaps he simply needed Annie to help; she could do that, right? She was happy to stir up a little more competition and low-stakes drama. "Now I don't want to give too much away," Grant teased the audience, taking a look inside, "but this little basket sure packs a punch that 'walnut' disappoint!"

"The puns are punning!" Annie cheered, attracting the scrutinizing gaze of a few nearby neighbors who were taking this event quite seriously.

"Can we start the bidding at twenty Simsbury Bucks?" Grant asked. "Remember, y'all, it goes to a great cause!"

"How?" Annie asked Nick. "Is Felix the great cause? Is there some kind of exchange rate for these?"

"I'll bid twenty!" Bailey's voice called out. There was a small round of polite applause, which she graciously accepted and beamed out.

"I think we can do better than that, folks, can't we?" Grant asked.

"I'll bid twenty-two!" Annie yelled proudly.

"Um, sure, okay, I don't think our bills come in anything less than twenty-dollar notes, but you know what, we'll figure something out!" Grant said. Nick gave Annie an exasperated eye roll.

"What? I don't want to bid too high now if I don't have to, maybe I can get more than one basket," Annie muttered defensively.

"Now I don't usually do this, but let me tell you about what you're missing here, friends. Inside this basket I see what looks to be a handcrafted nutcracker!" Grant exclaimed. Annie heard a loud gasp that quickly turned into a sob and turned to see Eve loudly weeping into Ferguson's jacket as he tried his best to comfort her. Ferguson patted her hair with one hand and used his other to present her with a royal handkerchief.

"Oh no," Annie whispered.

"What?" Nick asked, completely confused. "What happened? Why is Eve crying?"

"It's her dad," Annie said. "He was involved in some kind of nutcracker incident, and he died." Nick gave Annie a skeptical look before his face broke into a grin and he let out a loud laugh.

"That's a good one, Annie, but it's a bit much, don't you think?" Nick asked, continuing to laugh as Eve cried.

"I'm not joking, Nick," Annie hissed at him, swatting at his arm to get him to shut up. "She told me last night."

"Papa! Oh, Papa!" Eve yelled in anguish. Nick stopped laughing and looked around at the crowd. The momentum of the event stuttered to a complete stop as Eve let out more wails, and more people tried to comfort her.

"But what does a 'nutcracker incident' even mean? I don't understand, how is that a thing?" Nick asked. Grant looked desperate to draw the attention back to the event at hand.

"Well, Miss Annie, it looks like you'll take the basket if there are no other bids—" Grant began.

"I bid forty!" Bailey called out over Eve's howls.

"That's what I like to hear!" Grant smiled, and Eve seemed to regain some of her royal composure now and was only softly weeping next to Ferguson. Grant opened the other side of the basket to search for something else to advertise. "Do I see chestnuts?" Grant asked, and a horrified murmur broke out. Annie covered her face in her hands, already knowing what was coming next.

"What now?" Nick asked, looking scared. Annie didn't have to answer him because now Chris stood near Eve, who had decided to ramp her own crying back up so that she could match Chris's own wails. Holly broke loose from wherever she had been standing to sprint to her dad so that they could hold each other and weep. Obviously, most of the townspeople knew about Chris's wife's tragic death with a warm chestnut because most of them were now shaking their heads in disgust at the basket or clutching their hearts with wet eyes of their own.

"Please tell me you don't have some eggnog in there too," Annie whispered to Nick. His eyes went large with fear as a look of horror consumed his face. "I bid one hundred Simsbury Bucks!" Annie said, racing toward Grant, throwing all of her currency in his direction. He gave her a thankful look.

"Going, going, gone to Annie Meyers for one hundred Simsbury Bucks!" Grant said into the mic, though everyone's attention was still on Chris and Holly. And adjacently, Eve. Bailey shot Annie an angry look while trying her best to calm Chris by making soothing circles on his back with her mittened hand. "Please take this away," Grant begged Annie. "And maybe it's best you both get a head start on enjoying your brunch date?" Grant encouraged, and Annie took the basket and beelined for Nick.

"Let's go," Annie said through gritted teeth, and the two of them withdrew to the sounds of sobs. Once they were outside the gazebo's proximity, Annie stopped by a bench and let out a loud laugh. "Now that was fun," she cackled.

"It's not funny!" Nick cried.

"It's hilarious," Annie said, her laughter growing every time she replayed the scene in her mind. "That was the best thing that's happened here so far, my absolute favorite moment. How exactly did you put together your basket?" Annie asked when she was feeling a tad calmer and curious.

"Stuff was just there in my kitchen!" Nick exclaimed. "I didn't think to examine it; everything seemed holiday-inspired, so I had no idea it would be full of triggering items. What was all that?"

"Ah, where to begin?" Annie giggled, "Felix's wife, sweet Caroline, lost her life to 'bad eggnog,' Chris's wife passed away thanks to a large warm chestnut, and Eve's dad died after a tragic run-in with a nutcracker." Nick's eyes grew wide again before his face broke and he let out his own hoot of laughter, which made Annie laugh harder. When Nick thought he had gotten control of himself, he would give in to another spout of snickering, and his body shook from head to toe. The two looked at each other, their eyes both looking particularly twinkly, and laughed again before settling into a moment of quiet. "So now what? Should we break into this basket for a snack?" Annie asked him, wiggling her eyebrows in interest.

"Go ahead, it's probably safer if we consume or destroy it all before we unleash another round of emotional trauma on the town," Nick said, and Annie shook her head in agreement and placed the basket on the bench.

"Lukewarm eggnog?" Annie said, pulling out an unlabeled jar of thick white liquid. "This looks disgusting and would clearly kill us." Annie opened the jar and tossed the contents onto the road.

"Annie!" Nick scolded her, frantically looking around.

"What? What are you worried about, Nick? Are the police coming to arrest me for littering? The whole town is still at that gazebo, and if there's any type of crime community, you know it's a one-man operation of Felix. With, like, Chris as the head volunteer firefighter who has never actually had to do anything but save a kitten from a tree . . . I can't believe I paid a hundred Simsbury Bucks for this," Annie complained, and she was grateful that her body still didn't process feelings of being hungry here because she didn't find anything remotely appetizing. Suddenly, her hands pulled out a small silver tin, and her heart stopped. Unable to speak, Annie turned to Nick.

"Oh, yeah, I found one of your grandfather's tins. He used to leave us some of his lemon cookies in those every year; he'd put them in the mailbox," Nick said softly.

"He did?" Annie asked, moving to sit down as her voice cracked with emotion. Annie knew it was exactly something her sweet grandfather would do. Nick nodded slowly. Annie closed her eyes for a moment and could almost smell the familiar combination of lemon and sugar that would fill the kitchen when her grandfather baked his famous lemon cookies. As a proclaimed chocolate lover, even Annie had to admit the bliss these cookies brought to her taste buds. He had claimed he had learned the language of proper baking from watching his Italian grandmother, and he got emotional when Annie watched him bake, as if he was witnessing the true circle of life. Annie opened her eyes, and the tears she had been trying to keep in check finally spilled out.

"Oh, I'm so sorry, I didn't mean to upset you," Nick said, sitting next to her. He looked like he wanted to put his hand on her back to comfort her but couldn't build up enough courage to actually do it.

Annie tried to speak, to assure Nick she was fine, but the truth was, she wasn't. She hadn't seen one of those cookie tins since that last Christmas with her grandfather. And when he died, she had let her family sort and pack all of his things, unable to face the space he no longer occupied. But here it was with all the memories of that day coming crashing through now that the dam she had worked so tirelessly to build and maintain had broken.

When Annie's grandmother passed away from a chronic lower respiratory disease, her grandfather had moved in with her family, begrudgingly taking the small room that had once been an office as his bedroom. He hadn't wanted to inconvenience anyone. If it had been up to him, he would rather have passed away before his beloved wife, as he had never intended to live without her, but he had agreed to the idea on Annie's insistence. At the time, she had just passed the test for her driver's license, and her grandpa always let her borrow his car. It was more than car usage, though; of course, they needed him. He was the celebrator in the family, especially for Christmas.

Her grandfather had asked Annie if she'd sit and watch a holiday movie with him on Christmas Eve. He planned to call it an early night, since he was volunteering at McClean the next morning. Before the family gathered for breakfast and presents, he wanted to spread a little cheer for the seniors in the assisted living quarters, delivering his famous cookies and lending comfort to those who might otherwise spend Christmas Day alone.

Annie couldn't even remember why she brushed off the offer. She probably wanted to hang out with Marsha and whatever guy she was crushing on at the time. She asked her grandfather if they could put it off a few hours and promised they could watch movies once he returned from his Christmas morning plans.

"Annie," Nick said, breaking through her sobs.

"I should have spent Christmas Eve at home," Annie blurted to Nick. Her eyes continued to empty tears into her palms. Nick didn't say anything, but he watched her, ready to listen to any emotions she felt inclined to share until she allowed them to slip out, trusting they'd find a gentle place to land. "I didn't know," Annie sobbed as Nick put an arm around her and she cried into his chest.

On the morning of the twenty-fifth, her grandfather had passed out cookies, sung a few carols, and apparently, had even pretended to be Santa for a woman with dementia who asked if she could share her Christmas wish. Annie had learned that afterward.

When he was getting ready to drive back home, he sat down in his car and took a moment to ready himself. Before he could start the car, he had closed his eyes. On his favorite holiday, Christmas Day, her grandfather experienced a sudden cardiac arrest due to an arrhythmia and died instantly.

Waking up later on Christmas morning, sixteen-year-old Annie had gone straight to her grandfather's room. When he wasn't there, she assumed he must be waiting by the tree for the family to get up and get to celebrating. It was the lack of Christmas music that first gave her the sensation that something was off, the absence of brewed coffee and breakfast aromas next. Walking into the kitchen, her mother and father were sitting red-eyed at the table and her sister, Elise, was reaching for another tissue to cry into. Annie knew before anyone had to tell her. And in that moment, she knew she'd never be the same.

Annie continued crying on Nick's chest, but she opened an eye and happened to catch that rogue dog in the green bandana running toward them, or more specifically, toward the basket. Annie sat up, alerting Nick. The dog raced by in a blur, stopping to take the basket in its teeth before running away.

Nick and Annie paused before bursting into laughter. When they made eye contact, it only sparked another round.

"The Dougie look-alike," Nick smiled.

"I still can't believe you remembered Dougie . . . and it's very sweet you have memories of my grandparents," Annie said, her eyes filling with fresh tears. "It means a lot to me," Annie admitted, allowing the honesty to pour out of her now.

The loss of her grandparents had meant no more color and light, no more treats just for her. Each day since, but especially in December, she felt the vacancy their love had once filled. She loved her parents and her sister, obviously, but she struggled with their gazes of expectation of how she should be living her life. Each time her mother or father lobbed a loaded question about when she'd get serious and commit to "a real job" and a "real partner," it cut into her spirit. Those wounds were always the hardest to hide during the holiday season so, honestly, when they had decided to go away for Christmas, it was an easier way to pass the time of year she dreaded most.

"Does it hurt to talk about them?" Nick asked softly.

Annie thought about that. "I try to avoid thinking about it because it makes me sad, but then the idea of not thinking about them is also sad. Honestly, I don't know how to not be sad, and it's become so routine now that I don't even fight it," Annie said.

"Your grandfather really loved Christmas," Nick said.

"That's the understatement of the century," Annie said wryly.

"Why do you think it meant so much to him?" Nick asked.

"Hmm, well, for starters, he met my grandmother in mid-December. At a town Christmas candle walk event," Annie said, a fond smile fighting to make its way to her face.

"Watch out, Simsbury Celebrates, that sounds fun," Nick said.

"They also got married the next year, right around the holidays, they even had a Christmas-themed wedding, can you imagine? That's some made-for-TV movie magic right there," Annie said. "But Christmas was woven into their relationship from its inception, so it was, like, intertwined in its existence and their history. My grandfather, definitely the more sentimental of the two, reveled in all the festivities a little more every year, so by the time I came along, it had become a way of life for the entire family . . . but when we lost him, we all lost the celebration too. No one was up to carrying it on, not without him."

Nick nodded before meeting Annie's gaze and speaking again, "You're always going to miss him, Annie, but I think it's okay to celebrate Christmas again. Your grandfather would want you to be happy, especially during this time of year. You don't necessarily have to do all the things he did in order to enjoy the season, but maybe allowing a little Christmas magic into your life is a way to honor his spirit and keep the good memories close. I think he'd want you to find the parts you love and have fun making new moments," Nick said.

Annie's heart squeezed until he mentioned, "making new moments" and she had to laugh. She knew he was right, though, and for the first time, the idea of finding joy in a time of year that had previously been riddled with her grief didn't feel impossible. But it was still a bit complicated.

"It's hard to imagine celebrating a 'real' Christmas until we've escaped this place," Annie started and Nick gave a small nod of agreement. "Nick, why haven't you almost kissed Bailey yet?" Annie asked him, the words falling out of her mouth before she could second-guess them.

Nick broke their eye contact, wringing his hands together as if he were looking for the response in his fingers. When he met Annie's eyes again, the sound of a loud town bell rang and a small group of kids appeared to drop down to the street, declaring it was "the dress rehearsal bell" sounding. When they saw Annie and Nick, they gathered around them in an excited bunch, eager to escort their favorite costumer and set designer back to the school.

"Saved by the bell," Annie blurted as it continued to ring out, and Nick offered her a small half smile as two kids took his hands, skipping beside him. "Well, we can't let them win," Annie said, eyeing the two girls nearest to her and offering her open palms. "Let's go."

CHAPTER TWENTY-TWO

"Community, making amends, hospitality, metaphoric expansion, and Christmas magic," Perry preached passionately. "These are only a few of the defining principles that have led us here today to share this very special story with this beloved town," Perry paused dramatically and scanned the room with a meaningful, distant stare before locking eyes with Grant. Bailey and Chris were nodding enthusiastically, full of emotion. "Let's do this final dress rehearsal for us; tomorrow will be a true gift for all of Simsbury."

"I think you've created a full-fledged Christmas lover." Annie smiled at Grant once Chris invited the kids closer to the piano for warm-ups. Annie watched Grant's cheeks redden as he busied himself with a box of paper tickets.

"I don't know about that," Grant said, unable to hide the smile.

"Dare I say . . . presidential even?" Annie tried, knowing this Grant wouldn't recall their President's Day antics, but still unable to resist. Grant smiled, his head slightly cocked as if Annie had said something familiar, but his eyes returned to Perry before looking back to the tickets. "It looks good on you," Annie told him, and Grant looked back up.

"The show has come to mean a lot to me," Grant told her as he, again, let his gaze return to Perry.

"Well, Mr. President, you've got my support," Annie said, giving Grant's shoulder a quick squeeze.

As the kids sang through a series of scales, Annie made her way backstage to double-check that all the props were on the table and every costume piece was easily accessible. She planned to stay backstage in case of any last-minute issues and actually found herself looking forward to seeing what the show would look and feel like with an audience watching this classic story unfold before them. Annie still wasn't a fan of *A Christmas Carol*, but even she had to admit, she didn't hate this version of it. The kids were well-behaved little angels who acted and performed with such earnest hearts that it was almost impossible to feel anything but merry in their presence. They radiated joy, really, and Annie leaned into the warmth like a plant seeking the sun.

"Miss Annie," a small voice called out. Annie saw the boy who was cast as Tiny Tim looking into the dressing room.

"Hey, Jimmy," Annie said, impressed with herself for remembering his name. Jimmy Holiday wrung his hands nervously. Annie wondered, not for the first time, if he was actually a very old man trapped in the body of a first grader. "How're you doing?"

"I don't know if I can do it, miss," Jimmy said, shaking his head with worry.

Annie stepped closer and gestured for him to come inside. "Do what, Jimmy?" Annie asked, trying to make her voice as calm as possible.

"I believe it's a classic textbook case of stage fright, and I simply don't know what to do. You're the only person who can help me," Jimmy said, all in a rush, his small face twisted with concern.

Wow, Annie thought, *this kid is a solid actor . . . and I'm totally not equipped to assist him in any real way . . .*

"Huh," Annie said instead, taking a deep inhale. "You're the best Tiny Tim I've ever seen," Annie told him honestly. Jimmy didn't budge. *Okay*, Annie thought, *this may require a little more heavy lifting.*

"How do you do it, Miss Annie? When you're at your big-city job, I mean. Do you ever get nervous?" Jimmy asked. He sounded like he was on the verge of crying, and Annie really didn't want to have another person weeping away in her company if she could help it. Annie took another deep breath and tried to formulate a coherent response.

"Okay, Jimmy, well, I can tell you how I see things. The feelings of nervousness and excitement are almost identical. To your body, at least. You know, the fast heart rate and sweaty palms stuff. Your body is getting ready to take some kind of action based on some kind of unknown. When you're nervous, you're probably fearing the unknown, and when you're excited, you're looking forward to the unknown, but again, the physical feelings are so similar. So whenever I start feeling anxious about negotiating something or taking a risk, I try to remind my brain that what I'm feeling is totally normal, it's okay, and if I can focus on the excitement, rather than fear, it helps me," Annie said. Jimmy gave her a look of pure surprise, his eyes spellbound as he absorbed this concept. And then he leaped closer to Annie and threw his small arms around her neck.

"Thank you, Miss Annie," Jimmy said into her hair. And Annie's heart squeezed inside her chest.

"Everything okay, Jimmy? All set for the run-through?" Chris said, poking his head through the door.

"I'm ready now, Mr. Chris. Miss Annie was offering me some last-minute tips," Jimmy said, beaming at Annie and waving around two thumbs-up.

"I knew you would help," Chris whispered, giving Annie a very fond smile filled with warmth and genuine appreciation. Annie blushed, again uncomfortable with the amount of praise for doing what felt like so little.

"Anytime," Annie said with a small, encouraging smile at Jimmy. "Break a leg, okay? You're going to be spectacular out there, and I'm so excited for you," Annie told him, emphasizing the word "excited" so he'd hopefully take it with him. Jimmy nodded and gave Annie another quick hug before racing out of the room.

"I guess that means it's time for places then, huh?" Chris said, sheepishly grinning. "I'm looking forward to getting to spend some more time together at the Christmas festival," Chris told her with a meaningful glance.

"Sure, me too. What a day, huh?" Annie said, unsure of what else to say.

"What a day indeed," Chris nodded. A moment of silence hung between them. "Places!" Chris suddenly boomed out, and Annie had to cover her ears from the sudden explosion of sound.

"Thank you, places!" The murmur of kids' voices called out in response. And so, to places they escaped, and as far as Annie could tell from her spot backstage in the dressing room, the rest of the run-through passed without a hitch.

Once everything had been put away and prepped for the final performance, Annie was mid-exit when she caught Grant and Perry in a heated discussion. Both of them made exaggerated gestures, bordering on pantomime performance. As much as she wanted to eavesdrop, Nick, Chris, and Bailey were waiting for her by the exit. After crossing the street together, Eve and Ferguson were conveniently making their way to the festival too. Apparently, they would be attending the final night as a group.

"Tonight we can go sledding, drink hot cocoa, and walk through the ice sculpture gallery," Chris said, listing activity after activity on his fingers.

"An ice sculpture gallery?" Nick and Annie asked at the same time before glancing at each other and smiling.

"Like the one in *Groundhog Day*?" Annie asked.

"That's what I'm imagining too," Nick smiled.

"Groundhog Day?" Chris asked, looking to Bailey for clarification, but she gave him a puzzled look.

"What is a groundhog?" Eve asked, full of excitement. "How American!"

"It's an animal, kind of like a marmot. But it's also a movie," Nick explained. "And the ice sculpture bit Annie and I are thinking about is pretty romantic." Everyone leaned toward Nick, awaiting details of the scene in question. "Phil tells Rita that no matter what happens tomorrow—"

"He's happy in this moment—" Annie added.

"And that he loves her," Nick finished, and a wave of warmth crashed inside Annie's muscles, momentarily stiffening her in place for fear her legs wouldn't be able to carry her another step with the weight of her feelings.

"Where to? Sledding?" Chris asked. "Holly's probably there with Felix now."

Annie wasn't sure if her body was quite ready to be hurled down a hill in some sort of plastic vehicle, but she moved mindlessly with the rest of the group upward to the sledding point, where Jimmy was eagerly waving to her.

"Miss Annie! Miss Annie! Ride with me!" Jimmy yelled. His sled was absolutely massive and had two designated seats that allowed them both plenty of space between them to comfortably share. Annie crunched through the snow to get closer.

"See you 'snowpokes' at the bottom!" Annie waved. Once she stepped into her sled with Jimmy, they moved in glorious slow motion; her hair flowed in the wind, and Annie let her arms go up like she was on a roller coaster. For a few moments, she was weightless and free, and it was a glorious bliss that ended all too soon.

"Again!" Annie demanded once the sled had come to a complete stop. She stared at Jimmy, assuming he would be just as eager to return to the slope together too.

"Oh, sorry, Miss Annie, my mom's calling me," Jimmy shrugged, abandoning the sled.

"Tell your mom to wait," Annie demanded, her eyes wide and pleading. *God, I sound so creepy*, Annie cringed, *but I need one more fix*. A moment later, Bailey and Nick's sled stopped gracefully a few feet away.

"Oh, what fun!" Bailey smiled, her cheeks looking exceptionally rosy in the evening light. She stood up, managing to somehow exit the giant sled in such an elegant manner that it looked rehearsed. Just then, Chris and Holly came giggling down the hill, and Bailey put out her two arms for each of them to grab but by doing so they managed to pull her down with them, all of them erupting into buoyant laughter.

Annie was in no mood for silly antics; she needed to glide down that hill again. She narrowed her eyes and decided to haul the heavy sled back up by herself. But without saying a word, Nick took the entire sled from Annie and lifted it above his head, maneuvering it up the hill, not bothering to glance back at Annie's look of surprise as she stomped behind him. When they got to the top, Nick put the sled down and let out a breath, the only sign that carrying that beast back up alone had perhaps been a tad more challenging than he had let on.

"That was . . . wow . . . thank you," Annie finally stammered. "I wanted to try it one more time," she tried to explain, feeling foolish at her ferocity.

"Yeah, I could tell and was not about to get in the way," Nick said, making his way back down the hill, sans sled.

"Wait," Annie said, stopping him. "Do you want a ride down?"

"Yeah, honestly, I was hoping you'd ask," Nick said with a big smile.

"I'm taking the front seat," Annie warned him, and he nodded in understanding. When they were given the signal that they were clear to go, Nick held the sled and allowed Annie to get situated before pulling the sled back a bit farther.

"What are you doing?" Annie turned back to ask.

"Giving us a running start!" Nick exclaimed with a wicked grin. Annie's eyes widened in childish excitement. Nick ran, and the jolt of motion turned Annie forward.

After a few steps, he hurled himself inside the sled, almost missing the seat but landing with a loud triumphant laugh Annie couldn't help but echo.

And then they soared, the hill wide and endless beneath them. Annie could feel the grip she had spent so long clenching loosen in an exhilarating rush. She turned her head to see Nick behind her, laughing and radiating unbridled joy. Annie flushed with the feeling of flying. When they landed back at the bottom of the hill, giggling and shaking snowflakes from their clothes, it was all too clear and unavoidable. She had done it. She had fallen madly for not just the thrill of riding in a sled, but for the man who had shared it with her. Nick.

"That looked enchanting!" Eve called to Annie, coming closer to offer her gloved hands.

"It was!" Annie exclaimed, taking Eve's hands and stepping out of the sled. Annie turned to Nick, but he was literally rolling himself out of his position and into a pile of snow. After making a rogue snow angel, he jumped up to join them and grabbed the sled. Annie's heart raced, needing to share her revelation.

"Have you had the chance to ride yet?" Nick asked, and Eve shook her head, looking toward Ferguson. "You take this one and you and Ferguson can try it together."

Eve beamed at the idea and waved Ferguson closer.

"Have fun!" Annie cheered to Eve before stepping out of the designated sledding area and searching for a place to have a private conversation with Nick, the words desperate to free themselves from her chest.

"There you two are, you silly gooses!" Bailey laughed, running over to Nick. She looped her arm through Nick's to pull him closer.

"Pretty sure the plural of goose is geese," Annie said.

"We need to pick a Christmas tree!" Bailey exclaimed to Nick.

"Don't you already have several?" Annie asked, knowing full well there were decorated trees in every corner of town. Bailey continued to ignore Annie and dragged Nick to a lot of bare trees for sale, skipping all the way. "Oh, Nick, listen!" Bailey swooned, putting her head toward a speaker playing music. "It's our song!"

"An instrumental version of a random, vaguely Christmasy song is 'your song'?" Annie asked, but as expected, Bailey ignored her yet again, too lost in the moment. Instead, she hummed, already eyeing nearby tree options, deep in contemplation.

"I'm not like all the other girls," Bailey explained, slowly making her way through the first few trees, gracefully placing herself between trees like she was in some sort of elaborate ballet. "I'm all in on the Charlie Brown Christmas trees! I know, I know, I'm so quirky, right?" Bailey giggled, turning to admire a small tree. "But the sparser the better, if you ask me. It offers more space to love it. And it helps me to remember the more important parts of the holiday season—we're meant to be treasuring the simple things." Bailey stared off into the distance, allowing her eyes to go misty before she let out a laugh and turned down another row of trees.

"Is a Christmas tree monologue by a manic pixie dream girl needed for a made-for-TV Christmas movie, because Bailey just checked that off for us," Annie eyed Nick. "Seeking a Charlie Brown tree must be a requirement of every holiday heroine, right? I could have written that line, and I don't even watch Christmas movies."

"You don't watch Christmas movies?" Chris blinked at Annie, crestfallen at her admission as he suddenly stepped beside them.

"Whoa!" Annie said, jumping back. "You snuck up on me there . . . you kind of blend in with all the trees." Annie said, studying Chris in his green jacket and green hat, and standing taller than ever.

"We have thirty-five different tree variants in this lot, you know?" Chris beamed.

"I definitely did not know that," Annie said honestly.

"The balsam fir is the most popular, of course, and it's notably fragrant," Chris said, his voice sounding extra deep and full, the low register resonating in her ear. *Whoa, hold on, I don't have time to be hypnotized by a tree monologue*, Annie thought, desperate to signal to Nick as Bailey's happy squeal cut through the square.

"This is the one! Oh, it's perfect. But it needs to be chopped down!" Bailey cooed from her place among the pines.

"Why can't she pick one of the ones that's already been cut down?" Annie asked, gesturing to all of the cut trees around them being sold for the very purpose of making them easier to buy and transport home.

Chris grabbed a nearby ax that again seemed to appear out of nowhere, and his chest seemed to broaden before Annie's eyes. She wondered how on earth the buttons keeping his shirt together weren't popping off one by one from the pressure.

"Wow," Annie whispered, unable to stop herself from appreciating the lumberjack now sharing her space. Nick let out a sound half groan and half sigh, his eyes ready to roll, as Chris posed with the ax. Annie swore she heard

Nick mutter "spruce-bag" in a tone suspiciously similar to a less festive way to say a word that wouldn't be allowed here.

Chris walked briskly and tossed his jacket into the snow, rolling the already form-fitting flannel shirt up his forearms. His muscles bulged with each movement. Annie couldn't help but notice Bailey, too, had a look of dazed gratitude, but she also looked about ready to swoon, which Annie would have understood. Chris's display was both completely wholesome and somehow totally erotic. But he wasn't the man she wanted. She had to tell Nick how she was feeling; she couldn't wait another moment.

"Nick," Annie began, her throat tightened with nervous energy. *No,* she coached herself, *it's the same feeling as excitement.* Annie stared into Nick's eyes, and he wore the slightest knowing smirk, sparking her need to continue.

Then a bell chimed in the distance. Crystal clear and somehow unnerving, wiping any trace of a smile from Nick's face.

CHAPTER TWENTY-THREE

"What was that?" Annie frowned, watching Nick swallow, his eyes flickering from her into the distance. "Did someone try and swear?"

"Annie, I have to tell you something," Nick said.

"Me too!" Annie beamed. "Nick, I—"

"It was me, I made the wish that got us here," Nick confided in a rush.

"What do you mean?" Annie asked, her stomach dropping.

"That night, after you gave me the cookie, things got a little hazy—" Nick started.

"Do not blame an innocent cookie," Annie warned him.

"The guy with the bell, the one who may or may not be Felix, came back," Nick went on. "He said he was drawn back by the chair and asked if it was a trap to capture Santa." Nick ran his hands through his hair, clearly trying to make sense of the memory. "And then he asked what the girl next door and I wanted for Christmas this year," Nick said tentatively.

"What?" Annie asked, shaking her head in confusion.

"I didn't want us to spend Christmas alone," Nick said.

Annie narrowed her eyes at Nick, burning them into him. He raked a hand through his hair and cleared his throat, obviously knowing he had to continue or her glare might actually kill him.

"He asked me if that's what we'd wish for. I thought, wouldn't it be nice if we could have a Christmas like they do in the movies—"

"We?" Annie's voice crackled with tension.

"A holiday where we didn't have to be alone . . . He rang the bell. It was so loud," Nick shook his head, the sound seeming to bounce back into his brain. "When I looked up, he was gone, and a light from your house was beaming out the window, the TV was on—"

"You wished us here?" Annie blinked, the world tilting.

"I didn't know—" Nick winced.

"I thought we were on the same team. This whole time I thought this was happening *to* us, not *because* of you!" Annie erupted. "Why didn't you tell me from the beginning? You kept it from me, and now we're no closer to getting out!"

Then, as if to punctuate the moment, the tree Chris had been chopping made a loud cracking sound before leaning over, freeing itself from the ground. Annie's body went into fight or flight, unable to process Nick's words or their subtext.

"So, what? You got us stuck so we'd be here with these dummies?" Annie asked, gesturing in the direction of Chris and Bailey, the realization taking her breath away. If Nick had wished them here and they hadn't been able to kiss each other, then it had to be so that he could spend Christmas with his perfect movie heroine. "Bailey's your Esther, isn't she?" Annie asked him, trying to piece herself back together, her eyes still stinging with unshed tears and unsaid feelings.

"What?" Nick asked, taken aback. "No—" Nick's face was wrecked, caught between protest and guilt.

"You have to fix this. Right now."

"Annie, wait, is this what you want? You want to end up engaged to Chris?" Nick asked.

"I want to get out of here!" Annie yelled back at him.

"And what happens when you do?" Nick challenged. "Chris doesn't even know the real you, Annie—" Nick said. Annie's chest flushed with immediate defensiveness

"What's that supposed to mean? That he couldn't possibly fall for the real me?" Annie asked; the idea wounded her because it echoed how she already felt.

"No. That's not what I'm saying—" Nick said, shaking his head and letting out a frustrated sigh.

"We can't all be perfect like Bailey," Annie said, the words bubbling out of her and burning all the way. "She's a cookie-cutter mold of an ideal Christmas movie heroine, she's always so happy, and she loves this time of year. That's what you wanted, what you wished for, right?" Annie swallowed and it felt like she was being stabbed by a thousand Christmas tree needles. Bailey had all the qualities that Nick deserved in his rightful partner.

"Annie—" Nick tried again, but Annie shook her head. She had the chance to be a bigger person here, and that meant putting Nick's needs first, even if it made her heart feel like it was cracking apart.

"We need to get back to the plan," Annie said. "Complete the formula's steps."

"Is that really what you want, Annie?" Nick asked, his eyes pleading with her. Annie steeled herself and swallowed what she really wanted to say.

"I'm getting into the Christmas spirit!" Annie said instead. "I'm going to romance the pants off of Chris. Him and his rugged look and woodsy smell of the great outdoors!"

"We're outside, everything should smell like the great outdoors—" Nick said as Annie physically pushed Nick into Bailey's path. His eyes widened in surprise. He turned back to Annie, voice low and gravelly. "Annie. Please. This is what you want? This is *your* Christmas wish?"

This time Annie couldn't force the lie out and instead nudged Nick into Bailey.

"It's a beautiful tree. Can I carry it home for you?" Nick offered. His voice sounded robotic.

"Are you sure, big guy?" Chris asked with genuine concern. "She's a hefty lady," Chris said, gazing appreciatively at the tree.

"I'd love your help picking out my tree, Chris," Annie said, batting her eyelashes in a flirtatious effort.

"Well, if you're sure," Chris said, heaving the tree into Nick's chest.

"Thanks, Nick," Bailey smiled, but Annie caught a stiffness in her that she hadn't seen before.

"See you two tomorrow!" Annie waved before hissing in Nick's ear, "This is it, seal the deal!" Nick turned back to her, and his eyes were deep puddles. Annie gave him a small nod of her head before linking her arm through Chris's. When she was finally brave enough to turn back, Nick and Bailey were walking away. Annie fought the instinct to grab Nick again, beg him to stay by her side, and admit that what she really wanted was him. But she wouldn't keep him from his perfect made-for-TV Christmas movie girlfriend. He deserved all the things Bailey could give him, and Annie would fight for Nick's happy ending above her own if it meant he got one.

"I have the tree for you, Annie. The biggest balsam I can carry!" Chris said, puffing out his chest. Once he had slain the dragon and carried it home for her, they found a full box of ornaments and strings of lights ready to be used waiting for them on the living room table.

Annie mindlessly wove a string of lights around her fingers, imagining Nick around that darn bloody chair, trying to make his own Christmas treasure, unknowingly luring a mysterious man to them. *I mocked him*, Annie thought, feeling guilty. *I wasn't nice, and he only wished for us to not spend Christmas alone. It was a kindness, not a curse.* Annie clenched the lights, trying not to cry.

"Let me help you with those," Chris offered kindly and Annie blinked, wordlessly handing the lights over and allowing Chris to weave them around the tall tree. She explored the various decorations in the box. Most were generic, traditional adornments, but one caught her eye and she drew it closer to examine.

"Mistletoe was made for two," read the small circular ornament. And then with a sudden burst of memory, she recalled a neighborhood ornament exchange party from childhood.

Each household contributed a wrapped ornament to a communal Santa bag, and families took turns pulling out one and opening it. Annie's family had provided this one, the one she was now holding, but that year, she had also been the designated picker. She had selected the ornament that was on Nick's luggage now, the one with the snow people and the corny "You mean snow much to me" nonsense on the scarf.

That's not the ornament she took home, though, Annie recalled. Nick, after fighting with his older siblings to let him pick the wrapped ornament that year, had pulled out Mr. Heartgrave's contribution. The painfully dorky "Math puns are the first sine of madness." Instantly, the small thrill of being the one allowed to choose gave way to terrified little guy-logic that his siblings would tease him and kill his chances of ever being cool in their eyes.

Annie had been the first to notice him, completely distraught, the way only a small child can be, weeping alone on the staircase. He confided his fear of his older brother and sister (along with all the bigger neighborhood kids) reacting to him picking an ugly and, honestly, offensively nerdy decoration, so Annie had simply offered to trade. She didn't want Nick to cry or be so sad during Christmas time. She took the dorky decoration from his hands, the ornament that now sat on her magical suitcase upstairs, and switched them. He had taken the snow people scarf ornament and held it to his young heart, speechless with gratitude.

Annie was so lost now, trying to recall all the details of the party, that she didn't notice Chris had moved in closer to observe the ornament until he was reading it out loud.

"Mistletoe was made for two," Chris said slowly. Annie looked up to find his face nearly inches from her own, close enough to feel his warm breath, and he gave her the faintest smile. Instinctively, Annie angled her chin, as if daring Chris to finally kiss her. Chris moved a millimeter closer as his eyes slowly blinked in Annie's direction. Just when Annie thought their mouths would close the distance, she moved her hand and dropped the ornament, sending it rolling under the tree and cracking the moment between them.

Annie let out a breath of air. She was pretty sure she had actually done it. She had almost kissed Chris. And the only person she wanted to tell was Nick.

"Mistletoe was made for two," Chris repeated once they had placed themselves back at a comfortable distance.

"Are you reading the ornament again . . ." Annie began.

"I've loved this time we've spent together here," Chris said before letting out an audible sigh. "But Annie, what happens after Christmas? You'll be returning to your big fashion job in the big city. I doubt you'll even have time for a small-town guy like me," Chris finished sadly. Annie wasn't sure what to say to him. Should she try to reassure him that of course she'd stay if only he would ask or should she finally admit to him and to herself that, no, she didn't want any of this. Not in this made-for-TV Christmas movie, and not in real life.

Before she could properly formulate a response, Chris checked his watch and noticed the late hour. He said his quick goodbye, kissing Annie's cheek. In the past, his lips anywhere on her body had given her all types of fiery feelings, but this one left her cold, only solidifying her readiness to close the Chris chapter of her dating history. Annie walked Chris out and peered over at Nick's house. All the lights were dark. *He must be at Bailey's*, Annie thought, nibbling her lip. She crept to the window and willed him to walk down the block. Finally, when it was clear he wasn't returning, she gave up hope of his return and tried to fall asleep.

Her thoughts kept piling on top of each other. Letting herself imagine Nick as her partner filled her with fear. Simply being in the presence of another person who personified Christmas terrified her, because she didn't want to have to go through losing them again.

But what if it wasn't nervous energy her body was feeling? What if it was what she had tried to explain to Jimmy? What if it was actually excitement and something far more joyful and happy?

Maybe she didn't need to control the fireworks of feelings she had tried so hard to keep track of and tame. Maybe she didn't have to compartmentalize and neatly pack Nick away somewhere deep within her brain like she tried to do with every other crush she'd had throughout her life. She already knew how that story went; she had already done that with Chris and guys like him. Nick was different. He was so earnest and open, and it was all so refreshing considering almost every other interaction she had had with the male-identifying humans in her life. Maybe she was right where she needed to be, in a quaint winter wonderland, becoming the person she wanted to be and finally falling for the right person.

Hours later, Annie woke up and sat straight up in bed. It was Christmas Eve. The air was electric. She looked out the window at Nick's house, but there was still no trace of him, and the discomfort of the unknowing refused to budge from her body. Even after getting dressed for the day and walking outside, Nick didn't appear, and once a few minutes had passed, Annie made her way to the school alone. It was the day of the big show, after all, and she couldn't be late.

Chris and Bailey were buzzing around the cafeteria, wrangling kids. They seemed to be in their own nervous haze too, and Annie wondered if that was just how Christmas Eve felt for everyone here, though their apparent butterflies were doing nothing to settle the ones multiplying inside her.

Grant flew around the space in a frantic frenzy, jumping every time the door opened and fixed on the entrance.

"Morning, Grant," Annie said, Grant jolted in surprise. "Are you okay?"

"Of course," Grant said automatically. But when Annie's gaze pressed him, he cracked and shook his head. "He left." Annie knew he meant Perry. "We got into a little argument last night before the festival. The kids had been asking him if he'd be here to help with the play again next year."

Okay, rude, Annie thought, *no one has asked me that*. She nodded for Grant to continue.

"I said it would likely take another snowstorm or a direct order from corporate," Grant said, his voice thin. "I didn't want to admit that I hope the snow never melts, I don't want him to leave. But when I went back to the inn last night, all of his things were packed up!"

"Where would he go?" Annie asked, mostly wondering if she, too, could escape.

"I don't want to be alone for Christmas," Grant answered, his face threatening to break into a million pieces. "I put on a show of being unstoppable, but I'm fragile too." Annie nodded encouragingly, realizing this truth was likely something the real Grant might feel. "Perry sees me. The real me, behind the curtain. At first, it gave me stage fright. But losing him feels as devastating as making your entrance to an empty theater."

Annie pulled Grant into a hug, her own chest needing the support from a quickening heartbeat. She understood that fear, of someone seeing you in all your true colors and the ache and bleakness of a life without them. Grant's words (well, she could leave out the theater metaphors) could have been her own.

"Maybe being seen is the bravest thing we can do; it shows we still have a heart strong enough to keep putting ourselves out there," Annie said.

And with that, the front door burst open with a crash, Perry at the entrance, brushing snow from his shoulders, his smile wide. Grant saw him and let out a small, grateful gasp, and Annie nudged him closer.

"I thought you had left town," Grant said, tentatively taking steps to meet Perry.

"I would never leave before the show," Perry reassured him. "I was getting these." He grinned, pulling out a pair of keys and dangling them for Grant to see. "I'm taking over the dance studio and staying to run the business. This town, it's got a hold of me. I love Simsbury and I love all its residents."

"All its residents, huh?" Grant smiled, tilting his head.

"There is one especially who has taken permanent residence in my heart," Perry said softly. Grant reached into his pocket with a theatrical ease, flourishing a sprig of mistletoe, holding it between them.

"I'm certainly glad I came prepared," Grant told him.

Perry took the hand holding the mistletoe and rested it on his chest. The moment was so beautiful and intimate that Annie's eyes watered, and she turned to give them privacy to enjoy it together.

Annie poked her head into the dressing room where most of the kids were already dressed. Jimmy was meditating in a chair, and Annie tiptoed around him to make herself available to any of the kids who might need help zipping into a garment or completing their stage makeup.

Annie closed her eyes for a moment to try and steady her breathing. When she opened them again, she could see Nick and Bailey reviewing notes on a clipboard in the wings. Annie wanted to look away, but her eyes were fixed on the movie-montage-esque sweetness between them. Bailey laughed and gave Nick's arm a squeeze, a move that Annie could swear she felt across her own body as her muscles twinged. The warmth pouring out of Nick's eyes when he returned Bailey's stares was undeniable, and Annie physically ached to be the recipient of such a favorable gaze.

Annie watched Nick spot something on Bailey's face and lean in closer. For a moment, Annie was terrified she might witness an actual kiss between them, but Nick lifted his index finger to Bailey's cheek and pulled it back, revealing something now perched on his fingertip. Bailey beamed, dramatically closed her eyes, and puckered her lips to provide a steady stream of air to what Annie could now assume was an eyelash.

Looks like Bailey has everything she could wish for, Annie thought, watching Bailey reopen her eyes and laugh again next to Nick. *This is how it should be*, Annie reminded herself, *Nick deserves someone like Bailey*. But still, a lump lodged itself in her throat and her eyes prickled. She should have been celebrating. Nick had clearly succeeded in winning over Bailey and she had almost kissed Chris—they had to be nearing the finish line now, right?

It wasn't long before Chris was giving the final call for places. When the house lights dimmed and the hush of the audience filled the space, Annie felt her body's nervous energy buzz in a different direction. There was something about that moment before a performance that made the air spark as everyone willingly suspended their thoughts to a place alive with magic.

Chris played a short opening number on the piano before the stage lights slowly came up to reveal Scrooge, in all his glory, looking peak curmudgeonly. Annie gave herself a mental high five for his presentation. Even without the assistance of a YouTube tutorial on old age makeup, her efforts were pretty solid, and dear ole fourth grader looked like a true professional.

"A merry Christmas, Uncle!" the child playing Fred called out in a tiny, adorable, squeaky voice.

"Bah! Humbug!" Scrooge yelled back to him, and the audience burst out into applause. *Wow, two lines in and these kids are already bringing down the house*, Annie marveled.

"Christmas is a humbug, Uncle? I hope that's a joke," Child Fred said, clearly mugging to the audience like they were all in on this together. The crowd roared with laughter. Annie could already feel herself slowly slipping into the familiar story. She shifted her weight from one foot to the other, careful not to make a sound backstage, and moved a little closer to watch.

"Ah, what else can I be when I live in such a world of fools as this? Merry Christmas! Out with merry Christmas!" Scrooge cried out, and Annie sucked in a breath as if hearing the words for the first time, goosebumps covering her skin like an emotional cape. But she let the scene unfold before her eyes, unraveling itself to reveal a simple, beautiful story, free from any of her past expectations.

When it was Holly's turn to reveal herself as Christmas Past, Annie heard an audible collective gasp from the audience, clearly in awe of her costume and makeup. Annie warmed with pride, looking at Holly under the stage lights, illuminated like an angel. She was beautifully ethereal, like a doll given the chance to breathe life into the room around her. Holly wore a white lace dress with delicately placed iridescent sequins that projected their own sparkles across the stage. Her face had been painted with white and blue swirls around her eyes, and her hair had been woven into a series of delicate braids across her head.

"Holly is a perfect Christmas Past," a voice whispered into Annie's ear, causing her to jump in surprise, clasping a hand to her mouth to keep from yelling out.

CHAPTER TWENTY-FOUR

"Sorry!" Nick said. "I didn't mean to scare you."

Annie turned to him, catching a whiff of his aroma, which was a blend of earth and fire. Combined with the cozy, mixed scents backstage, it was enough to make Annie feel warm and safe, comfortable and connected. *There he is,* Annie thought, her breath catching in her chest, *this kid I casually referred to as my nerdy neighbor, all grown up into a kind, sensitive, adorable, silly, good-looking man.* This sweet guy, who watched made-for-TV Christmas movies with his aunt to bring them both some comfort and joy during a dark time, who preciously held all the memories they had shared growing up next door to each other, and had somehow done the impossible: provided Annie with the Christmas spirit she never imagined she'd feel again.

"Shouldn't you be up in the booth?" Annie asked, realizing she had been gawking at him in wonder. She desperately wanted to both interrogate Nick about each and every detail of where he had been the past several hours and plug her ears to hide from whatever had transpired between him and Bailey.

"Bailey has everything under control," Nick said simply.

"So you and Bailey . . . ?" Annie started, unable to meet his eyes.

"I'll fill you in after the show," Nick said, and all Annie could do was give him a nod. "Is it weird that I'll miss this play?" Nick asked, and Annie shook her head.

"I will never admit it again, but no, I don't think it's weird at all . . . I even think I like the show," Annie relented, and Nick gave her a playful nudge in mock shock.

"Why, Annie Meyers, you never cease to surprise me," Nick smiled, his eyes back to the stage so he couldn't see Annie blush.

"It turned out so well," Annie said, her hushed voice husky with feeling.

"Yeah, it did," Nick said and turned to Annie, offering her a small private smile. Annie smiled too and turned her attention back to the action onstage, already unable to look away from the familiar tale. *Maybe things like this get better depending on who you get to experience them with.* Annie thought of taking a quick look at Nick to see him completely engrossed in the play. He seemed to radiate his own light, and Annie couldn't help wanting to bask in it, him so in his element and contagiously happy.

And that's how Annie Meyers came to watch the entirety of *A Christmas Carol* without a single negative thought or critique. It played out how it always did, of course, but this time real tears traveled down Annie's face when Scrooge woke up to his real life, forever changed by magical

Christmas spirits. When Annie heard Jimmy's Tiny Tim call out the iconic "God bless us, every one!" she had to silence a small sob.

"Are you crying?" Nick asked, while also clearly crying.

"I hate this for me, but I guess I'm a theater person now," Annie said, unable to avoid letting out a small laugh of disbelief as the show neared its conclusion and the sounds of the piano playing picked up for the final number. "I'm forever destined for dorkiness."

"It's a good life," Nick smiled, and Annie wanted to say more, to hold this moment between them a little longer, but the sounds of cheering and clapping filled every nook of the cafeteria turned performance venue, and all Annie and Nick could do was add their own applause to the crowd.

When the kids finished their first series of bows, Chris took the mic to thank everyone for coming out, especially given the snowstorm that had first been an impossible challenge but had actually morphed into a beautiful opportunity to allow for some kind, local talents to come together in support of the production and the town, protecting the tradition for another tremendous year. When Chris called for Annie, Nick, Bailey, and Perry to join him onstage, Nick had to grab Annie's hand and pull her out. Holly and Jimmy handed each of them a bouquet of red roses before Annie could give a small wave and excuse herself from the spotlight so the children could enjoy another round of applause.

Next, it was time for the announcement of the local business that would be gifted with the play's proceeds. After a three-way tie between Déjà Brew, the Nutmeg Nest, and

Tinsel's Christmas Tree Farm, all three businesses decided to put the money into next year's holiday fund instead because the past few days, despite a "rampant" snowstorm, had revived their commerce. Another win for the Spirit of Christmas, though truthfully, Annie felt like it had been a tad anticlimactic.

At some point, the standing ovations ceased, and the kids returned to the dressing room area, jumping with the post-performance high and the general joy of being that much closer to Christmas. All the children wanted celebratory hugs from Annie, and she happily obliged, enjoying these small, costumed people who were much less smelly and sticky than any child she had encountered in the past.

As the kids changed out of their pristine costumes for the last time and handed them back to Annie, she made sure to organize them for optimal accessibility should they need to be laundered. She handled them with care and delicacy, even though they would likely disappear from existence should she ever leave this place, and tried to lose herself in the task of tidying up the makeup, props, and costume items.

Annie was about to zip the last garment bag when she heard Bailey's voice outside the door. Being the forever sneaky bitch that she was, Annie took a huge step closer to the exit and tried to hold her breath so she could focus on eavesdropping.

"I have to tell him. Today," Bailey said, full of an intimate intensity. Annie wondered who she could be talking to. "I came so close right before the show started, but I lost my nerve."

"There's still time," Felix told her.

"I love him," Bailey gushed, and Annie strained her neck, craning to get a better listen. "He needs to know as soon as possible."

"Bailey, you're doing the right thing," Felix encouraged her. "You two will make a wonderful married couple."

"Oh, Felix, I don't know if he's ready to propose," Bailey stuttered, but her voice twinkled with delight and hope.

"It's written all over his face every time you two are together," Felix said.

"To be honest, I've worried he's falling for Annie," Bailey admitted, and Annie felt like she was being dunked in ice. "She's so polished and cosmopolitan with her big fashion job in the big city, and I'm just a small-town girl," Bailey said demurely.

"Bailey," Felix said softly, holding her name in his mouth like it was a precious stone. "Annie is a wonderful woman," he began, and Annie dug her nails into her palms. "For the record, you're so much more than a small-town girl, and I'm happy to have it on proper authority that you are just what he wished for this Christmas." Annie let out a small gasp. Nick wanted his Christmas movie heroine, and Bailey fit the role.

"Thank you, Felix. I appreciate your sage wisdom and support. Can I share one last secret with you?" Bailey asked him, Annie's body becoming one with the door as she tried to listen. "If he doesn't propose, I'm prepared to do it myself," Bailey said, a newfound confidence taking hold. "I found a ring in some of my Great-Grandpa Wally Jones's collection of antiques and knew he was looking down on me to lend his support."

"I'm happy for you, Bailey," Felix said, and she heard Bailey say something in return, but it was muffled. Annie assumed they had hugged and perhaps Bailey's words had been lost to Felix's jacket. "Hopefully you'll save me a dance at the Annual Joyful Jovial Jingle Bell Ho-Ho-Hoedown of Yuletide Two-Stepping and Festive Fiddles Boogie Oogie Jig and Jangle?" Felix asked, and Annie put her ear directly to the door. What did he say?

"And if not there, then at the ball!" Bailey said, sounding like she was moving farther away and out of range of where Annie could eavesdrop.

"Dang it," Annie muttered. She wasn't ready for whatever event was happening next or for the impact of Bailey's words to fully sink in. Bailey was in love. Bailey was about to declare her feelings. Bailey wanted a proposal.

Annie opened the backstage door, wondering if she could sneak out and regroup, but Eve intercepted her with a warm hug before she could attempt an exit.

"Annie!" Eve said, her voice twinkling. "I'm so glad I could run into you! What a wonderful performance. I must say, it was quite moving. And the costumes!" Eve dramatically rolled her eyes up like she was about to faint. "You are so talented!" Eve beamed.

"Oh, I barely did anything," Annie muttered.

"Nonsense. American women are far too humble. I know your trademark high quality," Eve said, squeezing Annie's hand. "I'm heading back to the inn to pack and begin preparations for tonight's event," Eve said, suddenly serious. "It's my last night here in your beautiful Simsbury, Connecticut. They estimate the storm will have passed by tomorrow, and we should be cleared to fly home." Eve let out a wistful breath.

"How are you feeling about that?" Annie asked, and Eve caught Annie's eye before lightly biting her lip in thought.

"I need to break off my engagement with Nigel," Eve said softly.

"Oh, yeah, you go, girl," Annie encouraged.

"And I will share my true Christmas wish with my forever love, Ferguson. Even if he doesn't share my affections, I have to tell him tonight," Eve said, her eyes full of emotion. Annie's stomach twisted, thinking of Bailey's similar plan, and a buzz filled her ears. She had no way of knowing how tonight would unfold, and it was making her nervous. For the first time since she had slipped into this version of Simsbury, she wished she had more time to make a concrete game plan. "Oh, Annie, you must come and get ready with me before the ball. Please say yes. I have the perfect dress for you!" Eve said, dangling her words like a treat for a puppy who was being asked to do a trick.

"Hard to say no to that," Annie smiled.

"It's settled then! Come over as soon as you can," Eve said, giving Annie a quick goodbye hug. Annie took it in, grounding herself by closing her eyes and pretending it was the real Marsha holding her instead.

Entering the cafeteria space again, Annie audibly gulped. Everything had been transformed once more. The rows of chairs from the performance had been packed up and put away, and the walls were adorned with rodeo Christmas decorations.

"Welcome to the Annual Joyful Jovial Jingle Bell Ho-Ho-Hoedown of Yuletide Two-Stepping and Festive Fiddles Boogie Oogie Jig and Jangle!" Grant's voice called out. Sometime between the curtain call and getting everyone out of their costumes, he had been fully mic'd and was now wearing yet another bedazzled cowboy hat. Next to him, Perry stood proudly in a matching outfit, encouraging the crowd to listen. Annie saw Nick approaching, and she gave him a desperate stare.

"Wait, wait, wait. What in the Christmas heck is this now?" Annie asked. "I thought it was time to get ready for the ball. How could there possibly be another event?" Annie asked and Nick looked sheepish. "Nick! How is there another thing?!" Annie nearly spat.

"Yeah, I didn't think it was worth sharing the full schedule," Nick admitted.

"So we have a hoedown? An actual hoedown? Why are we pretending we live in the South again? Can I please sit this out?" Annie begged.

"No!" A chorus of townsfolk called out in unison, and a group of active fiddle players aggressively played a rendition of "We Wish You a Merry Christmas."

"No, absolutely not, I have to draw the line somewhere," Annie hissed to Nick, her eyes wildly searching for the exit.

"Why not draw it at *line* dancing?" Nick joked. "It can't be any worse than the dance card prank Esther plays in *Meet Me in St. Louis.*"

"How on earth are you encouraging this? A hoedown, Nick? A *hoedown*. Have some respect for yourself," Annie said, crossing her arms across her chest in defiance.

"It's my last dance in St. Louis, I feel like I'm going to cry," Nick said, batting his eyelashes at Annie in his best Judy Garland voice.

"Don't you dare pull that cute Esther routine on me, buddy," Annie told him. "We don't have time for this; we have too much to catch up on—"

"Nick," Bailey said urgently, appearing next to Nick's shoulder and looking up at him. "I need to talk to you," she said, her eyes moving to Annie.

"Of course," Nick said, nodding his head. "Is everything okay?"

Bailey offered a weak shrug, and her eyes looked big and glassy.

"Sorry, Bailey!" Annie interjected. "He needs to do this group number first," Annie said. The only thing she could think to do was pause whatever moment was happening or waiting to happen. Both Nick and Bailey stared at Annie in confusion, and she did a small marching jig in place. She needed a real moment with Nick.

"I understand, this is a truly tremendous tune," Bailey said earnestly before giving Nick a loaded look. Once she was out of eyeshot, Annie grabbed Nick's arm, delivering an urgent pinch. Nick let out a small yelp of pain and rubbed at the spot where Annie had grabbed him.

"Again, woman, you continue to be a walking weapon," Nick muttered. "This is going to leave a bruise."

"Everybody, line up!" Grant's voice echoed in the space. "Head couple at the top, please!" Grant sang out, winking at Perry, and the crowd parted to allow Felix and Noelle to take their place at the front of the line, women on Noelle's side and men on Felix's. "Now, as always at the Annual Joyful Jovial Jingle Bell Ho-Ho-Hoedown of Yuletide Two-Stepping and Festive Fiddles Boogie Oogie Jig and Jangle, the head couple will slide down the row and back again and everyone else will clap," Grant explained, but from what Annie could tell, everyone around them was laser focused and overly prepared to fully commit themselves by already loudly clapping along. Annie and Nick were across from each other, but the constant stomps and claps made it impossible to have a private conversation.

"Nick!" Annie cried to him, trying to convey with her eyes that she had something to get through to him. But it seemed Nick had caught whatever hoedown hum was intoxicating everyone else as he clapped along and grinned a goofy half smile.

"Step forward and bow to your partner!" Grant said on top of the loud fiddling music. Annie stepped forward too quickly and was instantly out of sync with the rest of the dancers. But when Nick got closer, she quickly tried for his attention again.

"Nick!" Annie said.

"Bow to your partner," Grant said.

"Listen, Nick, Bailey wants to marry you," Annie burst out during a break in sound and before half-heartedly bowing before Nick.

"What?" Nick asked, coming up from his own bow.

"Listen to me—" Annie started, but Grant was ready for the next move.

"Right elbow swing!" Grant called, and Annie put her arm out, allowing Nick to swing them in a small, contained circle amid a sea of other swingers.

"Oh, truck this," Annie muttered, her body still reluctantly participating in the dance.

"Left elbow swing!" Grant continued.

"Nick," Anne said sternly as she caught Nick's eyes before their arms switched spots. She tried to keep her eyes on Nick but just ended up twirling around again.

"Now do-si-do," Grant said.

"How do I do that?" Annie asked. The dancers around her stepped forward and passed right shoulder to right shoulder, continuing to move to the right and passing in back of their partner until they were faced away from each other. Everyone moved backward, passing their partner's left shoulder now before returning to their starting spot. "Oh, I did it," Annie said when she had completed the step. She felt a small surge of accomplishment; she should have known the made-for-TV Christmas movie puppeteers would take over.

"Make a bridge and let the head couple slide down!" Grant said, and Annie brought her hands to meet Nick's. They were warm and made her own tingle at the touch. Felix and Noelle rushed past them in a blur of red and green and took their new place at the end of the line, stomping and clapping along with the music until everyone else had followed their lead. Annie tried to get out a few more words in between claps.

"I (*clap*) heard (*clap*) Bailey (*clap*) talking (*clap*)—" Annie yelled.

"What?" Nick asked, continuing to clap along with the group. Annie groaned in angst and annoyance. After all her time in this bizarre universe, this event was starting to feel like the most absurd.

"Let's mix things up now! Everyone jump to the left, skip to the right, and set your sight on a new partner!" Grant called, and Annie saw Noelle wiggle her eyebrows at Nick before beelining for him.

"Sorry, Noelle, he's next on my dance card," Annie shrugged and took Nick's hand. Noelle gave a little scowl, but Annie was laser-focused, and she knew time was running out. "Nick, Bailey is in love with you, she wants you to propose tonight, and if you don't, she will—" Annie attempted again.

"Where are you getting this from?" Nick asked before another loud boom of laughter came from the crowd.

"Let's switch partners one more time!" Grant sang out, and Annie tried to move them away from the dancing and Noelle's line of sight.

"From the ghost of Wally Jones, okay?" Annie scowled, and Nick looked confused. Annie was overwhelmed by the tsunami of mixed emotions twirling inside her as everything around her moved with activity too. "Listen, Nick, if you marry Bailey, you're going to be with a woman who actively participates in doing that Elf on the Shelf nonsense for your kids," Annie blurted in a rush, unsure why that was the direction she had decided to take to get through to him but committing to it anyway. When Nick didn't answer, Annie continued, doubling down, "Is that what you want, Nick? A wife who puts energy and effort into Elf on the Shelf? And, like, writes stupid notes from the elf? Every year?!"

"Annie, we both know if someone was going to do that kind of thing for their kids, it would be me," Nick said neutrally. Annie gasped as if he had slapped her. She was close to slapping Nick herself if only to wake him up to the horror of life shared with an Elf on a Shelf and to how seriously he needed to be taking this issue. Annie could see Noelle coming closer, ready to claim Nick as her rightful partner.

"Annie, why don't you want me to talk to Bailey? This is what you wanted to get us out of here," Nick stated pointedly. A group of nearby fiddlers played their instruments so hard that it made it impossible to think. Noelle also loomed closer, ready to steal Nick away.

"Last night, I almost kissed Chris. I mean, I'm pretty sure we had our almost-kiss moment—" Annie said, probably the worst thing she could have said at that moment, short of "Go truck yourself." Nick's eyes expanded before they hardened. But before Annie could explain that it had only solidified that Chris was *not* the one she wanted to be with, Noelle scooped her arm through Nick's, sending him in a circle around Annie.

"Let's finish what we came here to do. I'll see you at the Christmas Ball, okay?" Nick said, not meeting Annie's gaze, as Noelle continued to spin him farther away.

"Wait! Nick—" Annie tried, but Nick and Noelle were caught in the wave of limbs, finding themselves at the center of the cyclone before Annie could do anything.

"Dig it forward," Grant called as Annie stayed still. "Now grab your Santa Sack!" Grant continued, and the rows of partners obediently pretended to lift large, invisible bags over their shoulders in glee.

"Merry Christmas," Annie said, her eyes filling with days' worth of pent-up feelings. "Dang it!" Annie muttered to herself, realizing that she had just participated in another made-for-TV Christmas movie cliché, and she was the one who had been left behind.

When Annie made it home, she stomped up to her room and collapsed into bed.

"What am I supposed to do now?" Annie wailed to Arthur. "I trucked everything up back there." Arthur looked at Annie and blinked. "Not helpful, bud."

Arthur pawed at the yearbooks by her side table, nudging the book on top with his head, growing more insistent with each contact.

"Whoa, what's in that thing? Catnip?" Annie asked, reaching for the book to have a closer look. "My junior year?" Arthur let out a loud meow that made Annie startle. "Dude, you are freaking me out," she muttered. Annie thumbed through the yearbook, and Arthur placed himself in Annie's lap to headbutt the passing pages until she stopped on the freshman class. For whatever reason, this settled Arthur, and he went back to staring at Annie. "This is Nick's class," Annie said as her eyes traveled the faces of young students until she found Nick's tiny headshot. Annie couldn't help but smile, placing a delicate finger over his round and familiar fourteen-year-old face. But an inscription written in tiny green hand-writing next to the image caught her attention. Annie brought the page closer to her face to get a better view.

"Much Ado About Annie," the note began, "with or without the mistletoe, I'm in a holiday mood. Love Always, Nick." Annie had to read it three times before bursting out into an equal combination of laughter and tears.

"That is the dorkiest thing I've ever seen," Annie squeaked, her voice already hoarse with the variety of sounds and experiences she was putting it through. "He loved me," Annie said, two tears making a getaway down her face. Even after losing her beloved grandfather that year and closing up her heart, Nick had seen all those sides to her then and liked her anyway.

Maybe the reason they had slipped into this strange snow globe world was to get Annie to this point, in love with the boy next door and finally ready to release some of the grief that she had been gripping on to for dear life these past sixteen years. Maybe it was finally time. Maybe she was ready for her happy ending.

"I have to get to the ball!" Annie yelled, hoping Arthur would use this opportunity to become something useful, like a carriage or whatever else Cinderella needed to get herself to her destiny. Instead, Arthur gave his paw a lazy lick before curling into a ball. Annie took a big breath, grabbed her things, and made her way to the inn, unable to spare another moment with love and Christmas on the line.

CHAPTER TWENTY-FIVE

Grant had outdone himself in preparing for the ball. Once again, the inn's reception hall had been transformed into a winter wonderland, white lights and candles glowing as artificial snow dusted the numerous Christmas trees guiding the way to the grand staircase. Annie couldn't help but note that this may be one of the last chances she'd have to experience this unrealistically full schedule, where time could stretch generously to accommodate each and every holiday whim.

Grant was lighting candles on the second floor, and Annie gave him a small wave.

"Annie! I've been wanting to thank you for your advice. I'm so happy you'll be attending tonight's ball," Grant said, coming closer.

"So tell me, what's the full name of tonight's event?" Annie asked, wanting to prepare herself for whatever absurdly long-winded title awaited.

"The Annual Simsbury Christmas Ball," Grant said simply. Annie waited for the hundred words that were supposed to follow it up. When Grant didn't go on, Annie raised her eyebrows in surprise.

"Huh, well, okay, then," Annie shrugged, seeing Perry in the corner, carefully placing mistletoe.

"You're trusting him with the mistletoe?" Annie joked. "Things must be serious."

"He's not going back to the big city," Grant gushed with visible glee.

"Perfect," Annie nodded. "I'm happy for you," she added. "You found love in a holiday place and you were brave enough not to let it get away."

Grant hugged Annie, and it was like being flooded with warm light.

"You're brave too," Grant assured her. Annie nodded. "Be with the one who *sees* you. And I'll see you at the ball," Grant smiled before pointing her to the white door labeled "The Sweetheart Suite" in white cursive inside a red heart. Before Annie could knock, Eve had opened the door, wearing a lush white robe, her fake wig hair of strawberry curls cascading down the back. Still, she looked every bit like her beautiful princess self.

"Oh, Annie! I'm so happy you're here!" Eve squealed in delight. "Shall I pour you a cup of cocoa?" Eve asked, and she took the smallest, daintiest sip from her own cup, her pinky pointed high.

"Maybe later," Annie smiled, the idea of yet another hot chocolate making her feel queasy.

"Wait until you see the dress I have for you," Eve purred, taking Annie's arm and closing the door behind them. When Eve selected the green velvet hanger and unzipped the garment bag, Annie expected to see something in holiday red, but instead, it was a light blue with an overlay of tiny pearls and crystals forming intricate snowflakes patterned from one shoulder down the entire floor-length dress. The back was sheer lace. It all looked impossibly delicate.

"Bury me in this dress," Annie whispered, and Eve let out a giggle that sounded like an angel receiving its wings. With steady fingers, she gingerly took the dress, with Eve's encouragement. She was so eager to put it on her body but wanted to give the dress the respect it deserved to ensure it would remain pristinely intact. Eve excused herself to the bathroom so Annie could change in privacy, and once the dress was safely on, Annie called for her to return.

"Annie, what a vision you are!" Eve squealed. "Now, let me do your makeup. I promise I have a skilled hand," Eve said, reaching for bags of cosmetics and helping Annie onto a white cushioned chair before Annie could object. It reminded Annie of all the times she and Marsha had taken turns doing each other's hair and makeup for various school dances, and she was grateful to have a familiar moment with a friend amid these crazy circumstances. Within mere moments and a few proficient strokes across her face, Eve turned Annie toward a mirror. Her eyes were covered in iridescent, sparkly eye shadow, and her cheekbones caught the flattering light, showcasing a beautifully blended highlighter. Annie's lips looked like they had been stained with raspberries. Eve released Annie's hair from a claw clip, and it fell perfectly down to her shoulders, loose waves cascading into place before she finished the look with a diamond snowflake hairpin. Annie wanted to cry. She was a magical Christmas queen. Annie had never felt so beautiful in her entire life. Since she had stopped bothering to carry a useless phone around, she couldn't take a picture. Instead, she tried to take a mental photograph to store in her mental files so she could hold on to this feeling for when she would inevitably cruelly criticize her appearance once she had been deposited back to real life in her true form.

"Could you help me with my tiara?" Eve asked Annie, interrupting her thoughts.

"I'd be honored," Annie breathed out, hoping her working-woman American fingers wouldn't do anything to compromise the coveted crown of a princess. Luckily, the tiara seemed to do most of the heavy lifting and landed on Eve's head with ease. Annie fought the compulsion to tug on Eve's hair just to see how well the obvious wig had been placed but didn't want to hurt her friend. In a green velvet dress with long sleeves and a grand, sweeping neckline, Eve joined Annie at the mirror and squeezed her hand.

"Shall we make our way down?" Eve asked hesitantly, her voice wavering.

"Are you okay, Eve?" Annie asked. "You've seriously never looked hotter in your life . . . but you'll feel better when you talk to Ferguson. Even though I think he may die when he sees you."

"Oh no, really?" Eve asked, sounding horrified.

"I mean, because you look so beautiful!" Annie assured her, and Eve let out a small, relieved laugh.

"You Americans and your expressions," Eve said with mock crossness.

"I'm going to tell Nick he's the one I want," Annie asserted to her mirror self. She saw Eve's reflection widen her eyes.

"Yes, Annie, you must! I'm enchanted to hear it," Eve said, turning to hug her.

"I need him to know how I feel . . . Even if Bailey managed to propose to him," Annie added, trying to convince herself that this was the necessary next step and she needed to take it.

"Look at us," Eve said encouragingly, "two strong women who have only become stronger with love. We can do this, we deserve our happily ever after." Annie pulled Eve into another strong hug. Annie savored the connection, her heart aching for the closeness she only shared with Marsha.

Annie wanted to walk into the ballroom, descend a golden staircase at half speed, and force the crowd to marvel at her beauty. If she was truly starring in a made-for-TV Christmas movie, she deserved her moment, ding dang it. She let Eve go first, in search of Ferguson, before she made her own way out of the Sweetheart Suite. Annie walked slowly, grasping the banister for support, and was swept into the crowd of formalwear swaying to the sounds of violin strings. There were couples dancing some sort of choreographed waltz, and Annie wondered when they had all had time to learn yet another dance routine.

The lights in the room had dimmed, making everything softer and dreamier, and Annie assumed cinnamon spice was being pumped into the air from a nearby vent because the scent was delightfully intoxicating. She searched the room for Nick, but when she couldn't find him, she wondered if she could get his attention another way.

"As—" Annie started and the sound of a bottle popping and its accompanying fizz echoed from somewhere nearby.

Annie strained her neck, hoping she'd see Nick and also see actual alcohol. After a moment, she tried again, "Sh—"

A dog's bark tore through the room, but, again, no sign of Nick. Time to bring out the big guns.

"Fu—" Annie said, mentally preparing for the Little Drummer Boy but instead hearing a loud whoopie cushion.

"Was that a whoopie cushion?"

Annie bumped right into Nick's chest, causing them both to step back.

"Hubba, hubba," Annie said, her mouth dropping open into a small O-shape of surprise. Nick looked gorgeous. Annie couldn't take her eyes off of him or make a coherent thought, let alone declare her love. He was wearing a black suit with a light blue bow tie. His hair had been styled back, and even his black shoes seemed sexy to Annie; they were so shiny.

"You look beautiful," Nick said softly.

"You look beautiful," Annie repeated back to him, dumbly. "I mean, wow, Nick, you look straight up Jack Dawson from *Titanic*."

"That's probably the best thing anyone has ever said to me. I may need to tattoo that on my body," Nick smiled.

"Please do," Annie said, her mouth involuntarily watering, imagining both Nick and Leonardo DiCaprio's (circa 1997) bodies.

"Why are your eyes doing that 'I've spotted something delicious I want to eat' look?" Nick asked, looking around the room. Annie blushed and let out a nervous laugh.

"I don't know what you're talking about. Listen, we have to talk—" Annie began as Bailey glided toward them. She was wearing a gorgeous lilac dress. It had a high neckline and a long skirt with layers of ruffled hems, giving her the appearance of a walking, elegant dessert set free from a bakery display case. When she turned, Annie could see that her back was bare except for a barely visible lace that sparkled and made her look ethereal.

"Merry Christmas," Bailey said in a serious voice when she reached them.

"Your dress," Annie breathed. "It's stunning."

"Thank you, Annie. I made it this morning. I was inspired by the Sugar Plum Fairy, of course," Bailey smiled modestly.

"Of course," Annie said, a smile tightly stretched across her face.

"Nick?" Bailey asked. "Since we couldn't chat earlier at the Annual Joyful Jovial Jingle Bell Ho-Ho-Hoedown of Yuletide Two-Stepping and Festive Fiddles Boogie Oogie Jig and Jangle—"

"Yeah, I'm sorry about that. Noelle wouldn't let me stop dancing, and when I tried to find you, Chris said you had left—" Nick explained.

"I need to speak with you privately, right away; it can't wait a moment longer," Bailey said in a hushed tone, not looking at Annie. Bailey used her incredibly talented, little, nimble fingers to grip Nick's arm.

"Oh, yeah, okay," Nick said, his voice now holding the slightest edge of unease. Nick gave Annie a shrug before following Bailey to the Land of Sweets. Or wherever Bailey could have this heart-to-heart inside this old, mysterious inn.

"No, no, no," Annie murmured, nervously scanning the crowd. She had no interest in talking to anyone other than Nick, but her eyes stopped on Chris. Her sweet and handsome made-for-TV Christmas movie hero. He clutched something in one hand and ran his other hand through his hair in a nervous gesture. Annie took a step, trying to get a better look at what he was holding, when she accidentally bumped into Felix.

"Good evening," Felix chuckled.

"Oh! Sorry, Felix, did I hurt you?" Annie asked. She was so ready to leave this clumsy-girl habit in Christmas past.

"No, my dear, I'm made of some pretty strong stuff. When you're in my line of work, you have to be," Felix said, his eyes twinkling. "Have you finalized your Christmas wish yet? There's still time," Felix said. Annie was about to answer when she saw something in Chris's hand. A red ring box. She gasped. Felix followed her stare.

"There's still time," Felix told her again, this time with more force. Annie shook her head in confusion. What was he talking about? That ring box couldn't be for her, could it? Was she supposed to get engaged to Chris tonight? Was the only way out of here an engagement, or was that the only way to stay? No, she had to talk to Nick first. Annie couldn't process the collision of thoughts coming in and out of her head to formulate any kind of rational response as the sound of someone tapping on glass pierced through the room and silenced everyone in it.

"Excuse me, excuse me!" A voice called out from the top of the staircase. It was Ferguson. He looked handsome but was definitely more bald Billy Zane than Leo. "I wanted to first congratulate my dearest new friend, Grant, on hosting his first Simsbury Christmas Ball at the inn. The decorations are gorgeous—and yes, the tinsel is straight Grant!" Ferguson joked, and the crowd laughed politely. "But there's another person I need to thank," Ferguson paused. "A woman who makes every day feel like Christmas. A soul who twinkles like the lights around us tonight. Someone I want to spend the rest of my life with . . . if she'll let me," Ferguson said as the crowd hushed in eager anticipation at his every word.

"Eve," Ferguson began as he wiped a supposed tear from one eye. "The royal family legacy of Wintermore is in your hands, and I know you had intended to be with Nigel. But I hope you'll take a different leap of faith with me and trust that our love will be the one written about in history books. You are the only one for me. Every moment with you is a song I wish would never end. It would be my great honor to live as your most loyal subject, your husband," Ferguson finished grandly.

"Oh, Ferguson!" Eve beckoned from the other side of the staircase, a small crowd parting to let the lovers grasp each other's hands. Ferguson dropped to one knee and opened his palm to reveal a red ring box of his own.

"Princess Eve, will you marry me?" Ferguson asked. Eve looked down at Ferguson, her eyes glittering.

"Before you answer, darling, I have something to say," an older woman's voice echoed throughout the room.

"Mama?" Eve gasped, leaping toward the woman dressed in a long-sleeved red velvet dress and wearing a huge crown covered in jewels.

"Whoa, are those real?" Annie whispered aloud. No one answered, of course, as everyone was captivated by the scene unfolding before them.

"Is it really you, Mama?" Eve asked.

"It is I, my child, the Queen of Wintermore," the Queen of Wintermore said in a deep, full voice. The crowd murmured, and someone let out a loud gasp. Annie recognized the queen as her second mom, Marsha's mother, June, and despite the absurdity of this whole thing, Annie was moved to watch her best friend get engaged with a treasured member of her family nearby.

"Is Nigel here?" Eve asked her mother in a somber whisper.

"Nigel ran off with the Countess of Aldovio; it's all been a bit of a scandal. But good riddance, I say," the queen quipped.

"Truly?" Eve asked, clearly unable to believe the amazing fortune of being off the hook from marrying that dweeb and instead getting to be with her true love. "But how did you get here? What about the snowstorm?"

"It cleared in time for me to fly here," the queen said. Annie wanted to stop everything and check to see if that meant her phone was now finally working. "Eve, please know you have my sincere approval to marry Ferguson. Along with the dear citizens of Wintermore. And lastly, I know your dear Papa approves. He would be so proud of you."

Ferguson, who was now at the queen's side, deeply focused on her every blink, gave her gloved hand a squeeze of support.

"Oh, Mama," Eve sobbed into her mother's bedazzled chest.

"Before we catch up, I think you owe someone a formal answer," the queen smiled, and those around gave a hearty laugh as if she had made the wittiest comment imaginable.

"Yes, you're right!" Eve exclaimed, no mascara streaks or any sign of her tears apparent on her beautiful face, and turned toward Ferguson. "Ferguson, I do love and adore you so. I'm proud of the man you've grown into during these past few days and can't imagine a life without your presence; it's been a true Christmas present. Of course, I'll marry you!" Eve cried, pulling Ferguson up and giving him a tight hug. Then, moving at a slower speed, Ferguson opened the box and took the ring out, fitting it seamlessly on Eve's ring finger as she beamed down at it. Once the ring was on and admired, Eve and Ferguson looked into each other's eyes and moved in slowly for a kiss.

The kiss was, in a word, basic. Annie squinted up at them, waiting for any sense of real passion to overtake them, but they appeared content with a very mediocre-looking, closed-mouth, dry, chaste smooch. Around them, people cheered. The trio retreated to a more private corner. Annie smiled, genuinely happy for Eve/Marsha.

"I don't want to steal the focus from that incredibly romantic, storybook love story moment!" A man's voice called, and it echoed across the room, once again silencing the crowd. Annie looked around and, to her horror, saw that Chris was now standing at the top of the stairs, taking Ferguson's spotlight. "But I was so moved by that raw, heartfelt emotion that I had to act, right here, right now. Surrounded by all of my closest friends," Chris stated before taking a dramatic pause. "As you all know, my heart has been absent since losing my beloved wife," Chris said solemnly. Those near him nodded, and one man reached over to squeeze his shoulder while fighting tears of his own. Chris nodded at the man appreciatively before continuing, "I didn't think I could ever love again. Even when Holly yearned for me to try, I never believed I could find someone to fit into our lives and approach this special holiday season with renewed hope."

"No, no, no," Annie whispered. Thankfully, no one seemed to notice Annie's looks of panic as they were completely transfixed by Chris's every word and thoughtful sigh. *This can't be happening*, Annie thought, desperately seeking an exit. *Nick, where are you?* Annie wondered, feeling truly terrified.

"This woman has taught the teacher," Chris chuckled softly. "Working alongside her these past few magical days has made them some of the best of my entire life. She's talented, beautiful, and so funny!" The crowd laughed, and Annie groaned, cursing herself for her hilarious sense of humor. "And tonight, I would like to ask her a very important question . . ." Chris trailed off.

"Stop!" Annie found herself yelling out. She instantly flushed, knowing that everyone's attention was now locked on her. "I can't marry you, Chris."

Around her, Annie could hear concerned and confused murmurs. Chris looked stuck in a state of surprise.

"I thought that was what I wanted. I daydreamed of you choosing me and seeing what would happen if we gave 'us' a real chance," Annie said. "Getting to know you this week has been eye-opening. You're better than I hoped for: kind, devoted to your community, tall, and very hot, and so strong, and, like, incredibly knowledgeable about trees, which isn't something I had ever cared about but is probably something I should unpack with my therapist . . ." Annie trailed off before suddenly remembering she was mid-speech in front of a waiting crowd. "Sorry, where was I? Chris, we're not meant for each other, I see that now," Annie said, feeling Felix's eyes focused on her. She braced herself and kept going. "I have stronger feelings for someone else . . . someone who makes me feel better when we're together, like I'm their valued partner, the best version of me." Annie's voice cracked with emotion, hoping to find Nick in the crowd, but when she couldn't locate him, she turned back to Chris. "I want you to be happy. You deserve someone who can appreciate having a bona fide hottie lumberjack widower dad of their own, but it's not me," Annie said, staring up at Chris.

"Oh, um, Annie, thank you, that was . . . something," Chris said, slowly trying to gather his wits. "But, actually, I was hoping to bring Bailey up here. Bailey?" Chris called out.

"What's that now?" Annie asked. Bailey was now at the bottom of the stairs, her own perfect pink O painted on her lips.

"Yes, Chris?" Bailey asked, her eyes as big as the moon. Chris glided down the staircase, taking the steps at least three at a time.

"Bailey Jones, I love you. You make me feel like every day is Christmas. Will you join Holly and me this holiday?" Chris asked, and Bailey nodded, releasing a single, silent tear to roll gently down her face. "As my wife?" Chris continued, gracefully dropping onto one knee. "I have it on good authority that your dear great-grandpa, the great Wally Jones, would approve, and I have his ring right here," Chris said and gave Felix a conspiratorial wink.

Bailey gasped in delight and hugged Chris fiercely, and like the couple before them, they stared lovingly at each other. Chris put a sparkly diamond ring on her finger, and then Bailey wrapped her arms around Chris's neck, and they kissed before the crowd erupted into happy applause.

What the truck is happening? Annie screamed internally. She was relieved, certainly, that her hand was not the one wearing a ring at the moment, but what had she missed? Chris and Bailey were in love? The whole time? Was Chris who Bailey had been talking about backstage? Not Nick? How and when did that happen?

"There's still time, Annie," Felix whispered, suddenly next to her. "Tell the boy how you feel. Be honest," Felix said. Annie could swear she could see actual stars now sparkling in his eyes. *Wow, staring too deeply into Santa's eyes is better than booze*, she thought, wishing she could bottle it up. "It's Christmas," Felix smiled warmly and backed away, revealing Nick. Her Nick. Annie nodded dumbly at Felix and offered a weak nod of understanding.

A flash of green streaked by Annie's knees, and she realized it was that darn, rogue dog. He was running straight for a Christmas tree.

"I'm sorry, who owns this dog?" Annie asked, exasperated, trying to follow him. He took a different turn when Annie got to the tree, snatched something off of it, and bolted upstairs. When Annie turned her head, Nick was striding closer to her. "I didn't know about Chris and Bailey. Are you okay?" Annie sputtered.

"Why wouldn't I be?" Nick asked. "Bailey told me she was in love with Chris and wanted my advice on how to tell him," Nick said casually as if this progression in the story wasn't the same complete shock to him that it was to Annie. She stared at him, her mouth open. "Wait. Are *you* okay? I know you and Chris had a big night—" Nick said.

"No, we didn't! I don't want to be with Chris. I wanted to tell you last night, but I thought you were too busy almost kissing Bailey," Annie said.

"What? No? I carried her tree home, she kissed me on the cheek, and I left. I fell asleep when I realized you were still out with Chris. I hoped you'd forgive me for landing us here . . . wait, you didn't suspect that Chris and Bailey were falling in love?" Nick asked, now surprised himself.

"Nick! What are you talking about? Bailey has been obsessed with you this whole time! When I saw you two backstage, you looked like a couple!" Annie yelled, her voice feeling stretched and raw.

"Wow, the hardest to learn was the least complicated," Nick muttered.

"Did you just Indigo Girls me?" Annie gasped. It might have been the sexiest thing she had ever experienced. Nick gave her a half-smile and a shrug. "What am I going to do with you?" Annie marveled. An ear-splitting bell started going off around them.

"The Christmas Chime!" a woman's voice cheered. "It's almost Christmas!" Annie scrunched her face and put a finger in one ear to drown out some of the sound.

"Midnight . . . hark! The time is drawing near," Annie heard Felix say.

"Nick!" Annie hollered.

"What?" Nick yelled back.

"There's so much I want to say—" Annie began, before getting cut off by a second bell. "I've never been in love before, not real love, not pure made-for-TV Christmas movie love, that's for sure—" Annie continued as a third bell blasted. "I've been terrified to celebrate Christmas again since my grandfather died, and I've been too afraid to believe in love because I didn't want to end up sad and alone. But I wanted to . . . I secretly wished for it, I know I did—" Annie said, her voice fighting to be heard as the sound of the fourth bell rang out.

"I wished for it too, Annie. I've been wishing for you for forever," Nick admitted. "And I definitely wished it when I saw you again with your Pringle can wine."

"I'm not a perfect made-for-TV Christmas movie heroine, though, and I'll *never* do Elf on the Shelf," Annie said.

"I don't want a made-for-TV Christmas movie, Annie. I never have. It's only been you from the moment you swapped your ornament for the math pun one," Nick said, his eyes warm.

"You remember that?" Annie gasped.

"Of course. You made my Christmas with that gesture. You were kind when you didn't have to be when no one else was watching. Why do you think I made my mom buy all those bus stop Pop-Tarts? I wanted you then exactly as you were, and I want you now, exactly as you are," Nick said alongside the fifth bell.

"What if it's us? What if we're the ones that are supposed to be together? The couple everyone's been waiting to get together this whole time?" Annie asked.

Nick grinned as the sixth bell chimed. "Big duh," Nick smiled.

The seventh bell rang. Annie looked to Felix for help, and he pointed to something angled above them. There was the rogue dog, his head poking between two balusters of the grand staircase, holding what appeared to be a sprig of mistletoe.

"I hope he doesn't eat that—isn't it poisonous?" Annie asked. People around them were counting along now with the final five bells as they approached midnight. Annie was pretty confused as to why that was happening, considering that it was definitely more a New Year's Eve than Christmas Eve activity, but she sensed that maybe this was it, maybe this was the end of their made-for-TV Christmas movie. So with that in mind and knowing she might only have seconds left, she put her arms on Nick's shoulders and pulled him in. She paused briefly right before their lips met to try and double-check that her advance was wanted, but he quickly closed the distance. When their mouths touched ever so briefly, Annie caught fire. There was the sensation of heat, and time stopped. And then everything faded to black.

CHAPTER TWENTY-SIX

Annie awoke and shot straight up in bed. At first, she didn't know where she was. She reached for Nick but only ran her hand into Arthur, who swiped a clawed paw, hissed, and then bit her flesh.

"You little bitch!" Annie yelled, pulling back her hand, realizing the absence of warning sounds to her verbal transgression. "Bitch," she whispered, looking around. "Bitch. Fuck. Fuck. Fuck! Oh my God, I can swear again!" Arthur let out a deep meow. "Shut the fuck up!" She giggled and clapped her hands. "Wait, what's happening? I'm back?" Annie grabbed her phone and saw that it looked like it always had, and she had eleven missed messages from Marsha. "Was that all a dream?" Annie asked Arthur, who only blinked at her. Annie stood up to examine her surroundings. With a broad, theatrical voice, she cried, "Yes! The bedpost is my own. The bed is my own. The room is my own. Best and happiest of all, the Time before me is my own, to make amends in!" Annie stopped her *Christmas Carol* tribute, and her stomach twisted. No, it couldn't all have been a dream, right? She'd had a very real experience with Nick. The idea that Nick hadn't actually been beside her these last few days made Annie's eyes sting with tears. She had to find him. Right now. Annie took a step to start her frantic run and immediately tripped on her pajamas and basically pantsed herself in the process. With her pajama bottoms now more off than on and tangled, she frantically removed them in a series of kicks and crawled her way out of the room to get downstairs.

"Nick, Nick!" Annie screamed before opening her front door. When she found herself outside, she yelped at the cold and let out a long string of profanity. Annie's body, mostly her bare and pantsless legs, begged to go back inside. But then she saw Nick scooting in leopard slippers toward her around the weird, bloody barber chair and she quickened her pace to get to him. "Nick, that was real, right? You were there too?" Annie asked, her voice breaking in desperation.

"Where?" Nick asked, his face a cloud of confusion. Annie gulped in some cold air before burying her face in her hands and choking out a small sob. No, this wasn't happening; this couldn't have all been for nothing. It's Christmas! "No, no, I'm kidding! Of course, I was there." Annie looked at him critically. "Sorry! I'm nervous, and I don't have ornaments to juggle. And I'm cold. But yes, Annie, we were in whatever that was together, and now we're back home." Nick reached out his arms and brought Annie closer. The touch was electric, and Annie caught her breath. She wanted to laugh, cry, and make out all at once. "You're pantsless in the snow? This is feeling very *Bridget Jones's*

Diary and, not gonna lie, that is a big fantasy of mine . . ." Nick admitted, and Annie chose to laugh first.

"Remember where we left off?" Annie asked, now needing to make out with him immediately.

"You in that dress? The dog and the mistletoe? Those trucking, deafening chimes? Yeah, I'll never forget that." Nick said softly, staring at her mouth.

"Oh, we can say 'fucking' again," Annie blurted out happily.

"I know, but to be honest, some of the alternatives may be worth keeping; like 'spruce-bag' is so much more fun—"

"Why aren't you trying to jump my bones yet?" Annie demanded, cutting him off and pulling his face in, inviting his warm lips to cover hers. It was tentative at first, both of them testing the boundaries, adjusting to their non-G-rated current circumstances. But it wasn't long until they revved it up.

Nick took Annie's bottom lip between his teeth, and she let out a surprised gasp at the unexpected force. It was on the right side of painful pleasure, and his growing confidence in mastering this make-out was absolutely a turn-on. Annie wrapped her lips around Nick's tongue, slowly sucking it into her warm mouth and using her lips to stroke it up and down.

Nick's eyes flew open, and Annie knew he was imagining that technique across other areas of his body as she felt him go hard where his pajama pants met her belly. Annie flushed at the realization that she had caused that reaction and was also thrilled that she was unlikely to find a Ken doll situation. Annie fingered the waistband of Nick's jammies, eager to remove them completely.

"Really hoping it's not going to be censored this time," Nick said, taking Annie's hand between his and pulling the elastic so they could both get a peek.

Annie's mouth involuntarily watered as she admired the sight. She stared back up at Nick's face, his eyes hungry with pressing need. It was hot as hell. She fisted his T-shirt and backed his body up to the wooden chair behind them until he was sitting. Annie's hand slapped the back and clamped the armrest, positioning her body so she could straddle Nick, desperate to feel him underneath her. Annie wrapped her arms around his neck, clawing at his back to remove any space between their bodies. She wanted him everywhere.

"Really glad I brought the chair out here," Nick murmured into Annie's hair before gripping her hips, inviting them closer.

Annie arched her back, grinding herself against him, already panting and ready to remove all their clothes but savoring the friction of the fabrics. Nick slipped a warm hand under Annie's flannel, teasing her breast before cupping it and burying himself in her neck.

"Annie," Nick breathed, clenching his teeth in an effort to control himself.

Before he could finish that sentiment or they could engage in some very not-made-for-TV Christmas movie shenanigans, a sudden blur of red caught their attention and they looked toward the street. Their garbage had been picked up, and the driver was peering out from behind the front seat.

"Stoned Santa," Annie whispered. "I don't know whether I want to scream at him or thank him."

"Felix?" Nick called. Stoned Santa Felix took his hands off the wheel. One hand was holding a bell, and the other looked like it was working overtime, holding the bong and beer. Stoned Santa Felix was making his way back down the street in the garbage truck, but before he turned a corner, he waved and called out to them from the window.

"Merry Christmas!" his voice boomed, followed by a loud hacking cough.

"Merry Christmas!" Annie and Nick yelled in response.

"As much as I want to continue this, it's freezing, and I'd rather not see people posting about it later on the town Facebook page," Nick said.

"Oh, is this the part of the movie where we can talk about our kinks? Because I have a Santa voyeurism fantasy I should tell you about," Annie teased. "Take me inside," she ordered, her eyes flashing with heat. Nick gave her a grin and picked her up in a fireman's carry.

She squealed in surprise as the cold temperature reminded her that she was indeed pantsless. "I feel like a Christmas tree," Annie laughed, but when Nick quickly covered the distance to his front door in strong, confident strides it made her breathless.

In an impressive act of horny heroism, Nick managed to open the door, kick it closed, and continue carrying Annie all the way up the stairs to his bedroom, depositing her on the bed.

The room wasn't the one where they had watched *Meet Me in St. Louis*, but it wasn't actually as different as Annie had expected, the bedspread festively adorned. Nick ripped his T-shirt off, standing above Annie.

"Fuck," Annie breathed. "You are hot as fuck," she marveled, very much enjoying the view of Nick's chest and well-defined biceps, reaching out to appreciate them. Nick was looking at her as though she were some sort of Greek statue, or like how she admired her first iced coffee in the morning.

"Annie," Nick began, breathless. "You have no idea how much I've dreamed of this. You. Here." Nick shook his head in awe and ran a hand across his stubbled chin. Annie was desperate to feel that stubble across her body. She dug her fingers into his upper arms and pulled him on top of her, ready to succumb right there with the weight of his body putting pressure and heat in all the places that were begging for it, aching for closeness.

Annie kissed Nick's neck until she reached his Adam's apple and sucked it into her mouth. Nick groaned at the sudden suction and his fingers tightened around her hair, his other hand hungrily trying to unbutton her flannel. Annie, impatient, ripped it open, mismatched buttons be damned.

Nick froze, gazing at her freed, braless breasts. After a moment, he looked back at Annie's face. "This is the stuff of dreams," he said, returning to worship her body, like he wanted to memorize every inch of it.

Annie traced a hand down his jaw, running her thumb across his bottom lip, parting his mouth open. His teeth nipped at her and she grabbed his face, inviting his tongue to find hers.

Nick quickly stood back up and removed his pants, presenting himself to her. He was naked, ready and wanting, awaiting her direction. Annie arched her back into the mattress, unsure how much more suspense she could take, then let out an impatient moan. Nick laughed, gently lowering himself back on top of her, and she kissed him with urgency.

"I want to do all the foreplay and sexy other stuff at some point very soon, but I swear Nick, if you don't get inside me right now, I may die."

"Should I get a condom?" Nick asked, nervously glancing around the room, seeming unsure if he even had one.

"I'm on birth control, and I've been recently tested, I'm clean," Annie said, urging him back to her.

"Me too," Nick said.

"Come on then, hurry," Annie whined. "Don't make me wait any longer."

"I want you so badly," Nick said, his tongue exploring her neck.

"Show me," Annie whimpered.

Nick pulled her hair with a little more force. He wrapped a thumb in the waistband of her underwear, and Annie, concerned her legs might give out in anticipation, helped pull them off, kicking them to the floor. Wrapping her limbs around him, Annie repositioned their bodies so that she was now on top of him, her legs spread open across his thighs, and lowered herself onto him, using a hand to guide him deeper inside her. The pleasure was immediate, Annie exploring how much closer they could get before she moved her hips to ride him.

"Annie," Nick gasped. "I'm not going to last long like this." Annie agreed as she started moving faster, up and down, each plunge taking her deliciously closer to the peak. As he thrust, she clenched tightly around him, her nails marking his shoulder blades until her muscles seized. Annie cried out first, a satisfied scream reverberating from deep in the back of her throat and bouncing off the wall. The sensation of mind-numbing waves violently crashing inside her, ready and willing to drown among them. Nick succumbed second, once he was confident she had her moment, in a quick rush, his own deep bellow escaping from the well within.

Breathless, Annie inched him out of her as Nick shuddered, still fresh from his own moment. She put her head on his chest, pulling the blanket they had just defiled over their naked, shivering bodies.

"I can't wait to do that again. And again. And again," Annie said, snuggling into his chest, her body still humming. Nick wrapped an arm around her, pulling her in so he could be the big spoon.

"I can't wait for this part too," Nick said into her hair, referring to the cuddling. "I don't know if I'll ever be able to leave this bed."

"I am starving, though," Annie told him. Nick groaned and squeezed her.

"Let me have a few more minutes, woman," Nick demanded and Annie grinned, sinking into the comfort and joy, her body relaxed and calm.

"We're driving, right?" Annie asked Nick an hour or so later, after they had enjoyed another moment, redressed and were back outside, met with an immediate gust of wind.

"Your car or mine?" Nick asked. Annie grabbed her keys, and they got in her car.

"Is your phone back to normal?" Annie asked, her eyes looking between Nick and the road. Nick grabbed his phone, opening various apps to make sure everything was intact.

"I think so," he said, waving it, but before he put it away, he opened up the phone's camera. He gasped and stared at the picture on his screen.

"What?" Annie asked, trying to get a look. He moved the phone a little closer to her so she could see, and she let out her own sound of surprise, accidentally letting out a short beep from the car's horn.

There they were in a beautiful selfie, the sky behind them something out of a literal dream. It had been their first day in the made-for-TV Christmas movie universe before they stopped bothering with their phones altogether because they were virtually useless.

"Stunning," Nick marveled, and Annie agreed.

"Send that to me immediately," Annie demanded, her focus back on the road. Main Street was gone, along with all the little shops on it. "It's almost a little sad," Annie sighed.

"Let's go get you an iced coffee," Nick offered, pointing to the closer of the Dunkin' locations on the road (because, obviously, there were multiple options). Annie lit up, pulling into the parking lot, ready to skip inside. Before she made it, though, she ran straight into someone carrying a large wreath. Annie fell to the ground in a messy heap.

"Oops, sorry!" a voice called down to her.

"Chris?" Annie said, standing up.

"C'mon, babe, we gotta go," a female voice said.

"Bailey?" Nick asked.

"Hey!" Bailey smiled, popping a piece of gum in her mouth while balancing a tray of drinks.

"You guys are a real couple?" Nick asked her, smiling.

"Um, well, we've never done labels. But we met a few years ago at a Phish cover band contest and ran into each other again a few months ago . . . and now me and this dum-dum are talking about a commitment ceremony next year at Burning Man if you can believe it," Bailey said, giving Chris a teasing look and sticking her tongue out at him. Chris looked momentarily nervous about Annie's reaction.

"Such a dum-dum," Annie laughed. "I'm happy for you, Chris."

"And I'm happy for you, Bailey," Nick said softly.

"Aw, thanks, Nick. It's so random to see you. But nice. And you look happy. Wait, are you two finally together?" Bailey asked. Nick and Annie looked at each other, unsure who would answer first. They laughed, opting to nod. "That's great!" Bailey gushed and then turned to Annie, "I always thought he had a crush on you in high school, even when he was technically my boyfriend. You and Marsha were always so cool . . ." Bailey trailed off, her thoughts drifting down her own memory lane. Annie beamed and looked warmly at Nick, letting Bailey's words fill her with butterflies. "Well, nice seeing you guys. We gotta hit the road. My parents are expecting us." Bailey gestured to the parking lot.

"What are your parents up to these days?" Nick asked.

"They're running a business—" Bailey began.

"Bakery?" Annie asked immediately.

"Oh, no. Though they do sell some baked goods . . ." Bailey said, her voice full of mischief. Annie and Nick stared at her, waiting for her to continue. "They own a store called Yes, You Cannabis."

"No way," Annie whispered as Chris got a text alert. "We are big fans of your work."

"Speaking of, it's my uncle again; he has a bunch of requests," Chris told Bailey.

"Your Uncle Felix?" Annie asked.

"How do you know my uncle?" Chris asked, his face clouded with confusion. "Wait, was Felix the guy in your Instagram story last night? He looked familiar."

"Please tell me he's dating Noelle," Annie said, ignoring his questions, her own voice too busy and full of hope and happiness.

"Noelle?" Chris asked, thinking it over before he lightened and laughed. "Yeah, I think that's one of the women who lives with them." Chris looked at Bailey, and the two of them shared a knowing look before letting out a little chuckle.

"One of the women?" Nick asked, unable to stop himself.

"My Uncle Felix is poly and lives in a commune nearby," Chris said, his mouth still stuck in a smile.

"Oh, I remember Noelle," Bailey said, nodding. "She's the outdoorsy goddess one?" Bailey asked Chris, and he nodded in recollection. "She invited us to bathe naked under the full moon once," Bailey recalled.

"Of course she did, such divine feminine witch energy," Annie admired.

"Do you know them?" Chris asked, returning to bewilderment at this strange relationship intersection. "No, seriously, why do you know them?"

"Oh, Chris, I couldn't even begin to tell you," Annie dismissed. "I'm glad you and Bailey found each other at that Phish cover band contest and got a second chance at love. It's been such a blessing to see you both again," Annie said, pulling both Chris and Bailey in for a hug.

"Uh, yeah," Chris said as Nick joined them in a warm group embrace.

"This has been pretty weird," Bailey smiled. "We'll see you guys. Have a great holiday."

Annie grinned and offered them her token finger-guns routine, complete with pew-pews, as a farewell. As Annie and Nick moved to the door, a young girl came stomping through holding a very large chestnut praline blended drink with mounds of whipped cream and spiced praline crumbs on the top and nearly ran into them.

"Holly?" Annie asked as Holly turned to glare at her and didn't say anything. "It's me, Miss Annie," Annie told her, reaching out her hand for a squeeze.

"Ew. Fuck off, hag," Holly grumbled and took a loud sip of her drink and viciously crunched a praline piece, her eyes still locked on Annie, threatening and daring her to respond before storming her way to a car and loudly slamming the door.

"That's my girl. I'm so proud," Annie told Nick, her eyes tearing.

"Let's stock up on your iced coffee and some snacks so we can go back home. We probably shouldn't be out in public much longer," Nick said.

"Can we watch a movie?" Annie asked.

"Only if it's the VHS copy of *Meet Me in St. Louis*." Nick smirked.

"That's the only thing I want to watch!" Annie beamed. Nick looked up, and his eyes caught what was hanging above them.

"Mistletoe," he whispered and pulled Annie in for another kiss. A small jolt of happiness moved through Annie as she realized she now had someone to kiss beneath every sprig of mistletoe that crossed her path going forward. And she realized with profound clarity that Nick was the only one she wanted to meet there, year after year.

After ordering two of the largest iced coffees known to man (Annie had to make up for lost time, after all) and as many snacks as they could carry from Cumberland Farms, Annie and Nick raced back to the car to get home to enjoy another "moment" before settling in to watch a movie.

"What the hell is happening here?" Marsha gasped, walking in on Annie and Nick cuddled up on Annie's couch a few hours and two more "moments" later. "Oh, my God, what's going on? Annie, you freaked me out! I thought something had happened to you, and then I saw a selfie Nick posted of you guys with 'Simsbury' tagged as the location!"

"You posted that?" Annie asked Nick.

"I guess I did. Is that okay?" Nick asked.

"Of course, it's a great picture—" Annie answered.

"Hello!" Marsha barked out. "What the hell is happening? And what the fuck is with that bloody chair next door?"

"Fake blood," Nick and Annie answered together.

"Hey, is that a barber's chair from Sweeney Todd?" Pete said as he jogged in.

"It is!" Nick grinned, standing up.

"Dude, it's awesome, can I touch it?" Pete asked Nick. "I'm Pete, by the way."

"Nick," Nick offered, pointing to himself. "Do you want to see the trap door mechanism?"

"Oh, my God, yes!" Pete grinned excitedly as Nick led him back outside, explaining the engineering that went into easily "disposing of bodies" onstage.

Annie and Marsha watched affectionately

"Okay, that was really cute," Annie said as Marsha moved to sit on the couch. When she had her best friend beside her, Annie turned to her with watery eyes. "Marsha, I missed you so much. More than you'll ever know."

"Annie, what's going on? What did I walk in on?! I haven't heard from you all day!" Marsha scolded.

"Honestly, I got so used to not having a working phone that I haven't thought about checking it," Annie explained.

"You got used to not having a phone for a few hours? What happened to you after you texted me last night?"

"Nick and I banged," Annie admitted sheepishly.

"Are you serious?" Marsha asked, shaking her head in confusion. "Annie, no, that's not funny. I told you to hook up with a high school crew team guy, not our childhood neighbor, *stage* crew guy . . . ew! He's probably going to take you into his improv team's lair," Marsha shuddered.

"How dare you, he's not a monster," Annie recoiled.

"Blink twice if you're okay," Marsha whispered to Annie, eyeing the entrance in case Nick returned. "Okay, you guys have been home for a few hours, but now you're what? Hooking up?"

"I'm in love," Annie admitted.

"Annie!" Marsha gasped. "In love? In love?! I mean, I always suspected Nick had a little crush or whatever in high school, but Annie, yesterday you were, like, glum about that douchebag, Chris—"

"That spruce-bag," Annie smiled before turning back to Marsha, "he's dating Bailey, Nick's high school girlfriend! And her parents own Yes, You Cannabis!" Annie squealed.

"Whoa, really?" Marsha asked, contemplating how this development might be able to benefit her.

"I know it all sounds unbelievable," Annie said before stopping herself. "Wait, Marsha, why are you and Pete here? I thought you'd be at his house by now? Learning about Hanukkah and possibly getting engaged."

"Annie," Marsha said seriously. "You are my family. My best friend. My true number one. No matter what is happening in my romantic relationship, I'm never letting you go. Nothing is ever going to change that," Marsha finished, and Annie couldn't help it, she burst into tears. The restless anxiety that had once twisted inside her had transformed into a comforting confidence: their unbreakable friendship would withstand anything. They didn't have to traverse separate paths; they could expand the forest together.

"I feel the same way, but thank you for saying it," Annie cried as Marsha hugged her closer.

"Marsh—Nick let me get ejected from the chair! It was incredible!" Pete squealed, running inside. Marsha and Annie shared a warm look. There was something endlessly delightful about her best friend's love befriending her own. Nick returned, his cheeks flushed with color and bashfully grinning. Marsha rifled through her purse before pulling out a bottle of champagne, a bag of popcorn, and a wrapped piece of brie.

"Nigel with the brie!" Annie cheered.

"Do you always carry that around?" Nick asked.

"Dinner," Annie and Marsha said together.

"What?" Nick asked, and Annie and Marsha rolled their eyes at his lack of understanding.

"Duh. In case I ever need dinner," Marsha said slowly as if Nick was the dumbest person on the planet.

"This is your life now," Pete sighed to Nick, giving him a knowing squeeze on the shoulder.

"I'm going to grab some things from my house—I had an idea. I want to try and make your grandfather's lemon cookies and something chocolate too . . ." Nick trailed off in thought.

"I love you," Annie blurted at him. "I've never said that to anyone first. And I've never meant it until now," Annie said, overflowing with feeling.

"It's always been you, Annie," Nick said, coming closer. "And now it'll always be us. I love you too," Nick told her before they kissed. "Now I'm really going to grab cookie stuff; I know the order of priorities," Nick said with a playful smirk.

"I love him," Annie said, overcome with emotion as Nick scurried to his house.

"I always knew you'd get your happy ending with the guy of your dreams," Marsha said. "I never thought it would be Nick Laurel or that it would happen immediately after I asked you what it would take to make you believe it could happen, but you know what, it's Christmas and I'm all in on you guys."

Annie gave Marsha another hug, and when Nick returned after multiple trips, they turned on a made-for-TV Christmas movie (after Nick put the remote back together) and transformed the space with cheer. Marsha and Pete stayed for a bit to enjoy the champagne and brie before eventually heading off on their own holiday adventure.

"Hey," Annie said to Nick a little while later, when it was just the two of them again, as he was mixing dry ingredients, "you know how you said some of the movies do a 'one year later' check-in right before the credits?"

"Yeah, I'm familiar. Aren't you a little star student?" Nick smirked.

"I learned from the best," Annie admitted, finding herself immediately distracted by his mouth and wanting to bite down on his lower lip. She took the opportunity to put a dab of flour on his nose. "You're so truckin' cute. Do we get one of those?"

"Do we get a check-in one year later?" Nick asked, putting his arms around Annie's shoulders and pulling her closer. "Truck yeah, we do," he grinned before putting his own dab of flour across Annie's lips and then covering her mouth with his.

There will never be a time I don't love this, Annie thought, letting herself sink into the kiss, tasting the sweetness of pure holiday joy. It was delicious.

"I love Christmas," Annie said, staring into Nick's eyes. She felt as splendid and illustrious as Scrooge himself upon realizing he could now live in the Past, the Present, and the Future.

EPILOGUE

One Year Later

Annie and Nick made out. Hard. The space was technically considered a closet, but it felt more like a narrow, mostly neglected nook, buzzing with the hum of nearby industrial freezers and crammed with boxes of canned eggnog concentrate.

If they had still been in their alternate universe made-for-TV Christmas movie world, this is the part where they'd speed through a year of happy moments to get to this specific point. No need to share the less-than-glamorous times or anything too boring, let's keep it to the good stuff.

After the new year, Nick nailed his interview with the Bushnell Theater and was hired to oversee the installation of the touring sets he had once helped to build in New York City. He moved in with Annie within a few weeks, and like Annie knew he would, he shared each and every one of his

Lilith Fair holiday playlists. Their parents were so delighted and made countless jokes about "cruising together more often" that eventually, they took advantage of a President's Day trip deal, and Annie and Nick enjoyed house-sitting for them again. Biblically speaking, of course.

"Are you two done yet?" Marsha asked, banging on the kitchen closet door. "I don't think I can fend Grant off much longer—"

"No, you cannot," Grant huffed, emphasizing each word as his shoes squeaked closer, that speed-strutter pace undeniably his.

"Hurry, he's coming," Marsha whispered as Grant planted himself in front of the door and immediately beat two fists against it.

"Passed hors d'oeuvres have started, and your photographer needs to finish the shot list."

"Sorry, Grant," Annie called back through the door, jumping up to straighten her dress.

"Grant! We'll be right there. You know how much we appreciate everything you're doing and how much we love you," Nick added earnestly.

"I need to check in with the DJ, so I'm leaving Marsha in charge of getting you two out of there in the next minute," Grant warned, but Annie could hear the corners of his mouth trying to suppress a smile. "Perry did not spend weeks choreographing your first dance for you to be late."

"Got it," Marsha nodded, her hands up in surrender. "Also, I passed a tray of gingerbread meatball skewers on our way over here and literally nothing will keep me from them," Marsha promised and Grant gave her a curt nod before marching out of the kitchen.

"Aw, is the parasite hungry?" Annie asked.

"Hey, that's our little niece or nephew in there," Nick said, zipping up his suit pants and retucking his shirt. He gave Annie a look to ensure she was decent enough to open the door, and when she nodded, he immediately beamed at Marsha's enormous belly. "Maybe they'll arrive on Christmas Day. Wouldn't that be the best?"

"As long as it's after tonight, they can arrive whenever," Marsha said, rubbing her stomach.

"Are you thinking it's a boy or a girl today?" Nick asked as they beelined toward the ballroom space.

"It better be a girl because Pete told me what his first name pick is for a boy and I don't love it," Marsha said. "Pete's middle name is Ferguson, which is apparently a big family name, and his mom wants us to go with that."

Annie and Nick looked at each other in surprise. Up until now, they had been unaware of Pete's full name.

"And what's the girl's name?" Annie asked, but she already knew the answer.

"I've always liked Eve, like the original first woman of the world; it has a nice ring to it," Marsha said assertively as Annie and Nick shared a knowing glance.

Similar to her made-for-TV Christmas movie counterpart, Marsha too got engaged on Christmas Eve (which coincided with the last night of Hanukkah!), but they decided to move up the wedding to that spring when, at the end of March, in the bathroom stall of their tiny office (of LaundryBae's increasingly successful quarter), Marsha realized she was pregnant and joking around about birth control is not funny.

Nick proposed to Annie on July 4th (during a July made-for-TV Christmas movie marathon), and Annie had surprised Nick on Halloween with "an early Christmas gift": a shaggy shelter dog they named Mistletoe. And because Annie wanted to see Nick look like a *Titanic* character again, the threesome spent their first holiday together dressed as Jack, Rose, and the infamous door (played by Annie).

Their decision to have a Christmas Eve wedding was instantaneous. Annie and Nick had lovingly borrowed ideas from their time in the made-for-TV Christmas movie Simsbury for inspiration and were excited to share an ice sculpture gallery and sleigh rides through town with their guests. They had an assortment of cookies waiting to be unveiled (half of which were provided by Yes, You Cannabis), and at the end of the night, guests would enjoy a candle walk, in honor of her grandparents, with a Christmas tin of cookies and candles to take home.

Annie had also had custom red silk pajamas made for their wedding night. Nick's with an "N" and "L" stitched on the front pocket and hers with an "A" and "L." Annie knew it would be sexier and more appreciated than any other holiday lingerie and looked forward to "making another moment" with her husband later that night.

They also had their eyes on Mr. Heartgrave's house once it officially went on the market. They happened to pass by him when they were out with Mistletoe on a post–Thanksgiving dinner walk, and after he made a joke about "reducing square roots" that Annie hadn't understood, he clarified that he would be downsizing to a nearby condo.

"Okay, newlyweds, this is where I leave you," Marsha said once they had entered the ballroom and saw Pete proudly showing off an assortment of goodies he had procured for her. "See you on the dance floor!" Marsha called, her hands already reaching to double-fist some bacon-wrapped dates.

"I can't believe we managed to have sex in that tiny closet before Grant could find us," Nick marveled. "Or before he could get a quickie in with Perry first."

"I think our wedding planner will forgive us. I heard at least three people ask for his info before the ceremony. When he's not planning his own, he's going to be booked and busy next year," Annie assured him.

"More importantly," Nick said, turning to Annie and slipping his arms around her waist, "I got to marry my dream girl,"

"How can I ignore the boy next door? I love him more than I can say," Annie sang into Nick's ear in her best Judy Garland voice, and Nick let out a little growl.

"You know I can't resist that jam; I must have you now," Nick said, grabbing her hand and rushing her back toward the kitchen.

"Nick!" Annie laughed. "I don't know if we can pull that off again!" She could see their guests eyeing them, eager to celebrate the happy couple.

"I love you, Annie Meyers, my girl next door. I always have and I always will. You make every day feel like Christmas morning," Nick said instead.

Annie wanted to let herself melt into a loving mess of warm goo; she couldn't imagine a happier ending. She looked up to see mistletoe hanging right above them, and she nudged Nick. So they kissed. Again. And a lot. In front of a solid group of townspeople from Simsbury too. And Annie Meyers's love for Christmas lived on for always.

ACKNOWLEDGMENTS

There are people in this world who love you because you are a weird girl, not in spite of it. If you are lucky enough to find them, hold on tight and never, ever let go. Leaning into your whimsy, it turns out, is one of the greatest gifts you can give yourself.

To my agent, Claire Cavanagh: Not Another Christmas Movie is so much stronger because of you, your editorial eye, your instincts, and your tireless belief in what this book could be. Thank you for always being in on my very particular brand of joke, and for giving me the confidence to take it further than I ever could have on my own, a sure sign the universe had been taking very good notes. This story found its home with you, and for that, and for so much, I am endlessly grateful and excited for all that is to come.

To Maria Donatti and Amina Chaudhry of The Rights Factory, whose early insight brought such care and craft to this manuscript, thank you.

To Jess Verdi, who championed this book with generosity and enthusiasm, whose early notes live between the lines, and whose belief in acquiring this story was a dream come true. To Faith Black Ross, who stepped in and wrapped her arms around this project with such tenderness and vision, thank you for everything you brought to these pages. To the wonderful team at Alcove Press, including Thaisheemarie Fantauzzi Perez, Julia Abbott, Dulce Botello, Beata Garrett, and Lindsey Staub, whose work brought this story into the world in ways that will forever humble and delight me.

To my honey, Will: I love you more with each and every dad joke. Getting to live out our happily ever after, one terrible pun at a time, is the greatest romcom. To our girls, Scarlett, Violet, and Ruby, a chapter I hoped for long before I had the words. I will spend the rest of my life trying to be worthy of how proud you make me every single day as your mama.

Mom and Dad, thank you for gifting me with your heart, your humor, and the greatest gift of all: my siblings. Kate and Kevin, so much of our childhood, our neighborhood, our world found its way onto these pages, and I carry our family with me in everything I write. Kate, thank you for consulting the cards, for welcoming retrograde plot twists, and for encouraging me to lean into my Leo Rising the way only a Sagittarius Rising could. Alongside my bonus siblings Patrick and Dana, you four were some of my earliest readers, my cheerleaders, the people who always encouraged me to stay authentic.

Dearest Dana Piechowski, you've been with me from the very first sentences of this writing life, one of the people I trusted with the stories that scared me most to share.

Our Facts and Feelings walks, where you bring the clarity and I bring the chaos, have shaped not just this book but who I am as a storyteller. Forever grateful to be on this path with you.

To Carrie Firestone, who was always ready with kindness and wisdom whenever this wide-eyed debut author came calling, thank you for lighting the way. To my Babbledeeboos, Alex Harris, Allison Page, and Mariah Castle, you made me laugh when rejections made me cry, workshopped scenes at all hours, and never once let me believe this goal was too grand. I'm so grateful for our group chat. To Lexi Bazoukas, my partner in crime and co-conspirator in the art of the perfectly timed punchline, who has been beside me through the work and beyond it, lending her talents wherever they were needed most, thank you. To Lauren Graczyk and Betsy Maguire, my creative pillars, on the stage and off it, thank you for pouring your hearts into every artistic endeavor we have shared and for making this creator a little braver. Theater is my heartbeat, and its pulse is steadier with you in the wings.

To Past Ashley: Hang in there. Keep going. Get the bangs, why not. And don't you dare stop dreaming. One day you are going to hold this book in your hands, and it is going to feel like the best kind of magic, the kind you made yourself.

And finally, to you. Yes, you, the one holding this book right now. Thank you for making room on your shelf for a proud weird girl's story. It's been the truest gift to share a little whimsy with you.